Praise for *Last*

'What lifts the novel above bei
empathetic portrayal of lives spent in the shadow of coercion
and abuse.'

— *The Times*

'As cinematic as it is gripping.'

— *Peterborough Telegraph*

'There's a path this novel could follow, but there are twists and surprises that make it a more intriguing read. The who and the how is more subtle than the usual.'

— Crime Time FM

'I was gripped by Simon McCleave's dark, whodunnit, captivating in every way... You can feel the hum of the cicadas and the corrupting beauty of the Italian landscape. A perfect summer read.'

— Abi Morgan, Emmy- and BAFTA-winning screenwriter of Netflix hit *Eric* and BBC's *The Split*

'Smart, evocative... full of the kinds of twist and surprises that makes a first-time reader into a lifelong fan. Terrific!'

— Gregg Olsen

'Had me gripped from the first page to the last, outstanding!'

– J M Dalgliesh

'Absolutely loved it. It was totally absorbing, and I didn't want to put it down. The setting was perfect and just superbly crafted… satisfying, stunning and stylish.'

– Rachel Lynch

FIVE DAYS IN PROVENCE

SIMON MCCLEAVE

This is a work of fiction. Names, characters, businesses, places, events and incidents are either the products of the author's imagination or used in a fictitious manner. Any resemblance to actual persons, living or dead, or actual events is purely coincidental.

Copyright © Simon McCleave, 2025

The moral right of the author has been asserted.

All rights reserved. No part of this book may be reproduced or used in any manner without the prior written permission of the copyright owner. This prohibition includes, but is not limited to, any reproduction or use for the purpose of training artificial intelligence technologies or systems.

To request permissions, contact the publisher at rights@stormpublishing.co

Ebook ISBN: 978-1-80508-905-6
Paperback ISBN: 978-1-80508-907-0

Cover design: Lisa Horton
Cover images: Adobe Stock, Shutterstock

Published by Storm Publishing.
For further information, visit:
www.stormpublishing.co

ALSO BY SIMON MCCLEAVE

Last Night at Villa Lucia

DI Ruth Hunter Crime Thriller

The Snowdonia Killings
The Harlech Beach Killings
The Dee Valley Killings
The Devil's Cliff Killings
The Berwyn River Killings
The White Forest Killings
The Solace Farm Killings
The Menai Bridge Killings
The Conway Harbour Killings
The River Seine Killings
The Lake Vyrnwy Killings
The Chirk Castle Killings
The Portmeirion Killings
The Llandudno Pier Killings
The Denbigh Asylum Killings
The Wrexham Killings
The Colwyn Bay Killings
The Chester Killings
The Llangollen Killings

DC Ruth Hunter Murder Cases

Diary of a War Crime
The Razor Gang Murder
An Imitation of Darkness
London, SE15

Anglesey Series

The Dark Tide
In Too Deep
Blood on the Shore
The Drowning Isle
Dead in the Water

NOW
STEPH

1 August 2022

A shadowy figure emerges slowly from a bank of acrid smoke. It looks otherworldly. Ethereal. I can't see who it is yet.

I cough as the smoke catches on my throat. My eyes are stinging and raw. I don't care.

We have to find her.

What the hell happened? How could she just vanish? I ask myself. Nothing feels real.

I rub my eyes, blink frantically and look around.

The view from halfway up Mont Ventoux is completely obscured by a thick carpet of smoke from the wildfires below us. As the noisy wind picks up, it blows the smoke into frightening, circular twists like a mini hurricane. The horizon has all but disappeared.

This is all my fault. It was my idea. My trip. My fiftieth birthday we were all celebrating.

The figure is now only ten yards away. I can see it's Shaun, the Irishman who is renovating the farmhouse opposite from where we are staying. He and Tom, the guy working with him, had been out cycling when I rang them for help.

'What is it?' I ask anxiously.

'Tom's found her,' he replies.

My whole body reacts with relief.

But then I can see that there's something wrong. He has a grim expression on his face.

Why does he look so serious? It's good that they've found her, isn't it?

'Is she all right?' I ask nervously.

Shaun gestures to the ridge. 'Tom's trying to get down to her now,' he explains sounding a little flustered.

'Show me,' I say, my pulse racing.

I follow Shaun through the smoke, waving my hands in front of my face as if this would somehow disperse it.

'Have you seen the others?' he asks.

'Not yet.' I point to our right. 'I assume they're still up the other path.'

Another figure appears, coming towards us. It's Tom.

The smoke catches on my throat again. I start to cough.

As Tom reaches us, he pulls off his rucksack, takes a large steel water bottle from a side pocket and hands it to me. 'Here you go, Steph.'

'Thanks,' I splutter as I take a few sips which seem to clear my throat. 'Can you see her?'

Tom nods but he wears the same sombre expression as Shaun. 'She's about fifty yards down the slope. But it's really steep.'

I spot another furtive glance between Tom and Shaun.

'What?' I ask in a curt but anxious tone. 'What is it?'

Shaun looks at me. 'From the way she's lying...' He stops.

I frown with a growing sense of dread deep in the pit of my stomach. 'What?'

'I think... she might be dead.'

ONE

DARCIE

31 July 2022

'Where's that fucking wine?' Darcie checks her watch again. Ten minutes since she'd asked the flight attendant to bring more white wine. Her fingers drum against the armrest, fighting the urge to press the call button. The diazepam she'd taken before boarding isn't quite cutting through her flight anxiety, and she needs something stronger than travel-sized wine to dull the edge.

'You're not in business class now, you snob,' Abi laughs.

Darcie starts to unbuckle her seatbelt. *I'll go and get it myself then*, she thinks.

'Where are you going?' Abi says with a quizzical frown.

Darcie shrugs. 'If Mohammed won't come to the mountain.'

Abi rolls her eyes. 'It's "If the mountain won't come to Mohammed..."'

'Is it? Well, whatever.' Darcie sighs. 'Who was Mohammed?'

'No idea.'

Darcie sees the spindly young steward Wayne coming

down the aisle of their budget aeroplane with four miniature bottles of white wine and a card machine. 'Ah, about time,' she mutters under her breath.

'Here we go,' Wayne says, placing down the bottles on their grey, plastic fold-out trays. He starts to tap at the card machine.

'I thought you'd forgotten all about us,' Darcie says in a spiky tone. *How long does it take to retrieve four tiny bottles and ferry them back, for God's sake? I could train a monkey to do that.*

'Oh, right. Sorry,' Wayne says, looking embarrassed.

Darcie feels Abi giving her a sharp nudge with her elbow.

'You've forgotten my ice.' Darcie sighs again. The only way to drink the horrible, cheap plonk that they served on this substandard airline was to put ice in it and get it to a temperature where she couldn't really taste it.

Wayne pulls an apologetic face. 'Have I?'

'Yes,' Darcie replies in a tone that leaves him in no doubt that she isn't impressed. She doesn't care. That was his job.

'I'm sorry.' Wayne seems flustered. 'This machine is playing up today.'

'Don't worry at all.' Abi jumps in with a warm smile, touching his arm. 'Wi-Fi is always terrible on flights. And you've been run off your feet.'

Darcie rolls her eyes. Classic Abi – always smoothing things over, just like she had when they were eleven years old at Milton Hall and Darcie had reduced a supply teacher to tears. Some things never change.

'Not your fault,' Abi reassures him.

'Right, got it.' Wayne sighs with relief.

Darcie slides her business debit card across the tray with a practised flick. The shiny black Amex with 'Darcie Miller Media' embossed in silver. Her accountant's voice echoes in her head: *Just run everything through the business, darling. First class, Champagne, the lot. I'll sort out what's kosher later.*

The same delicious thrill she gets every time she signs off an 'influencer lunch' or 'content research trip' – that little dance on the edge of what's legal. Like shoplifting expensive lipsticks as a teenager, but now with better clothes and a better alibi.

'There we go,' Wayne says politely as he hands Darcie her card. Then he turns and walks back down towards the front of the plane.

'Christ, he was exceptionally inept, wasn't he?' Darcie says in her best withering tone.

'Oh, Darcie, does it really matter?' Same old Abi, still trying to smooth her friend's sharp edges after all these years.

'Yes, it bloody well does. And bollocks to you,' Darcie cackles. 'Cheers.'

'Santé,' Abi says as they click their 'glasses' together.

'This plastic has such a lovely ring to it, doesn't it?' Darcie snorts caustically. She then takes a long glug of wine.

That's better.

'Such a snob.' Abi's eye-roll holds nearly forty years of affectionate exasperation.

Darcie grins. She plays up to be that way just for the effect. 'That's why you love me.'

Abi points over at Steph. 'Last of us to turn fifty.' Then she gives Darcie a sarcastic smile. 'You didn't even celebrate your fiftieth. We went for that little dinner and you banned us from posting any photos.'

'That's because I'm actually in my mid to late forties.' Darcie forces a smile. 'Remember?'

'All about your brand, is it?' Abi says knowingly.

'I can't have the yummy mummies of metropolitan London thinking that I'm in my fifties now. That would never do.'

'No, God forbid,' Abi snorts.

They fall into silence as they drink.

Darcie then leans in and whispers the burning secret that

has been on her lips for the past two hours. 'I slept with someone else.'

Abi's eyes widen as she splutters into her wine. 'You slept with someone else *again*? Jesus!' she exclaims. 'I thought you were going to stop shagging random people.'

Darcie has been married to Hugo for over twenty years.

'Shsh.' Darcie puts her finger to her lips. 'Say it a bit louder, I don't think the pilot heard.'

'When?'

'About a month ago. We spent a few nights together, actually.'

'That's not like you, is it?'

'No.' Darcie shrugs. 'It felt different this time.'

'Really?'

Darcie nods. 'Really.'

The tension in her body evaporates now she's told her oldest, best friend. It might be childish, but she also gets a frisson of excitement at sharing the secret and Abi's reaction.

Abi looks at her in disbelief. 'Who the hell was it?' she asks as her voice drops to a whisper.

Darcie nods with a smirk. *I know that smirking about this is incredibly childish, but I can't help it. I'm happy to have got it off my chest.*

'Come on,' Darcie says. 'You can't be that surprised. I've told you about me and Hugo. The last three years have been particularly horrible since he started drinking too much. What am I meant to do?'

'Why don't you just leave him?' Abi suggests – not for the first time.

'I don't know,' Darcie groans. 'I know I should.' What she doesn't like to admit, especially to herself, is that she and Hugo are a brand. She gets invited to film premieres and parties because she's married to Hugo, even if his star is on the wane. If they divorce, she can no longer play at 'happy families' and being a celebrity couple for her online fans. It's not a risk she wants to take after all the hard work she's put in over the years.

'I saw him on that panel show last week,' Abi says carefully. 'He seemed...'

'Drunk? Slurring his words?' Darcie gives a bitter laugh. 'The producers had to edit around him. His agent has suggested a stint in rehab. He just sits there every night drowning his sorrows, full of self-pity, banging on about that BAFTA he won twenty years ago and how no one's offering him proper acting roles anymore.' She takes a long swig of wine. 'You know what he said when that psycho broke into our house and held a knife to my throat? Nothing. Because he was passed out on the sofa with an empty bottle of Scotch. Thank God Bella's away at uni and doesn't have to watch her father destroy himself.'

There are a few seconds of silence. Abi finishes her wine and then looks at Darcie.

'I knew you'd had a few one-night stands recently,' Abi says, wide-eyed, in a hushed voice. 'But another affair, Darcie? I thought you said never again.'

'It's not an affair.' Darcie gives her a shrug. 'But Hugo and I haven't shagged for three years, Abs. What am I meant to do, not have sex from now until the day I die? And I don't want to have to pay for it. But I do love sex.'

A woman in her sixties who's sitting in the row in front of them turns around as Darcie says the last phrase a little too loudly.

'Oh, hello?' Darcie says to the woman in a sarcastically chirpy tone that's intended to suggest *Turn the fuck around and mind your own business.*

Abi gives her another dig in the ribs. 'Darcie.'

'Oops,' Darcie sniggers.

'Who is he?' Abi asks.

Darcie isn't about to divulge this information. Well, not yet.

'I can't tell you,' she admits.

'What? You tell me everything,' Abi protests.

Darcie shakes her head and mimes zipping her lips shut. 'I can't.'

Abi frowns. 'Bloody hell! You can't tell me that you're having an affair with someone and then *not* tell me who it's with.'

'I can't tell you.' Darcie pulls a face. 'But it's a bit of a shocker, to be honest.'

'You mean I know him?' Abi asks.

'Yes. I'll probably crack and tell you when I'm shit-faced in the next few days.' Darcie sighs. 'And don't tell the others.'

The air steward Wayne appears at Darcie's side, smiles and hands her a plastic beaker with ice cubes inside. 'There you go.'

'Thanks,' Darcie says.

Abi gives her a pressing look. 'Darcie, you cow! Tell me!'

Darcie undoes her seatbelt, hands Abi her glass, pushes up the tray and stands up. 'Hold that. I'm going for a pee.'

TWO
STEPH

My fiftieth-birthday celebration. All of us girls together again. Me, Darcie, Abi, Ruby and Katie. Five days in a farmhouse in Provence. A little town called Bédoin at the foot of Mont Ventoux. I can't wait. So excited.

The white Mercedes 4x4 rental purrs as I take another bend, the limestone cliffs of Provence rising ahead of us. The calming beats of Morcheeba's 'The Sea' fill the car. My hands grip the wheel a little too tightly. Behind me, Darcie and Abi are passed out from airport Champagne, while Ruby's sitting next to me, buried in her latest crime novel. Katie stares at her phone, uncharacteristically quiet.

'You sure you don't want me to drive?' Katie asks, catching my eye in the rear-view mirror. 'It is your birthday.'

I shake my head, focusing on the road. 'I like driving. Especially here.' What I don't say is that I need the distraction. Fifty. How did that happen?

The farmhouse website promised perfection – turquoise shutters, wooden beams, our own en-suite rooms so we don't have to suffer each other's snoring. I've planned everything down to the last detail: the local wine already chilling, ingredients for tonight's dinner carefully sourced by Shaun, the caretaker who lives opposite. Tomorrow we'll tackle Mont Ventoux, like we did Snowdon for Ruby's fiftieth. But right now, all I can think about is getting us safely to Bédoin.

I catch another glimpse of Katie in the mirror. Something's off with her today. She's barely said two words since Gatwick, and that tension between her and Darcie... I push the thought away, focusing instead on the navigation screen. Two hours to go. The road winds ahead like a ribbon, and for a moment I feel that familiar flutter of anxiety – the weight of being responsible for everyone's good time.

'You've got that look,' Ruby says, lowering her book.

'What look?'

'The one that says you're overthinking everything.'

I force a smile. 'Just want it to be perfect.'

'It will be,' Ruby says, but there's something in her tone that makes me wonder if she believes it.

I've done my research, obviously. It's all part of the fun of booking a trip like this. I'm the uber-organised one out of our little girlie gang. Except we're no longer girls. Women of a certain age. That makes me feel so bloody old.

The sun is blazing down from the azure sky above us so I pull down the visor to shield my eyes.

I peer out to our left as we speed north up the A7. The landscape is incredible. A small range of limestone mountains called La Chaîne des Alpilles – Chain of Little Alps. I love the name!

The peaks of the low mountains are white limestone but it makes them appear as if they're snow-capped. Against the rich blue of the sky, the undulating line of mountain tops is stunning. Below that, the landscape is bare rock and stony ground that is covered with scrub. It's the kind of landscape you see on those old spaghetti Westerns with Clint Eastwood. My father used to watch *The Good, the Bad and the Ugly* at least four or five times a year.

And then lower down, close to where I'm now driving, there are dark green olive and almond trees. I read in one of my books on Provence that Vincent van Gogh had painted this landscape, especially Les Alpilles, many times when he lived here in the 1880s. I can see why he was so inspired. The light and colours are so incredibly striking.

I spot what looks like a huge bird of prey hovering in the sky above us. It bobs and soars majestically on the currents of wind, tilting its wings to adjust its position. Maybe it's a snake eagle. Apparently they're native to the area. He looks so regal. And then, suddenly, he swoops and heads towards the ground over to my right like a rocket. It's astonishing to see the speed of his descent towards whatever prey he's spotted. He disappears behind a huddle of tall trees. I'm transfixed.

Keep your eyes on the road!

Then he reappears with something small like a vole in his beak and soars away up into the sky before vanishing. Was it okay to find joy in watching him hurtle down like the ultimate killing machine? To marvel at how he plucked the small, unaware creature and carried it away to murder and eat? It was natural law, wasn't it? He was killing to survive, not for any other reason.

I glance in my rear-view mirror and see that now all four of my passengers are asleep. And Ruby is snoring!

Charming.

It's hardly surprising though. Most of us were up at 5.30 a.m. We'd met at a bar on the other side of passport control at Gatwick. Darcie had arrived clutching a hardback copy of her debut novel, *Confessions of an Internet Influencer*.

'That was my dream when the publishers asked me to write it,' Darcie told us. 'Walk through an airport and see "my little ole book" sitting there on the shelves. I just had to buy a copy and post about it.'

Of course you did, I'd thought with an element of jealousy. Sometimes Darcie is a little too pleased with herself. But she's been through a lot in recent years so I'm more than happy to give her a bit of slack.

Darcie's book is an amusing romp through all the stories of her meteoric rise to internet fame. She has well over a million followers on Instagram. Her posts are mainly fashion, beauty and interior decorating tips. Sometimes restaurant reviews. Travel.

But Darcie's book skims past the parts we all know about – the first threatening DM that popped up on her Instagram Live three years ago, the way her hands had shaken as she'd shown us his messages at Ruby's New Year's party. The posts had grown darker after that. Photos of her house in Notting Hill. Her morning coffee route. The knife he'd left on her doorstep. The night Hugo had found her curled in the corner of their kitchen, phone clutched to her chest, tears streaming down her face.

But those weren't the kind of stories that sold lifestyle books.

At the airport, me, Katie and Ruby had sipped at our flat whites and picked at our croissants. Of course, Darcie and Abi had to order breakfast Champagne to celebrate the fact that she'd found her book! Jesus.

I look up and there's a hairpin bend coming towards us. I'm going too fast so I have to brake hard and the car jolts.

'Fucking hell, Steph! Are you trying to kill us?' Darcie shrieks playfully.

A burst of Darcie's laughter cuts through the car – that throaty, confident sound that always draws people in. Abi joins in immediately, like she always has since they were eleven years old at Milton Hall. I glance in the rear-view mirror and catch Ruby's eye-roll. The older sister who's seen it all before.

Bomb the Bass is playing and Darcie starts humming along to it. Then we all join in dancing and throwing silly shapes. 'Everybody in the street...'

'Remember when your dad caught us smoking behind the chapel?' Abi asks Darcie, wiping tears of laughter from her eyes. 'We thought we were the business, with our mini ghetto-blaster blaring out the tunes. What were we thinking with our little rave-up?'

'He made me copy out Bible verses for a week,' Darcie says. 'Ruby got away with murder though – perfect daughter who could do no wrong.'

Ruby stiffens slightly.

'Someone had to keep them happy.'

The temperature in the car seems to drop a few degrees.

I've seen this dynamic play out a hundred times – Darcie performing, Abi her devoted audience, Ruby watching from the sidelines with that mix of protectiveness and exasperation. But there's something else there too, something darker underneath all that shared history.

When Abi's alone, without Darcie's spotlight to reflect in, she's different. Quieter. More thoughtful. But right now she's already laughing at Darcie's next joke, before she's even finished telling it.

A sign for Avignon: 35 km. The views on both sides are staggering. I slow down as we drive through a small village and have to stop at a set of temporary traffic lights. It's just as I had always imagined a sleepy, Provençal village would look. Roofs of rust-coloured terracotta tiles and bleached white walls. Pastel-coloured shutters closed against the heat of the late morning. An old man with a leathery face, flat cap, is shuffling along the pavement with two heavy wicker shopping baskets. A grey cat dozes in the sunshine on a doorstop. A woman in a headscarf cycles past on a black bicycle with a basket attached to the handlebars. There's even a little church over to my right. I think it's Romanesque in style. I did some kind of module on church architecture at uni, but I can't remember much. Romanesque churches have a telltale rounded arch at the front whereas Gothic churches have a pointed arch. *Crikey, I didn't know that was stored away in the dusty recesses of my memory.*

And then the lights change to green and I pull away.

I'm hit with a twinge of anxiety. What if people don't enjoy themselves? What if the farmhouse is a big disappointment? It's my trip, my birthday and so my responsibility.

Stop being so silly and enjoy yourself.

We try to go away at least once a year. It started when we all turned forty and went to Ibiza. That was our first girls' holiday. I love how we just fall back into that easy friendship and patter. It doesn't matter how long we've been apart.

'Remember this?' Ruby reaches forward to turn up the car stereo as the Verve's 'Bittersweet Symphony' fills the car.

'Urban Hymns tour, '98,' Abi says immediately. 'Remember queuing outside Brixton Academy in the rain?'

'That was before your time, Steph,' Darcie says, and there's that slight edge to her voice – the one that sometimes creeps in when she's reminding me I wasn't there for their glory days.

I force a smile, though something tightens in my chest. Even all this time, there are moments when I still feel like the new girl. The outsider who joined their story halfway through.

'Pretty sure I was already at the firm by then,' I say to Ruby. 'Remember that hellish corporate takeover? Us practically living in the office?'

'God yes,' Ruby laughs. 'You saved my sanity that month. Unlike some people' – she shoots a look at Darcie – 'who were too busy stealing their best friend's boyfriend.'

Abi suddenly becomes very interested in her phone.

'Ancient history,' Darcie says breezily, but I catch Katie's eye in the mirror. I know she's thinking about her own history too – the carefully constructed marriage to Justin, the beautiful wedding in Thailand we'd all flown out for. The façade that had finally cracked last year when she'd told us that she was gay and always had been as she'd fought back tears.

The string section of 'Bittersweet Symphony' swells, and for a moment we're all lost in our own versions of the past.

'Are we nearly there yet, Mum?' calls out a voice in a silly, childlike tone.

It's Darcie.

I chortle. 'Nearly. Don't worry, darling, I'll wake you up when we get there,' I say, playing along.

'Thanks, Mum.'

In the rear-view mirror, I spot Darcie's grinning face. But I notice that as she glances over at Katie, it changes to a strange expression that I can't quite read. At a guess, I'd say that Darcie looks guilty, even upset.

THREE
RUBY

Ruby tries to drag her wheeled designer suitcase up the stony path to the farmhouse. It's impossible. It keeps catching on the stones. *For fuck's sake! This cost a fortune!* Maybe it's because she's so tired, but she's not even sure that she wants to be here. It's hot and she's feeling menopausal. Plus there's a swimming pool, so Ruby is already starting to dread wearing a swimming costume in front of the others. They're all so horribly slim. They have personal trainers, do hot yoga, run half-marathons, blah blah blah. And two of them have had eating disorders in the past.

Ruby's suitcase catches on a stone with a crack. *Bollocks.*

'Lift it up, you silly cow,' Darcie yells from behind her.

Ruby bristles, takes a breath and ignores Darcie. *My sister is so loud and irritating.*

She's nearly three years older than her sister, Darcie. And to say that they're chalk and cheese would be an understatement. Ruby has always been the sensible, smart and responsible one. Classic traits of the first-born child.

Darcie was a bit of a teenager tearaway – booze, drugs, sex. Clichés of the second-born and youngest.

'Jesus, it's hot,' Katie sighs as they reach the front door. 'Not that I'm complaining, just that it's hard to know if I'm having a hot flush or it's the sodding weather.'

'Oh, to be a woman, eh?' Ruby jokes.

'It's all right,' Katie scoffs. 'I read an article about the male menopause the other day. Anxiety, depression, low sex drive, irritability.'

'Isn't that just being middle-aged?' Ruby sighs.

'Exactly. It's enough to turn you gay,' Katie jokes with a wry smile.

Ruby laughs. It's lunchtime and the temperature has hit mid-thirties Celsius. She can feel the sweat on the top of her lip and on the back of her neck. *This place had better have air-conditioning. I'm sure Steph said there was.*

Menopause has hit Ruby hard. Hot flushes, hair loss, broken sleep, irritability. It's a total nightmare. Katie told her that HRT has literally saved her life, but Ruby isn't sure she wants to go down that route. Pumping herself full of oestrogen is just delaying the course of nature. She is trying herbal remedies instead which have helped a little.

Steph uses the code on a key box and opens the front door to the farmhouse. Ruby already longs to be sitting in her air-conditioned office on the eighteenth floor of a building that overlooks the Thames close to St Paul's Cathedral.

Her phone buzzes – another email from Singapore needs immediate attention. She shifts on the hot stone step, the familiar tension creeping into her shoulders. A multibillion-dollar merger waits for no one, not even on holiday.

'You're not working, surely?' Steph asks, wheeling her suitcase into the generous hallway.

'Just checking my flight's confirmed for next week. Hong Kong this time.' Ruby tries to sound casual about it, like first-class lounges and five-star hotels haven't become her real home. Better than the echoing mansion in Hampstead, anyway.

Her phone pings again.

NIGEL:

> Running low on coffee. Can you order some?

She stares at the message. Three weeks since she's actually seen her husband, though they've shared the same house. He'll be on the golf course now, like always, while she's here trying to remember why they ever got married. These days, they communicate mainly through grocery lists and utility bills, two strangers orchestrating their careful dance of avoidance.

'You okay?' Steph asks gently, noticing something in her expression.

Ruby forces a smile. 'Fine. Just tired.' The same answer she gives everyone lately, easier than admitting the truth: that she's spent fifteen years building a perfect career to escape a perfectly dead marriage. That she can't remember the last time she and Nigel even sat in the same room together, let alone shared a bed.

Bédoin in Provence? What were they doing here, anyway? This place was famous as a stop on the Tour de France. They don't cycle. It's one of Steph's little plans to desperately keep her friendship group together.

For a moment, Ruby stops to peer at the farmhouse they're going to be staying in. The honey-coloured stone walls. The creeper and ivy entwined in wooden trellises. The terracotta-coloured slates on the roof. *To be fair, it does look nice*, she admits. *Maybe this weekend won't be quite as awful as I'm expecting it to be.*

FOUR
SHAUN

Shaun steps back from the wall to inspect his handiwork. *Not too shabby, fella.* Second coat of paint. He has been renovating a small holiday cottage in Bédoin whilst living in it for nearly two months. He loves it. There's a strong smell of paint, but he's used to it by now. 'My Honest Face' by the band Inhaler is playing from his Spotify on a small Bluetooth speaker. He loves them. They're from his hometown. Dublin. The lead singer is Bono's son. But Shaun thinks Bono is a bit of prick. There's a joke in Dublin. 'What's the difference between God and Bono? God doesn't walk the streets of Dublin thinking he's Bono.' Genius.

It's nearly midday and the heat in the first-floor bedroom is intense. Shaun takes his white vest and dabs the sweat from his face. He blows out his cheeks and checks his phone. Tom is arriving today. The agency told him to expect him around lunchtime. They've never met. Shaun hopes he's not a feckin' eejit.

There's also a new intake of guests due to arrive across the road. He gazes out of the window. The countryside is a beauty. Stunning. *Better than feckin' Parkview, that's for sure.*

Home is originally Ballymun, Dublin. A rough inner-city area at the northern edge of Northside.

Shaun is employed by a London-based employment agency who find people who are willing to live and work in locations around Europe. Fruit picking, renovations, nannies. The cottage is owned by Simon and Jennifer Barnes, a wealthy couple from Fulham who had bought it as another investment and holiday rental. They just need it to be renovated. The Barneses already owned a luxury farmhouse rental with a swimming pool directly opposite the cottage where Shaun is working and pay him a weekly retainer to do any maintenance, shopping, repairs, washing and generally keep an eye on the place. As far as Shaun is concerned, he's living his best life.

He glances at his phone: 11.55 a.m. The party of guests are due to arrive any minute now. Shaun doesn't have much information. Five women celebrating a fiftieth birthday or something. He'll get them to fill out the relevant forms when they arrive.

There are definite pros and cons to looking after a luxury farmhouse in Provence. It is so expensive that there is rarely any trouble. But the guests always reek of money. And that makes them very demanding. A right feckin' dose. Shaun has to be patient and smile even if he wants to lamp them.

There's a sound outside. A car arriving at the farmhouse. Shaun goes over to the window to check out the new guests. If it's a fiftieth birthday, he's not holding out much hope that there'll be anyone worth bagging. He's just turned thirty.

A white Mercedes pulls up slowly and then turns right. There's a shaded car parking space. He'll give them ten minutes to settle then make an appearance. It's a shame they've arrived. Shaun's been cooling off in the farmhouse pool for the past two days as it's been empty. Then he gets a little twinkle in his eye. *Maybe the older ladies won't mind a bit of me in their pool?*

Shaun drove over to Avignon in his van the day before to

pick up the guests' order for food and booze. Nothing unusual, really. Breads, cured meats, local *Banon* and *brousse du Rove* cheeses, artichokes, olives, vine tomatoes and so on. And enough fizz and rosé to sink a ship.

Out of the corner of his eye, Shaun spots a small car parked just up the road. It's a Fiat 500. It looks like a rental car. The driver is sitting inside. *Maybe they're lost,* he concludes as he turns away.

He takes a quick shower. He's not going over there smelling all manky. Then he grabs a white V-neck T-shirt which shows off his tan perfectly. Blue shorts and black slides. He combs his coal-black hair in the small mirror in the unrenovated bathroom. The bathroom is the next job. That's why Tom is arriving. To give him a hand.

Shaun gives himself a wink at his reflection. *Lookin' sweet, fella.*

He marches downstairs and strolls across the road to meet the new guests.

'Hello? Hello?' he calls out in a chirpy tone as he enters through the front door. The hallway is lovely and cool. He came over to the farmhouse two hours ago to put the air-conditioning on full blast for their arrival. What he'd give for some air-conditioning across the road in the cottage. Sometimes it feels hotter than Kabul.

'Hi,' says a small woman with brunette hair pulled back in a ponytail. She has those big seventies-style sunglasses up on her head and beautiful chestnut-coloured eyes. She gives him a lovely smile which lights up her face.

Fair play. She's all right.

Shaun gives her his best sexy smile. 'Stephanie?' he asks.

'Yes. Well, Steph,' she says with a little laugh. 'Shaun? Is that right?' Her face crimples a little as she squints at him. It's cute. And she's got long eyelashes. Maybe false but they look great.

'Yes, yes,' he replies. 'Journey okay?'

'Fine. No problem.' They walk down to the huge kitchen and living space. 'This place is fantastic,' she chirps enthusiastically.

'Oh, good. I'm really glad you like it,' Shaun says, catching himself using his best, polite voice. *If only the lads back home could hear me talk like this,* he chortles to himself.

Another woman is walking around holding up her iPhone. 'I can't seem to get the Wi-Fi,' she says in an incredibly posh voice. She's wearing a navy designer baseball cap, tight T-shirt and grey joggers. Her Gucci sunglasses are hanging on the neckline of her T-shirt. She clearly looks after herself. But she's definitely had work done on her face. Shaun doesn't know what. Not really his area of expertise. Botox, fillers, lift, whatever. The skin around her eyes and mouth just looks a bit weird.

Shaun frowns. 'Should be okay. It comes up as "Château Cardou Guest",' he explained.

'Château?' the woman snorts pompously. 'It's hardly a château, is it?'

Snooty bitch.

'I've found it, Darcie,' Steph says as she points to her phone.

Jaysus, they've not even bothered to look around yet. Straight on the phone.

Darcie looks at Shaun and raises a haughty, manicured eyebrow. 'Password,' she asks snootily.

Why don't you click yer wee fingers at me too, yer stuck-up hoor?

'Sorry?' Shaun replies. He knows exactly what Darcie is asking for. The Wi-Fi password for the farmhouse. But he isn't prepared to dignify her rudeness with an answer.

'It's fine,' calls over a voice.

An attractive woman in a flowing summer dress saunters in.

'It's fine. I've got it,' she says, waving the information booklet that explains in detail everything about the farmhouse, how things work, where rubbish and recycling goes, taxis and so on. 'It's all in here, guys.'

'Thanks, Rubes,' Steph says with a smile.

Darcie waltzes over and points to the booklet. 'Can you show me?'

'Jesus, Darcie,' says a woman who has just come in from the double doors that lead out to the patio and pool. She has blonde hair, fair skin and green eyes. 'Nothing is going to happen if you don't have Wi-Fi for two minutes.' She laughs, but Darcie isn't listening.

'The pool is out through there,' Shaun explains. 'I can heat it if you need, but to be honest, it doesn't need it this time of year. And I'll be over every couple of days to test the water for you.'

'Thank you,' Steph says. 'What's it like out there, Katie?'

'Lovely,' Katie says, but she seems distracted.

'So, everything is in that folder,' Shaun says. 'But I live just across the road in the small cottage.' He looks directly at Steph. 'Anything you need, please don't hesitate to ask. I drive into Avignon everything other day so it's no bother to pick stuff up. Just ask.'

'Aw, isn't he a sweety,' Darcie says as she peers over at him. Shaun can't work out if she's being sarcastic or not. 'I love the Irish accent. It's very sexy, isn't it?'

What the hell is she doing? he wonders. He'd forgotten that there are women out there like this. Overtly flirtatious, needing to seduce every man they meet, as if it is a competitive sport.

Shaun shrugs. 'Not for me to say.'

A woman with red, curly hair comes down the stairs. She's diminutive, wearing a turquoise bathing suit. A large white towel is draped over her shoulder.

'Right, who's up for a swim right now?' she says in a cheery voice. Then she spots Shaun and looks a little embarrassed. 'Oh, I didn't know anyone was here.'

'Abi, this is Shaun,' Steph says.

'Hi.' He averts his eyes. His presence has clearly made her feel self-conscious about being in a bathing suit. 'I hear you guys are climbing up the mountain tomorrow?'

Steph nods. 'That's the plan.'

'Is it quite easy?' Ruby asks. She sounds concerned.

Shaun smirks. 'Erm, I wouldn't describe hiking up there as easy. It's called "the Beast of Provence" for a reason. But if you leave nice and early, take plenty of water and take it steady, you'll be fine.'

'Bloody hell, Ruby.' Darcie shakes her head and gives her a withering look. 'We're not a bunch of pensioners quite yet. We climbed up Snowdon and that was okay.'

Shaun shrugs. 'It's no harder than that. You'll be fine.'

'But it's very windy, isn't it?' Ruby says as she pops herself on one of the chrome stools by the enormous breakfast bar.

'Why do you think it's called Mont Ventoux?' Darcie scoffs. 'The windy mountain.'

'Actually, that's not why it's called Mont Ventoux,' Shaun explains, happy to put Darcie in her place and make her appear foolish. 'It comes from the ancient god Vintur. A Celtic tribe lived in this area, called the Albiques.' Darcie shoots Shaun a sceptical look. 'Don't worry,' he reassures her. 'Lots of tourists make that mistake.' He watches Darcie take a breath. She's clearly not used to being corrected or patronised. Then Shaun looks over at Ruby. 'And the famous mistral winds that you're referring to? Legend has it that these violent winds are Vintur's son having a wild tantrum. And if you climb to the top of the mountain with a dark secret that you've kept to yourself, the noise of the howling wind will drive you insane. Le vent qui rend fou. And then you'll throw yourself from the top of the mountain.' He laughs. 'But I'm sure that's a load of old French blarney.'

'Well, you're a barrel of laughs,' Darcie snorts derisively. 'Any more lovely local tales of madness and death?'

'Hey, I like hearing all the local legends and history,' Steph protests.

'Me too,' Ruby agrees.

Shaun ignores Darcie. *She's still salty because I corrected her about the name of the mountain.*

'I might stay by the pool,' Ruby grumbles.

FIVE
STEPH

Now

I can see her lying there. Motionless. Her body twisted against a rock, the trees towering above us. I can't bear to look.

The ridge down to where she's positioned is steep and treacherous. No wonder she fell so far.

I stare at Tom and Shaun.

This can't be happening.

Shaun is on his phone speaking in French to someone.

This was meant to be a perfect long weekend away for all of us. My head is a whirl of thoughts. Did she stumble and fall? Why isn't she moving? She has to be unconscious, doesn't she? Then I fear the worst. The thought makes me feel physically sick.

It's my fault. It was my idea to hike up this sodding mountain. And now this...

Shaun ends the call. 'Mountain rescue are on their way, but they've told me they could be a long time because of the fires. The emergency services are being swamped by calls.'

'We can't just leave her down there,' I say. There's a lump in my throat. I'm going to cry. My pulse is hammering, my stomach tight and knotted.

'Usually they'd bring up a helicopter,' Shaun explained. 'But the smoke and the wind means that visibility is too poor and it's dangerous.'

I burst into floods of tears.

'Hey, it's okay.' Tom takes a step towards me and puts his arms around me. 'Shaun and I will find a way of getting down to her. She's probably just banged her head in the fall. That's all.' He's trying to reassure me.

Shaun jogs to the road and flags down a passing pickup truck. He waves at us.

'This guy's got some rope we can use,' Shaun shouts.

'Grand,' Tom says.

Tom and I rush over as the motorist – a rugged man in his sixties – retrieves a coil of thick rope from the back of his truck.

I glance at my phone and try calling the others. No reply. God, the anxiety is unbearable.

The man reverses his truck to the edge of the road where the steep slope begins. Shaun ties one end of the rope to the steel tow bar while the man helps secure it.

'I can't believe this is happening,' I mumble, fighting tears.

'It's okay,' Tom reassures me. 'We're going to get to her.'

'Anything I can do?' I ask.

Tom shakes his head. 'No, we've got this.'

Shaun loops the rope around Tom's waist. They're going to use the truck to lower him down the slope.

I peer down the ridge. I can't see her face properly because of that baseball cap. God, she's just not moving. I pray she's only knocked herself unconscious. That we'll have drinks tomorrow and laugh about this.

Shaun speaks in French to the driver, who starts the engine. Tom goes backwards over the edge of the slope as Shaun helps guide the rope.

'Slowly does it, lad,' Shaun says.

Tom makes his way down the ridge until he's only yards from where she's lying. He looks up at me with a reassuring nod before taking the final few steps to reach her.

I hold my breath.

Tom crouches down, touches her face. He frowns and blinks. I don't like the way he's reacted.

With his two fingers, Tom goes to feel for a pulse just below her ear.

Then he stops for a second.

Oh God, no. Please.

My whole body tenses.

'What is it?' Shaun shouts down.

Tom looks up at us with a dark expression. He gives a little shake of his head.

For a moment, I don't want to believe what he's telling us. But I know from his expression and from the shake of his head what he means.

She's dead.

SIX
DARCIE

31 July 2022

This mirror is perfect, Darcie thinks to herself. She's put on her white Hunza G designer two-piece and checks herself in the full-length mirror in the bedroom. *Not many fifty-year-olds can pull off a bikini like this,* she reassures herself. And for a few seconds, she actually feels proud of her figure in the reflection. It's an unusual feeling for her.

Darcie has bagsied the only bedroom with a full-length mirror. That's what matters to her. Not the view, not the size of the room or even the bespoke en-suite bathroom. No. Her 1.7 million followers will be expecting regular posts of her in various outfits from her luxury holiday in Provence. And so will the companies that she has endorsement deals with. So, the full-length mirror is a deal-breaker. And none of the others really seem to care.

As Darcie continues to look at her reflection, she suddenly feels repulsed by what she sees. Her stomach is podgy for starters. *How do certain women my age get washboard stomachs?* Former Spice Girl Mel C has a body to die for and she's fifty! Then Darcie makes a resolution. More sits-ups, planks and yoga. No carbs. Then she turns to the side. *Has my bum sagged overnight? For fuck's sake.* More squats. She's recently researched the surgery to give her a bum lift and implant. About £8,000 to have it done properly in London. A BBL – a Brazilian butt lift. Darcie has always assumed that it was called this because all the beautiful women who roamed the Copacabana beach in Rio de Janeiro had perfect rounded buttocks. Apparently that's not the case. It's named after Dr Ivo Pitanguy, a famous plastic surgeon from Brazil who developed the surgery. Who knew? Darcie would never consider going abroad to have it done cheaper. She's heard too many horror stories. In fact, she is pretty sure that several British women have actually died after doing that.

Popping on her Gucci sunglasses, Darcie pouts her lips and gives the mirror her best sultry look. Then flash. A mirror selfie with something pithy and witty about her first swim of the holiday, along with a mention of the Hunza G and Gucci brands that she is wearing.

Darcie gazes out of the window and lets out an audible sigh. Everyone is just sitting around the pool relaxing – reading, listening to music, sunbathing. Katie is swimming lengths of the pool, of course. But Darcie doesn't want to sit and do nothing. She feels restless.

Why do I get so bored and uncomfortable in my own company?

It's a question that has plagued Darcie for decades. She can't think of anything worse than sitting still, with her own thoughts, with herself. She knows it's not normal. The inability to be still. Be quiet. Be in the moment. Maybe she has ADHD – the restlessness, the constant need for stimulation, the way her thoughts scatter like startled birds. She's read about it late at night, recognising herself in every symptom, but something stops her from seeking diagnosis. Easier to keep running than to look too closely at why she can't be still.

Taking her hammam towel, Gucci sunglasses and gifted DeMellier beach bag, Darcie goes out of the bedroom, down the stairs and out towards the pool. If she's honest, she isn't particularly impressed with the farmhouse. The decor is all a bit obvious. Clichéd. A beginner's guide to French shabby chic. And the pool is a bit old and tired around the edges. Darcie is used to beautiful, azure infinity pools at bespoke million-pound villas in the hills of Ibiza. Before she and Hugo, her loser of a husband, had hit their 'rocky patch', they'd had a plan to have a villa built in Ibiza. It's been shelved. She has no intention of spending time with Hugo anywhere while he's a barely functioning alcoholic.

Grabbing a sunbed, Darcie moves it so that it's directly in the sun. She knows the sunshine ages her skin, but there's nothing like a golden tan. Especially when you're posting photos of yourself in a white bikini.

For a few minutes, Darcie closes her eyes against the glare. *Breathe in, hold, out. Just like the therapist taught you.* But the sun burns red through her eyelids and suddenly she's back in her kitchen, evening light bleeding across the tiles, that moment when the air changed and—

Her eyes snap open. Her fingernails have left half-moons in her palms. The taste of metal floods her mouth as if the knife is there again, pressed against her throat, the wool of his balaclava scratching her cheek, the whisper of his breath—

'How's Bella doing, Darcie?'

Steph's voice yanks her back to the present, to safety. But her heart still hammers against her ribs. Darcie takes a second to gather herself before sitting up and putting on a bright voice.

'You know. Twenty-one and knows everything,' she groans. 'Still reading Economics at Bath.' Darcie is actually very proud of her daughter, but it's not really tactful to brag. Especially to someone who doesn't have kids. She catches herself reaching for her phone – her thumb automatically finding the photo she took last month, Bella asleep on their sofa, textbooks scattered around her like fallen leaves. Just like when she was little, that same tiny frown of concentration, that same loose dark curl falling across her cheek.

Darcie swallows hard, locks the screen before anyone notices. Even now, watching Bella sleep makes her chest ache with that fierce, frightening love that started the moment they placed her daughter in her arms.

'Does she like it?' Steph asks curiously, her book resting on her lap.

Darcie can't always work out Steph's agenda or even if she has one. She seems like an open book on the surface. But that makes Darcie feel wary. What would it be like to just not have an agenda?

She studies Steph for a few seconds. There is a fine line between being confident and comfortable in your own skin – and being a pompous arse.

'I think so,' Darcie replies with a shrug. 'I don't really get to see her that much. She's got a boyfriend. They stay down in Bath for a lot of the holidays. But I'm happy that she's getting on with her own life.' Even as she says this, she senses her words feel and sound hollow.

What she just said isn't strictly true. She isn't happy about her relationship with her only child. In fact, she and Bella seem to have grown apart in recent years. Darcie pushes away the memory, but it comes anyway: Bella standing in their pristine kitchen three weeks ago, her university essays spread across the marble island where Darcie films her cooking reels. 'God, Mum, do you have to document everything? My friends follow you as a joke – they call you "Desperate Darcie".' The way Bella's voice caught between contempt and pity. 'You do know that's what everyone thinks, right? That you're just... embarrassingly vacuous?' The words still burn. Darcie had kept filming that day, her hands shaking as she measured ingredients into her favourite Le Creuset bowl, posting three perfect stories before crying in her walk-in wardrobe where no one could hear. Two hundred thousand likes, and her daughter couldn't stand to be in the same room with her. But she pastes on her influencer smile for Steph.

'Of course,' Steph replies with a polite smile. 'Growing up.'

They fall into an awkward silence for a moment then Steph picks up her book and Darcie pulls her shades on before lowering herself onto the sunbed.

Darcie feels sorry for Steph. No kids. No husband. Steph would be mortified if she knew Darcie pitied her. It doesn't make any sense to Darcie. Steph is attractive. Very attractive. She is funny. Granted she is a bit wet and straitlaced sometimes. A bit wishy-washy. But she has a good career. Top lawyer at a huge international charity. Owns her own flat in Clapham which has to be worth a cool £500,000 in today's market. But Steph has never found 'the one'. And she seems to have given up. The years of potentially having children have passed her by.

Picking up her phone, Darcie holds it up to take a selfie on the sunlounger. It's all about high angles. Never low angles. The best is high and slightly left. Lead with a cheekbone as if it's been drawn to the camera by a thread. Look directly into the camera. Pout the lips but not so you'd notice. If you can, leave a tiny gap between the lips at the centre so a tiny fleck of tooth is showing. Apparently very sexy. It's called the 'keyhole pout'. See Angelina Jolie, Scarlett Johansson and Kylie Jenner. *And* it can be done, like her bum, surgically. Darcie is also considering having this done permanently.

'Feeding the machine?' Steph says as she glances over.

'Something like that,' Darcie replies with a fake laugh.

Don't judge me, she thinks angrily.

'And what about you, Steph?' Darcie asks with a tiny hint of forced pity. 'Anyone special in your life at the moment?'

Darcie knows there isn't anyone significant, otherwise all the others would have been texting about it. It would be such major news if Steph had found a man whom she didn't think was 'a freak' or 'a sociopath'. Darcie thinks there is something distinctly strange about a woman like Steph who is single but also so incredibly fussy and cuttingly negative about every man she meets. Steph is definitely scared of something. Maybe commitment or intimacy.

Steph laughs. 'Oh, I've accepted that I'm going to be alone forever. But at least my body will provide food for my two cats.' She grins wickedly at her. 'Because it's going to take a good few months before anyone finds me.'

Darcie laughs, recognising the practised lightness in Steph's dark humour. But before she can probe deeper, her phone buzzes, and the moment breaks.

She sees it's a text message from Detective Inspector Darren Baker from Notting Hill CID. Her mouth goes dry and her pulse quickens. He's the officer in charge of her ongoing stalker case. It's been going on for nearly three terrifying years now.

'Are you all right, gorgeous?' says a voice from behind her.

It's Katie. She comes over and sits down on the end of Darcie's sunlounger.

Darcie catches herself staring at Katie's pretty, symmetrical face. 'Hey,' she says with a smile.

'I haven't even talked to you properly yet,' Katie says. Then she puts on a silly American accent as she gently prods Darcie's forearm. 'So, tell me, what's going on with you?'

Darcie laughs, her skin prickling with familiar awareness.

'Not a lot really,' she says. 'My publisher has asked me to write them another book, which is nice.'

'Nice?' Katie exclaims. 'That's fantastic.'

Darcie can't help but feel delighted by Katie's reaction.

'I love that bracelet,' she says, pointing to the delicate jewellery on Katie's wrist.

'Christmas present from Sophie,' Katie explains. 'What about Hugo?' she asks with a tone that implies she dislikes him intently.

'Usual trainwreck.' Darcie shrugs. 'But he just won't help himself.'

Katie shrugs back. 'Kick him out.'

Darcie narrows her eyes. She knows how much Katie cares about her, but she doesn't seem to understand the complexity of her marriage.

'It's not as simple as that,' she sighs.

'It is from where I'm sitting. He's a drunken leach,' Katie snipes. 'You deserve so much better. It breaks my heart to see how you are at home when he's there. You're just not yourself.'

'I know, I know,' Darcie sighs and reaches out to take Katie's hand. 'And it's so sweet of you to care so much.'

Katie looks at her. 'You know I'd do anything for you.' Then she smiles. 'Kick him out and I'll move in to keep you company if you're worried about being lonely.'

'Now, that would be fun,' Darcie laughs. 'I'm hoping Hugo is just going to drink himself to death very soon.'

Katie holds up her fingers that are crossed as she raises an eyebrow. 'Anyone mention that a journalist has been digging around and asking questions about him?'

'There are always journalists digging around,' Darcie snorts. 'They never find anything. Hugo's not interesting enough to have any dark secrets.'

Katie gives her a quizzical frown.

But then Darcie remembers why she's holding her phone and her expression completely changes.

'Everything all right?' Katie asks, her voice etched with concern. *She can read me like a book.*

Darcie pulls a face to indicate that everything isn't quite right and then gestures to her phone. 'Text message from the police. It's just thrown me a bit.'

'What does it say?'

'I haven't read it properly yet,' Darcie admits. 'I'll take a look later.'

The stalking had started on Instagram three years ago. It ended with a man in a mask waltzing into her flat and holding a knife to her throat. Patrick Brennan. Although she isn't sure that's even his real name. The police told her that he is using a whole range of aliases. Most of the threats had been online to start with. He'd used the handle @DarcieMillerRIP. Strange accusations, death threats, suicide threats. Darcie wasn't easily scared but it had totally freaked her out. The letters, tweets, Instagram DMs and Facebook messages had then progressed to his appearing at her front door and in her back garden. Brennan always wore a balaclava so Darcie didn't even know what he looked like.

For a few seconds, she is transported back to a warm summer's night a year ago. Darcie was happily cooking, drinking wine and singing to music in their south London home. The back door was open. Suddenly she was aware that someone was standing behind her. She froze in utter terror. As she turned, to her horror she saw a man in a balaclava holding a knife. He pulled her roughly by the hair. Putting her in a neck lock, he held the knife to her throat. She could feel the cold metal of the knife against her skin. He pushed it so hard that she was convinced he was going to slit her throat. She was going to die. Her whole body shook violently, her heart hammering against her chest. In that moment, Darcie struggled but knew he was going to kill her. Images from her life flashed across her mind. She could smell his sweat. Then the man just let her go, turned and left through the back door. She had no idea why.

Darcie collapsed onto the kitchen floor and sobbed. She called for Hugo, but he'd drunk himself unconscious on the sofa.

Katie puts a reassuring hand on Darcie's foot. 'I don't know how you've kept it all together so well.'

'I haven't,' Darcie admits. 'Trust me, there have been some very dark days.'

What Darcie hasn't admitted to anyone is how dark. That there have been times when she's thought about ending it all.

SEVEN

SHAUN

'Seventeen Going Under' hammers through the cottage, Sam Fender's voice bouncing off bare walls as Shaun lines up the chrome switch plate. His hands know what they're doing – they've done this since he was a wee lad nicking tools from sites around Ballymun. The wiring in here isn't half as bad as he'd thought. Just needed someone with the right touch, like.

You're a bright lad, why don't you use that head of yours? His da's voice, thick with drink, echoes somewhere in the back of his mind. Shaun's fingers tighten on the screwdriver. The old bastard's voice crawls into his head uninvited.

The screw slips, scratching the chrome.

'Feckin' hell,' he mutters, forcing his grip to loosen. Patience, that's what you need with electrics. Something his da never had, unless it was patience for holding a grudge.

'Hello?' calls a voice. 'Anyone about?'

It makes Shaun jump out of his skin.

He turns to see a man, early thirties, coming up the stairs with a large rucksack on his back. His hooded blue eyes are twinkling. Very short, sandy-coloured hair, fair skin and broad shoulders.

'Jaysus!' Shaun exclaims with a startled laugh. 'You scared the shite outta me!'

'Oh, sorry, mate,' the young man says pulling an apologetic face. He has a Cockney accent which Shaun is trying to place. 'Front door was open. I heard the music.'

'Tom?' Shaun asks as he wipes his sweaty hands on his jeans and goes to shake his hand.

'Yeah. You Shaun?' Tom asks to clarify.

'I'm trying to place your accent,' Shaun says with a frown. 'Londoner?'

'Sort of. Watford,' Tom replies as he takes the heavy rucksack from his shoulder. 'You sound like you're from Dublin?'

Shaun nods. He's impressed that Tom has recognised it. 'Up on the Northside. Ballymun to be precise.'

He can see from Tom's face that he doesn't know about Ballymun's nefarious reputation. 'I've been on a couple of stag dos. But we stuck to the centre,' he admits.

'So, your email said you've been in London?'

Tom nods. 'I was in Kilburn for a bit. Then Camden.'

'What were you doing?'

'This and that.' Tom shrugs and then grins. 'Ducking and diving, fucking and skiving, as the saying goes.'

Shaun laughs and shakes his head. 'I don't know London really. I've got an auntie in Shepherd's Bush, but I've never been.'

'You're not missing much. London is full of people up their own arses, if you know what I mean.'

Shaun gestures over to the farmhouse. 'Yeah, we've just got a load in about an hour ago. Five women.'

'Oh yeah?' Tom gives Shaun a knowing look.

Shaun shakes his head. 'All old enough to be your ma.'

I'll take my chances,' he jokes.

Even from where Shaun is standing, he can smell booze on Tom.

'You've been on the lash?' Shaun asks, trying to make it casual.

'Couple of pints at the airport,' Tom reassures him as he stands back and looks around the room. 'I can see why they've asked me out here. Lots to do.'

Shaun nodded. 'And no feckin' air-con... Come on, I'll show you where to put your gear and give you the grand tour.'

They go out of the room, onto the landing and head towards one of the bedrooms where Tom will sleep. The floors are just bare paint-splattered boards at the moment. They creak a little under their feet.

'This is you,' Shaun says and then sees that he's left his .22 rifle over in the corner of the room. He's used it to do a bit of hunting in the dense forest that covers the foothills of Mont Ventoux. Nothing big like. Just hares and rabbits. His uncle Liam used to take him out of Dublin when he was a kid and they'd go shooting down in County Kildare. It had been a blissful escape from the dreary and sometimes scary life in Ballymun.

'Looks like a .22 to me,' Tom says as he gestures to the rifle. 'Browning, bolt action.'

Shaun raises his eyebrow. He's impressed. 'You know your guns then?'

Tom pulls up the sleeve of his T-shirt to reveal an intricate regimental tattoo. A large cannon with a crown on top and a scroll of Latin writing underneath.

'Royal Artillery?' Shaun asks.

Tom points. '*Ubique* and *Quo fas et gloria ducunt.*'

Shaun nods. 'Everywhere. Where right and Glory lead.'

'Blimey.' Tom raises a quizzical eyebrow. 'You served?'

'Two tours. Royal Irish Rangers,' Shaun says with a smile and points. 'I've got my tattoo on my back.'

'When did you leave?' Tom asks.

'2018,' Shaun explains. He doesn't like to talk about his time in the Rangers. He still carries around the demons of what happened during his two tours of Afghanistan.

'You guys were in Helmand, weren't you?' Tom says.

Shaun gives him a dark nod and pulls up his T-shirt. He has three thick shrapnel scars across his stomach. 'IED in 2011. We lost our sergeant in the attack. He was sitting next to me in the APC. You?'

'We helped with the evacuation of Kabul,' Tom replied. 'I'm glad we didn't have to go to Helmand.'

Shaun nods and then takes a breath. He can sense that recalling his time in Helmand is affecting his PTSD. His pulse has quickened and his breathing is shallow.

'I'll let you get your stuff sorted then,' he says. 'You hungry?'

Tom nods. 'Yeah, starving.'

'No bother. Come down the kitchen when you're ready.' Shaun wanders away and walks slowly down the stairs. What he hasn't told Tom is that while he was in Helmand he took a life. Killed a Taliban soldier who was no more than a teenage boy with his bare hands during a fire fight. His rifle was out of ammunition. The boy raised his Kalashnikov to shoot him, but it jammed. And then Shaun was on him, hands around his throat, choking the life out of him.

It's not something to boast about or even mention. Taking a person's life is a dark place from where there is no escape. It just never leaves you. A profound change somewhere deep inside that damages your soul forever. Shaun can still see the boy's terrified face as he struggled to breathe and survive. For a split second after the boy went limp, Shaun had felt it – that surge of savage triumph, that animal thrill of survival. His hands still locked around the boy's throat, heart hammering victory drums against his ribs. *I'm alive, I'm alive, I'm alive*.

Then he'd looked down at his trembling fingers, at the

marks they'd left in young flesh, and the shame had crashed over him like napalm. That moment of primal joy would haunt him more than the killing itself.

EIGHT
RUBY

Ruby glances up the big old-fashioned clock that sits on the wall of the enormous kitchen. 4 p.m. Steph is pottering around, getting out all the ingredients for dinner later and starting to prep. Ruby has offered to help her, but Steph is being vague. Classic Steph! She doesn't really want any help, but she'll ask Ruby to chop something just to make her feel involved. Steph's a loveable control freak.

Ruby glances around the kitchen. The work surfaces are black, rolled marble. There are wooden cabinets and shelves that carry orange-coloured Le Creuset pots and pans. A large black pot is packed full of wooden cooking utensils. There is an American-style double-doored fridge with an ice-maker and filtered cold water facility. And naturally, there's a state-of-the-art coffee machine with a packet of fresh coffee beside it as part of their welcome pack from the owners, along with local cheese, biscuits, red wine and chocolate.

The air-con means that the interior of the villa is lovely and cool. Steph goes over to the Bluetooth speaker, turns it on and then looks at her phone. The opening refrain of the song 'Mysterons' by Portishead from their seminal nineties album *Dummy* begins to play.

'Oh wow,' Ruby says with delight. 'I haven't heard this for ages.'

'It takes me right back,' Steph says as she twirls around the kitchen. 'That little flat we had in Clapham South. Do you remember it?'

'Jesus, it was tiny,' Ruby laughs. 'I think I smoked a pack of Marlboro Lights every day. And drank like a bloody fish.'

'We all did,' Steph says as they're both taken back to a completely different lifetime. 'You were the first person I ever knew that got a mobile phone.'

'Yes, that Motorola that flipped open and had a little aerial,' Ruby chirped happily.

Steph goes over to the fridge, gets out a few things and brings them over to the large wooden breakfast bar where Ruby is standing.

'And we were desperate to be living an episode of *Sex and the City*,' Steph recalls with a smirk. 'Except we didn't have the money.'

'That's right,' Ruby snorts. 'You were Carrie, of course.'

'And you were Miranda,' Steph says.

Ruby pulls a face. 'Yeah, the boring lawyer one.'

'Not at all,' Steph remonstrates as she goes and fetches a heavy-looking wooden chopping board. 'Katie was Charlotte.'

'And Darcie was Samantha Jones,' they both say in unison and then roar with laughter.

'Of course she was!' Ruby howl.

Steph's phone vibrates with a text. Ruby watches her as she goes over and looks at the phone. Her expression is thoughtful as she reads the screen.

'At the risk of being nosy,' Ruby says, '… anything interesting?'

Steph gives her a wry smile. 'You mean is it a man?'

Ruby arches an eyebrow. 'Is it?'

Steph nods unenthusiastically. 'Mark. Rich, very handsome, kind, owns his own publishing business. Divorced but gets on with his ex-wife. Two grown-up children. Funny.'

Ruby narrows her eyes. 'Erm, he sounds too good to be true.'

'He is,' Steph admits.

'So, what's the problem?' Ruby asks, feeling frustrated. It doesn't take a world-class psychotherapist to work out that Steph is terrified of actually having a meaningful relationship. Instead, she's attracted to unavailable men like François, a slimy fifty-five-year-old French advertising director, who Steph had had a toxic on-off affair with for the past fifteen years. They'd meet and have sex about five or six times a year, with François declaring his undying love and promising to leave his wife and kids. And then he'd just go off radar until the next time.

Steph shrugged with a helpless expression. 'I don't know. There's just no spark.'

Ruby rolls her eyes. 'I'm pretty sure you've said that about the last ten men you've been on dates with. What are you scared of?'

'I don't know,' Steph mutters, looking flustered. 'Can we change the subject?'

'Sorry,' Ruby apologises. 'I just think you deserve to be with someone really nice.'

There are a few seconds of silence.

Steph's expression changes as if she wants to broach something serious. She lowers her voice and glances around her before she says, 'Has Darcie said anything about Hugo?'

'Apart from he's a drunk and a waste of space, no,' Ruby sighs. 'Why?'

'Don't tell her, but I had a message from a journalist asking me if Hugo had ever been accused of sexually inappropriate behaviour or of making sexual comments when he was working at our company,' Steph explains.

Ruby raises her eyebrow. 'And had he?'

Steph flinches as she nods. 'Yes. But I don't think that's a huge surprise, is it? He's got an ego the size of planet. He used to think he was untouchable back in the day.'

'Was this journalist running an exposé on Hugo?' Ruby asks, dropping her voice to a virtual whisper. *What a bastard.*

'I don't know. He didn't elaborate and I said that I wasn't prepared to talk to him,' Steph says anxiously. 'Should I tell her?'

Ruby shakes her head. 'No. If you didn't say anything, there's no point.'

'Oh, what are you two gossiping about like schoolgirls?' Darcie asks as she swans into the kitchen with Abi.

'Just reminiscing, that's all,' Steph replies a bit too brightly, turning to open the fridge.

Ruby hates the way everyone has to watch what they say and appease her sister in case she reacts. If Darcie is in one of her moods, everyone has to walk on eggshells, and she's definitely getting worse the older she gets.

'I've started to read your book, Darcie,' Steph says enthusiastically as she starts to chop the garlic.

Here we go.

'It's great. Really great,' Steph says encouragingly. 'So funny.'

Ruby ignores all this and goes over to Steph. 'Right. I can't stand here and watch you do everything. Give me something to do.'

Steph points at some red onions. 'Chop up those as finely as you can.'

Ruby gives a salute. 'Right away, chef.' Darcie is hovering by the large kitchen island.

'Yes, my publisher was so pleased with the reviews,' Darcie says. 'I had a great one in the *Times*.'

'What did you think of it, Ruby?' Steph asks as she crushes another clove of garlic with the back of a knife.

There's an awkward silence.

'My sister hasn't bothered to read it,' Darcie snaps. 'Have you, Ruby?'

'No... But I hardly have any time to read and when I do, I prefer fiction. I like a good murder,' Ruby replies caustically.

'What the hell is that meant to mean?' The words slice through the air between them.

'Do you want me to cut all the onions?' Ruby asks, keen not to get into it. She needs to ignore Darcie and her ego as much as she can if she's going to survive the weekend.

'Please,' Steph says with a smile as she starts to finely chop the chives.

Darcie fixes Ruby with an icy stare. She can feel her sister's eyes burrowing into her.

Ignore her. Don't bite, she tells herself as she focuses on chopping the onions.

'What the hell does that mean?' Darcie repeats loudly.

Ruby doesn't look up. 'I'm not going to talk to you when you're like this, Darcie.'

'Sorry,' Darcie snarls. 'When I'm like what?'

'Guys,' Steph says with an imploring expression.

They fall into an awkward silence, while Portishead's 'Strangers' plays over the speaker.

Darcie storms over. 'I won't have you ignore me! What did you mean by that?'

'Oh, Jesus, Darcie. You are such a fucking drama queen.' Ruby sighs in the kind of withering tone that she knows pushes her little sister's buttons. Putting down the knife, she moves her eyes to meet Darcie's glare. Unlike most people, she's not scared of her. Darcie's her younger sibling.

'Come on, Darcie. Half the stuff in the book is made-up.

And the other half is embellished,' Ruby states calmly. 'But that's fine.'

'You wouldn't know, would you?' Darcie virtually spits out her words. 'You haven't even read it!'

'Please, guys,' Steph says again. 'Let's try not to do this here. We've only just arrived.'

But Ruby is now on the warpath. She's made the decision to confront Darcie and she's not going to back down.

'I don't need to read it!' Ruby shouted. 'Half of the people I know have for me! *Oh, your sister's book is hilarious. Isn't she clever and witty?* Yes, she is. But she's also a deluded fantasist.'

Steph makes a T shape with her hands. 'Whoa. Sisters, time-out please.'

'Oh, fuck off, Ruby!' Darcie yells.

'Right,' Steph says loudly, her voice cracking. She's upset as she puts up her hands in a dismissive way. 'Please, can you take this outside. It's not fair.'

Ruby feels bad. She doesn't want to upset Steph. She glances at Darcie and nods towards the double doors that lead out to the patio and then the pool.

Darcie rolls her eyes like a child.

Ruby follows her sister outside. It reminds her of when their mother used to send them outside when they argued. But that was over forty years ago!

Darcie goes to speak, but Ruby gets in first. 'I've read the reviews. I've had people coming up to me at work and asking about our parents and our childhood. You made it up.' Ruby taps her temple with her forefinger. 'That's fucked up, Darcie. Don't you get it? Dad's still alive. And you've portrayed our childhood like we were in some terrible cult.'

'We were,' Darcie protests. 'Just because we went to the church down the road, doesn't mean that Mum and Dad didn't treat us as if we were in a bloody cult. Dad rang the school because we were studying *The Picture of Dorian Grey* for Alevel Lit and it was by Oscar Wilde who was gay. You bought me the single "Victims" by Culture Club for Christmas and Dad put it in the bin! They were fucking Nazis, Ruby.'

'They weren't Nazis. They were just strict and Christian,' Ruby protests, but even as she says it, the memory ambushes her: their father's face twisted with fury that night they'd snuck out to a house party. Darcie, reeking of cigarettes and cheap vodka, defiant until he grabbed her by her clothes and shook her. The sound of her sister's bedroom door slamming, those racking sobs that Ruby had pretended not to hear.

Darcie shakes her head angrily. 'No. I refuse to accept that. We all know the Philip Larkin poem. *They fuck you up, your mum and dad.* Larkin got that spot-on.'

Ruby frowns at her sister. 'You do understand what the word *hypocrisy* means, don't you?' she says sharply.

'What the hell are you talking about?'

Ruby's jaw tightens as she thinks of Darcie's latest performance – all concerned daughter at their father's house, helping him sort through Mum's clothes five years too late. The same father she'd sworn she'd never forgive, whose name she wouldn't even let her daughter say. Now suddenly she's there every weekend. Each visit ending with another cheque, another transfer, another piece of their inheritance carved away.

The worst part is how easily he falls for it. Their battle-axe of a father, reduced to this grey, hollow man who'll buy anything that feels like love. And Darcie knows exactly what she's doing – she always has. Even at their mother's funeral, she'd known which buttons to push, which wounds to press.

'You've got Dad to pay for Bella's university tuition fees for starters,' Ruby says angrily. 'He paid for her flight to America last summer. And he bought her a car. I've not had a penny from him.'

'That's because you don't go to see him,' Darcie says, narrowing her eyes.

'And why don't you think I go and see him?' Ruby asks.

Darcie doesn't respond.

'You know why,' Ruby continues, feeling herself getting agitated. 'He's a cold, manipulative bastard. He's never going to change. And when Mum died, he told us that it was "God's will" and that we didn't need to get upset because she was now in the arms of the Lord. He didn't even cry at her bloody funeral!'

'I know. I was there,' Darcie snaps. 'You think I don't know what kind of person he is?'

'What, so you're creeping around Dad, even though you detest him, to tap him up for his money?' Ruby asks, taking a breath to control her growing fury. 'What's wrong with you?'

'He owes me!' Darcie shouts. 'He owes me because of the damage he did.'

'But you don't even need the money, Darcie!' Ruby exclaims. 'You and Hugo are loaded. So, why go and see him? Why try and get his money?'

'It's compensation, Ruby,' Darcie snaps. 'Emotional compensation.'

Ruby narrows her eyes. 'I bet he doesn't have a clue what you've written in your book about him and Mum. I'm pretty sure he wouldn't be handing out the cash left, right and centre for you and your kids if he knew.'

Darcie screws up her face angrily. 'What? And you're going to tell him, are you?'

Ruby shrugs. She has no intention of telling their father, but she wants to hurt Darcie. 'Maybe.'

Darcie grits her teeth. 'Do it then.'

'Okay.'

'But if you do say anything, I'll kill you.'

Ruby watches as Darcie turns and storms off towards the pool.

NINE
DARCIE

An hour later, Darcie sprawls across her king-size bed, one hand clutching her third glass of Prosecco. She's still fuming. Ruby's words play on loop in her mind as she tries to calm her breathing. Once she's checked her social media and finished posting on Instagram, she'll try to do a meditation from one of the apps she's paid to promote. The problem is she finds meditation very difficult. The internal chatter in her head often just doesn't stop so the lovely Canadian man with his soothing voice might as well be speaking underwater. She'll start counting breaths only to surface twenty minutes later, more anxious than before, having absorbed nothing but the final instruction to wiggle her extremities.

Not that her followers need to know that. Tomorrow she'll orchestrate the perfect wellness scene by the pool: designer activewear carefully arranged, sunrise lighting calculated, meditation app conspicuously displayed. She'll film herself flowing through yoga poses, then edit out the wobbles and speed up the footage. Caption it with something about 'finding her centre' and tag her sponsorships. The comments will flood in, praising her authenticity, her dedication to mindfulness. Darcie takes another long sip of Prosecco, a bitter smile playing at her lips. The irony isn't lost on her.

For a moment, Darcie remembers the text message from the police in Notting Hill. Then she banishes it from her mind and instead checks her bikini posts from earlier. *650 likes and 95 comments. I'll take that.* Then she takes out the white Zara designer dress and gifted Soru statement necklace that she's going to wear to the evening birthday meal by the pool. Maybe she'll wash her hair and go for a mermaid hair look? And Oran designer sandals. That will be part of her evening post. Mixing high street and designer. Maybe a few tips about how to pack light for a summer holiday. Or a recommendation for a summer destination thriller.

There's a quiet knock at the door.

'Hello?' Darcie says in a sing-song voice.

'Hello? Hello?' Katie says as she opens the door slowly. Then she gives Darcie a concerned expression. 'Are you okay? Abi said that you and Ruby had a horrible row earlier? I didn't hear it because I had my headphones on by the pool.'

'It's fine,' Darcie says with a shrug. 'Just sister stuff. We'll be the best of friends later. Don't worry.'

'Okay,' Katie says and then pulls Darcie into a hug. Darcie feels the tension in her body start to melt away.

As Darcie squeezes Katie back, she can feel her eyes fill with tears. Ruby's words, along with the recollections of their childhood, seem to have stirred up her emotions.

'Oh God,' Darcie says, taking a step back and wiping her eyes. 'Sorry.'

'What are you apologising for, silly?' Katie shakes her head, goes over to the bedside table, takes a couple of tissues from a box and returns. 'Here you go.'

'Thanks,' Darcie says with a sniff as she dabs at her eyes.

Katie looks at Darcie with a quizzical expression. 'Are *we* okay?' she asks.

Darcie nods, a beat too quickly. 'Yeah, of course.' Then she frowns. 'Aren't we?'

'Of course,' Katie snorts, her laugh a little too loud. 'More than okay.'

They hug again and Katie kisses Darcie on the cheek.

'I'm not sure what I would have done without you this last year,' Darcie whispers. She can feel her chest heave with emotion.

'It's okay,' Katie reassures her. 'I'm here for you. Anytime. It's just—'

There's another knock at the door and Abi peers in.

'Oh, sorry,' Abi laughs. 'Not interrupting anything, am I?' she jokes.

Katie lets go of Darcie. 'She's just a bit upset, that's all.'

'Yeah, well, you've been through a lot of crap recently,' Abi says. 'And your sister can be a bit of cow sometimes.'

'She means well,' Darcie says and then gives them a knowing shrug. 'Most of the time.'

They all laugh. Ruby has always had a reputation for being a bit bossy. And Darcie enjoys the mocking laughter at her sister's expense after their row. She can't believe that her sister actually threatened to tell their father that Darcie was manipulating him for money. What's wrong with her? It's none of her business anyway.

'I get the feeling sometimes that Ruby doesn't want to be with us when we go on these trips,' Katie says.

'I think she just likes to use them as a power trip,' Darcie groans.

Katie gets up and heads for the door. 'I'm going to grab some fizz.'

'I'll see you down by the pool in ten minutes,' Darcie says as her phone rings. The caller ID comes up as *Notting Hill police station*. Her pulse instantly speeds up and her stomach tenses. She takes a breath.

Her thumb hovers over 'decline'. Let them leave another useless voicemail about 'investigating' the stalker while he's still out there, still watching Darcie and her family. She jabs the red button and tosses the phone onto her bed. Not this weekend. Not one more second of her time.

She spots Abi hovering by the bedroom door, clearly wanting to talk. Darcie snatches up her phone. 'Right, I'd better get a few shots of this outfit to post.' She wants Abi to go so she can get on with it. She doesn't want an audience while she takes photos for her Instagram page.

'I thought we could do that thing we talked about a few months ago,' Abi says a little tentatively.

I'd forgotten all about that.

When Darcie and Abi had been horribly drunk and high on cocaine in the hospitality area of Glastonbury, Darcie had suggested that Abi should start her own online presence. She claimed she had lots to post about. For starters, she was a founding member of her local wild swimming club, the Bromley Blue Tits. Abi had pestered her about helping her a couple of times since Glastonbury. Darcie completely regretted ever mentioning it, but she was off her face and she and Abi were having such a great time.

I'm going to have to try and let her down gently.

'Yeah, I've been thinking about that,' Darcie says. 'You're so busy, Abs. It takes so much work and there are no guarantees.'

Abi frowns. 'You said you'd help me. You said that you'd use your name to promote my page.' She lowers her head, looking crestfallen. 'I don't understand.'

Darcie forces her grimace into something more friendly. 'Thing is, my agent has told me that I can't just go around endorsing other people's online presence just like that. I'm a brand. So I have to be very careful who I support.'

Abi takes a visible breath. She's clearly angry. 'But I'm not just anyone, am I? I'm your best friend.'

'I know,' Darcie says apologetically. 'But...'

Abi shakes her head in disbelief. 'So you're not going to help me?'

'Sorry, I don't think I can,' Darcie says, feeling a bit guilty. She doesn't want to upset Abi. 'Don't hate me, Abs.'

'Oh, fuck off, Darcie,' Abi growls as she heads for the door.

Darcie sits down on the bed and sighs. *She'll get over it.* Darcie resolves not to make anyone any promises when she's off her face on booze and drugs.

Just as she's about to get up to begin taking photos, her phone rings again.

Notting Hill police station.

'For fuck's sake.' She sighs frustratedly.

Fuck it.

She hits the reply button in annoyance. 'Yes?' she says in an irritated voice.

'Is that Darcie?' asks a male voice that she recognises.

'Yes.'

'It's DI Darren Baker from Notting Hill CID,' he explains.

'Hello, Darren. I'm on holiday. Is this important?' she asks with growing anxiety.

'I sent you an email and a couple of text messages. I explained that I needed to speak to you urgently?' Darren says with a questioning tone.

'I've just told you,' Darcie says. 'I'm on holiday.'

'Okay,' Darren says.

'Why do you need to speak to me so urgently?' Darcie asked. His tone is making her feel uneasy.

'It's Patrick Brennan,' Daniel says.

Oh God.

She feels sick at the very mention of his name. Her stomach turns.

'What is it?' she asks, dreading whatever Darren is about to tell her.

'We've had a report from emergency services in Bethnal Green,' Darren explains. 'Officers attended a fire last night in the garden of the property that we have as Patrick Brennan's current address.'

'A fire?' Darcie is wondering how this is relevant and why he's called her.

'A garden shed was set alight,' Darren continues.

Jesus! What the hell is he telling me this for?

'And the remains of a body were found inside.'

What?

Darcie starts to leap forward in the hope that it's him. That fucking monstrous freak.

'Is it Brennan?' she says, hardly daring to ask the question.

'We think so,' Darren replies.

'Oh my God,' Darcie exclaims, trying to process his answer. She doesn't want to allow herself to believe that he's dead. It's too much to hope for.

'The body was badly damaged in the fire so identification will have to be made with dental records or DNA,' Darren explains. 'But there are various things in the shed and the surrounding area that lead us to believe that it's Brennan. Plus there was a note left in the kitchen which we believe is in his handwriting.'

'A suicide note?'

'I haven't seen it,' Darren admits. 'But yes, I'm led to believe that it was some kind of suicide note.'

Silence.

Darcie is so overwhelmed by what Darren has told her that she's lost for words for a moment.

'Darcie?' Darren says eventually.

'Yes. Sorry,' she whispers.

'As I said, we can't make a positive identification of the body without more evidence,' Darren says. 'But there is a strong chance that Patrick Brennan killed himself last night in a fire at his address. And I wanted to let you know.'

Darcie sinks into the bed, the phone shaking in her hand. After all this time, could she finally be free?

TEN

STEPH

I check that everything is in order in the kitchen. Glancing up at the clock, I see that it's 7 p.m. on the dot. I told the girls that dinner would be at 7.30 p.m. They're all either getting ready upstairs or sitting down by the pool. That's how I like it. I like cooking on my own. No one getting under my feet or distracting me. Nice glass of rosé with a cube of ice. Everything under control. The chopping boards, knives and plates are all perfectly symmetrical. I feel uncomfortable unless everything is neat and ordered. I know that might be weird, but it's just how I am.

'I love this song,' Katie says as she comes in.

'Feel The Need' by Anita Baker is playing.

My plan to have the kitchen to myself hasn't lasted long, but I don't mind.

Katie's wearing a beautiful turquoise maxi dress. Her lovely blonde hair has been curled so that the tresses fall onto her shoulders.

Wow, she looks incredible.

'Gosh, Katie,' I say with a sigh. 'You look stunning.'

'Aw, thanks.' Katie laughs a little self-consciously. 'Oh, this old thing,' she jokes, pointing to her new Matteau dress. She told me at the airport that she'd bought it from Harvey Nichols especially for the holiday. A present to herself.

I'm so pleased to see Katie happy. Coming out hasn't been an easy road – even after she'd hinted at questioning things a few years back, it still took her until last year to come out. She had a husband, Justin, and two grown-up children, Max and Sophie. None of them had a clue. Justin has actually been very supportive of Katie. He admitted that he knew something hadn't been right between them for a long time but assumed that she was having an affair when they stopped sleeping together. He said that it was a relief that Katie had been struggling with her sexuality rather than cheating on him.

'I'm serious,' I say to Katie and then raise my eyebrow. 'If I was gay, I'd definitely go for you.'

Katie gives a booming laugh. 'Sure you can't be tempted?'

'Nope,' I giggle. 'I am strickily dickily.'

'Well, you wouldn't be the first straight woman I've turned,' she says with a tone of mock bravado. 'I reckon most of you are curious at least.'

I shake my head, but it makes me think for a second.

'What is that amazing smell?' Katie asks as she breezes around the kitchen.

'Garlic, onions, rosemary, lemon, chicken,' I say as I go over to the steel pan that's just browning off and crisping the chicken thighs.

Katie follows me over. 'Wow, they look amazing. How did you do them?'

'I just slow roasted them in the oven. Now I'm browning them off with butter and a dash of local olive oil to stop the butter from burning. And a glass of white wine.'

Katie shakes her head. 'You're such an incredible chef, Steph. You should open your own restaurant. We've been telling you that for years.'

I shrug with slight embarrassment, but her words are music to my ears. I take such pride in my cooking. 'I've got my granny Dot to thank for that,' I explain. 'When I was growing up, I used to spend most weekends staying at hers. We'd cook together. She'd play me all her favourite Elvis or Dean Martin songs and we'd sing along. It was bliss. We were so close. I used to fantasise that I lived with her all the time and not at home.'

Katie looks at me thoughtfully. 'You didn't really get on with your parents, did you?'

'No, not really,' I admit sadly.

'Do you see them or speak to them much?' Katie asks.

'Phone call every month or two. I pop in for a few hours at Christmas. That's it.' I feel a twinge of loss at the reality of my relationship with my parents.

Katie can see that I look a little upset. 'What are we having then?' she asks, changing the subject.

'Chicken Provençal. And a green salad with local goat's cheese, sliced grapes and walnuts. Not too much dressing,' I say, still feeling saddened by our previous conversation. 'And I've got some crusty baguettes that I'm warming up in the oven.'

'Very rustic. Sounds perfect,' Katie says, looking impressed.

'Parfait.' I laugh, thinking how lucky I am to have friends like these. As the saying goes: 'Friends are God's apology for families.'

'When I saw the chicken thighs earlier, I thought you were cooking coq au vin,' Katie explains.

'No. No cock tonight, Katie,' I giggle childishly.

'No cock ever,' Katie chortles.

'What are you two witches cackling about?' calls a loud voice.

Darcie waltzes in. She's wearing a lovely white summer dress. I think it looks like Zara.

'Wow, Darcie. You look amazing,' Katie says, going over to her and touches her forearm.

'Katie was just telling me that she's managed to turn a couple of straight women,' I joke.

Darcie snorts. 'Not me. I tried it once a long time ago and it's not for me.'

Katie frowns. 'What? You never told me that!'

'I never told any of you lot,' Darcie laughs. 'Usual story. Too much booze, too much coke. All a bit of blur. Around 2002, I think.'

'Bloody hell, Darcie,' I groan.

'It's not a big deal,' Darcie says with a shrug.

I notice that Katie is bristling and annoyed. She goes over to the table where I've laid out some glasses. Taking one, she goes to the fridge, pours a glass of rosé and heads for the doors outside.

'Think I'll go to the pool and see where the others are,' she says quietly.

Something is definitely up with her.

'Are you okay, Katie?' I ask, trying to catch her eye.

'Yeah, I'm fine,' she replies with a forced laugh and disappears.

'What the hell was that all about?' Darcie asks dismissively.

'No idea,' I admit. 'I was rather hoping you might tell me. Maybe it was me making gay jokes and taking it too far.'

Darcie shakes her head. 'No, it wasn't that.'

I have a thought and, as I've had three glasses of wine this afternoon, I say it out loud without enough thought. 'That time in 2002,' I say to Darcie. 'It wasn't with Katie, was it?'

Darcie's eyes widen and she lets out a huge laugh. 'Katie! God no.'

'Sorry. Stupid question. Ignore me,' I bumble, wishing I'd never said anything now.

Ruby enters wearing white linen trousers and a pink shirt. 'Have you calmed down yet?' she says to Darcie.

'No. Well, not with you,' Darcie snorts. Then she goes over

to Ruby and hugs her. 'Of course I have. I'm sorry. I can be such a cow sometimes.'

'I'm sorry too,' Ruby says gently.

They hold each other for a few seconds which melts my heart.

ELEVEN
RUBY

Ruby uses her fork to cut Steph's birthday cake but pushes the plate to one side and blows out her cheeks. 'Okay, I've officially eaten so much I can hardly move.'

So far, the evening has gone without a hitch. They drank Champagne as the sun set and watched as it cast a deep tangerine haze across the horizon. It had been stunning. There were more obligatory Ibiza chilled sounds. 'All I Need' by Air. They had all reminisced about how they'd met and their wild times in the late nineties and early noughties. Drunken escapades and boys. The air filled with raucous laughter. As the daylight faded, a couple of lights from farmhouses in the distance came on like small smudges on the horizon. The noise of the cicadas had started to dissipate. The air smelled of rosemary and wild garlic. They'd then lit candles and little lanterns and placed them all around where they were sitting.

The food that Steph had prepared was fabulous. Ruby feels a little envious that Steph is such a good cook. She remembers the days when the only dish she could cook was spaghetti carbonara. But that was over twenty years ago.

Abi and Darcie had disappeared and returned with a small

cake, candles, and everyone sang happy birthday. Steph blew out the candles and Katie opened more fizz. Now, Ruby looks around at her oldest friends, all varying degrees of drunk. Her sister, Darcie, is more hammered than she's seen her in a long time. And that's saying something.

'Speech,' Darcie yells at Steph.

Steph shakes her head. 'No. I'm not doing a stupid speech.'

'Don't be such a fucking bore, Steph,' Darcie snaps.

Then Darcie, Katie and Abi start to chant, 'Speech, speech, speech!' like drunken football fans, banging on the table. The cutlery bounces with a clatter.

Steph smiles and gives a shrug. 'Okay, okay,' she says as she stands up and looks at them all.

In her drunkenness, Ruby can't help but be overwhelmed by love for her old friends. They've all been through so much. She glances at Abi and her heart aches, remembering how they'd all shown up day after day when Abi's brother died. No one knew what to say, but they were there. Always there. And that's how it had been through all of it – Katie crying on her kitchen floor during the divorce. Hell, they'd sat in too many hospital waiting rooms together, holding hands through the health scares. Ruby looks around at their familiar faces and thinks, *We're still here. Still standing. Still together.*

'Thank you all for coming,' Steph says, holding her glass of Champagne. 'It really does mean so much to have you all here. You guys are like my family. You *are* my family, actually. I've known you all for over thirty years. Can you believe that? And you've shaped the person that I am today.' She looks a little overwhelmed. 'I think I've drunk too much,' she giggles as she wipes a tear from her eye.

'Awww,' Katie says.

'Anyway,' Steph sighs. 'I love you all so very much. Even if you are a bunch of weirdos. Cheers.'

Everyone says cheers and they clink the lovely crystal Champagne flutes.

'Presents!' Ruby shouts as she gets up and goes over to a series of gift bags that are lined up by the wall.

Steph looks embarrassed again as Ruby hands them to her.

'Open mine first. Open mine first,' Ruby insists, getting excited. She can't wait to see Steph's face when she opens the envelope that she's popped into the gift bag and covered in pink tissue paper.

Steph delves into the bag.

Ruby grins with anticipation as Steph pulls out the envelope.

Steph looks at what's inside. Her jaw drops.

It's exactly the reaction that Ruby wanted.

'Ruby!' Steph gasps in protest.

'What is it?' Katie asks.

Abi leans forward over the table and gestures. 'What does it say, Steph?'

Steph looks at Ruby and shakes her head in disbelief. 'It's two return business class tickets to New York, and three nights at the Four Seasons Hotel.'

'Wow,' Abi gasps. 'That's incredible.'

Ruby clocks that Darcie isn't saying anything. Just glaring at her.

Oh, great. Here we go.

Katie laughs. 'Yeah, thanks, Ruby, for making us all look bad.'

Steph reaches over and touches Ruby's hand. 'I don't know what to say.' She looks overwhelmed.

'Don't bloody cry again,' Darcie groans.

Please, Darcie. Don't cause a scene.

'Yeah, you're setting me off,' Abi sighs as she dabs a tear away with a napkin.

Darcie looks directly at Ruby and gives a slow, deliberate hand clap.

There's an awkward silence.

'Way to go, sis,' Darcie sneers. 'Upstage everyone and make yourself the centre of attention.'

'Darcie,' Abi says in a cautionary tone.

I knew this was coming.

'That's not what I was doing,' Ruby protests. 'And it's very unfair of you to do this. You're making everyone feel uncomfortable, Darcie.'

'Really?' Darcie reaches over, takes a bottle of red wine and pours herself yet another large glass.

'Can we not do this tonight?' Katie groans. 'It's Steph's birthday, for God's sake.'

Darcie looks at them all. 'I'm just saying what you're all thinking. Well, not you, Steph. But sometimes I just get so tired of all this bullshit.'

'What bullshit?' Ruby growls. She's not going to let her sister ruin the evening.

'Steph going on about how much she loves us all. Everyone so bloody happy to be here. Everyone is finger-popping each other's immaculately bleached arseholes,' Darcie says, her voice now slurring. 'It's bullshit. Utter bollocks.' She turns to look at Ruby. 'You don't even want to be here, for fuck's sake, Ruby.' Then she looks at Abi. 'You need to stop crawling up my arsehole and get a life.' She glances at Katie. 'You need to stop feeling sorry for yourself because now you're "gay".' And then she finally turns to Steph. 'And, Steph, darling, the reason we're so special and like a family to you is because you don't have one.'

'Shut the fuck up, Darcie,' Katie snarls.

'For your information, I do want to be here. But I was afraid that this was how the weekend was going to go.' Ruby can feel her blood boiling. 'Yet again. You've drunk too much. You're angry and bitter. You're alienating all of us. And I've no idea why.'

'You think I have the perfect life, do you?' Darcie asks and then swigs her wine.

'I think your capacity for self-pity and an inability for any perspective are astonishing,' Ruby says in a withering tone. 'But given that you pimp yourself, and your family, out, and have done for years, it's not all that surprising that you have no grasp on reality.'

Katie smiles at this.

'What the fuck are you smiling at?' Darcie demands.

'I think she's got a point,' Katie says with a shrug.

'Oh, fuck off, all of you!' Darcie snaps, getting up from the table and looking at them. Her eyes are wild. Her breathing is heavy as if she's about to hyperventilate.

Steph leans forward. 'Are you okay, Darce?'

'No, not really.' She laughs in a fake, unhinged way. 'I had a phone call from Notting Hill police station this afternoon. Apparently Patrick Brennan has killed himself.'

Silence.

'Why didn't you tell us?' Steph asks.

Darcie puts her hands up dramatically. 'I just don't want to talk about it. It's Steph's night. We can talk about it tomorrow.'

She then points to the cottage across the street. 'Right, I'm going over to invite Shaun over here for a drink and to get this party started. Anyone got a problem with that?'

Darcie turns and then waltzes away.

TWELVE

STEPH

Now

I rush forward and crouch down. 'Can you hear me? It's Steph,' I say urgently.

Nothing.

Grabbing her hand, I can feel it's warm. I put my two fingers on her wrist to check for a pulse. Even though I've done the first aider's course at work, I don't really know what I'm doing. I can't feel anything under my fingers, but I'm not medically trained.

I look up at Tom and Shaun in hope. 'She's warm.'

She's definitely still alive. I know she is. My instinct is telling me that she's unconscious.

I reach up and take off her baseball cap. I'm going to perform CPR. I pinch her nose, trying desperately to recall how long to breathe and how many pumps of the chest. My worsening anxiety is preventing me from thinking clearly.

How can this be happening?

My thoughts are just jumping around and I'm unable to focus.

Come on, Steph. Let's do this.

I push against her mouth, feeling her teeth under my fingers, so that her mouth opens. I pull her chin gently up so that her windpipe is straight.

I put the flat of my hand against her forehead. It's still damp from sweat.

I lower my head so that my left ear is just above her mouth.

Please be breathing. Please be breathing.

Nothing.

I hear the first aid trainer's voice in my head. *One rescue breath every five to six seconds.*

I move back, look at her face and pinch her nostrils tight to form a seal. My heart is thumping so hard against my chest that I think it's going to explode. The voice in my head is telling me to keep calm, but I'm terrified.

'Hello? Hello?' says a loud voice in a French accent.

I glance up. A young man in his late twenties in yellow and blue cycling clothes is rushing over from where he's dropped his racing bike to the ground.

'This is your friend?' the man asks me as he looks down at me with a concerned frown.

Why are you interrupting me to ask that? I think angrily.

'Yes,' I reply. I'm still holding her nose closed. I try to ignore him.

'Let me,' he says as he gestures. 'I am a doctor.'

'Okay,' I say gratefully as the young doctor moves in quickly. He uses two fingers to feel for a pulse on her neck just below her ear. Then he places his ear to her chest. 'This is not good,' he seems to mutter to himself.

Then I watch in horror as he starts to breathe slowly into her mouth twice before pumping her chest rhythmically. I try to reassure myself that if he's a doctor, she's now in good hands.

'Allez. Allez,' the young doctor says in frustration as he

moves swiftly up to her mouth again, takes her nose and breathes again.

Then he pumps at her chest.

The young doctor seems agitated as he listens to her chest and then mouth again.

He breathes into her mouth.

I can tell from his expression that he's concerned. The CPR isn't working.

Oh my God! She's not going to make it, I think to myself. My whole body is trembling.

Tom scratches his head nervously and then catches my eye. Shaun puts his hand to his mouth, shakes his head and takes a few steps away.

'Come on,' I whisper as I crouch down and stroke her hair. I can feel that her scalp is still warm under her hair. *How can she be gone?*

The young doctor pumps at her chest again. He looks at me stony-faced.

I heave a desperate sigh. 'Come on, please,' I plead. I keep stroking her hair as if this will help revive her.

Then my hand comes to my mouth as I blink and my eyes fill with tears.

The young doctor sits back down and looks at her for a moment. His eyes move up to meet mine. 'I am sorry. There is nothing more I can do.'

'No, no.' I can barely choke out the words. My body trembles. The pain is unbearable.

Tom comes over, squats down on his haunches and puts a comforting hand on my arm. 'I'm so, so sorry,' he whispers gently.

'You need to keep trying!' I implore the young doctor.

'I am very sorry, but she is gone,' he says very gently.

I'm having an out-of-body experience. Like I'm sitting in the middle of some terrible dream. *This just can't be happening.*

Then I notice that the young doctor is leaning over her, inspecting her neck and touching her skin.

What the hell is he doing? It feels wrong for him to be touching her now.

'What are you doing?' I snap angrily.

He points to her neck. 'Do you know what these are?' he asks.

A series of dark, purple circular marks around her throat that are no bigger than ten-pence pieces.

Shaun comes over and stands by her feet. He peers at what we're all looking at.

'I know what those are,' Shaun admits with a dark, heavy look on his face.

'Yes.' The young doctor nods. 'I think it is from someone's fingers.' He mimes something with his hands that sends a terrible shiver down my spine. I go cold.

The dark bruises are the marks of someone's fingertips.

He's miming someone choking or strangling with his hands.

'No,' I gasp. This is just too much.

Why is he saying that? That's not true. She fell.

'He's right,' Shaun says softly as he gazes over at me.

I'm suddenly disassociating from everything around me. My world is fuzzy and in soft focus. It's as if my brain is trying to protect me from what they're both telling me. I'm going to be sick.

'I'm really sorry, Steph,' Shaun says. 'I saw this when I was in the army. She's been strangled.'

THIRTEEN

SHAUN

31 July 2022

Shaun and Tom have been sitting drinking beers in the back garden, putting the world to rights. They've been trading amusing stories about their time in the army. Shaun told him that he once won a very drunken daffodil-eating competition in the barracks' pub.

Tom chortles and sips from his bottle of beer. 'I was once out on Dartmoor doing marksmen training. We've been hiding in the undergrowth for hours, freezing our bollocks off. We needed to stay there undiscovered to pass the course. This civvy bloke comes out of nowhere, walking along with his sodding labrador. Must have got lost cos we're on MOD land. This dog comes right over to where I'm lying, sniffs me out and gets all frisky. You know, he's shagging my fucking leg to death. And I'm trying to keep still. Meanwhile, my CO is bollocking me for all the movement and rustling. I tell him what's going on and that I'm trying to fight off this frisky dog. And so he says...' Tom does a public school accent. '"Well, Wilkins, put your cock away and leave the poor dog alone. But remember, as your commanding officer I do have first pick of the litter when it arrives." Sarky twat.'

Shaun laughs. He's relieved that he and Tom get on so well.

'One for the frog?' Tom asks as he leans forward on the creaky wooden garden chair and points to the empty bottle of Stella that Shaun is holding.

'Frog and toad,' Shaun says, nodding. 'Cockney rhyming slang?'

'Spot-on,' Tom laughs. 'My old man told me that when they were gonna hang someone over at Tyburn in London, the wagon they were travelling in used to stop at a roadside pub on the way. The prisoners were allowed to have one drink before making the last part of the journey. I guess getting a bit pissed might have made the journey to the gallows a bit easier. And that was "one for the road".'

Shaun smiles. The five bottles of Stella have given him a nice warm glow. 'I like it,' he admits. 'And in answer to your wee question, yes, I'd love another beer, my friend.'

'Great stuff,' Tom says as he disappears into the cottage.

There is silence as Shaun gazes out at the view. Tom has put his playlist on the Bluetooth speaker – 'God's Plan' by Drake. Shaun's not normally a fan of rap or hip-hop, but Tom's playlist is chilled and suits the mood of the evening.

Shaun looks up. The moon seems bigger than usual and it's throwing down a lovely honey-coloured light onto the roof of the cottage. Over to their left – which is west – there are shadowy hills and vineyards. Lights from other cottages and farmhouses are dotted across the vista and twinkle like distant stars. The air smells of lavender and honeysuckle and there is the soft, rhythmic tone of the cicadas.

Shaun likes Tom. He seems like a decent fella with a good sense of humour. Tom has admitted that he's not a real Cockney. He's from a place called Hemel Hempstead, near Watford, which is north of London.

Tom wanders out and hands Shaun a cold beer. 'Here you go, mate. Get that down your Gregory.'

'Nope.' Shaun grins and shakes his head. 'No idea what you just said there.'

'Gregory Peck, neck. Get that beer down your neck,' Tom explains as he sits down on the chair.

Shaun snorts. 'I like that.' Then he gestures to where they're sitting and the garden. 'So, what do you think of this place? Not too shabby, is it?'

'No. Christ, this certainly beats working as a panel beater in the local garage. That was my last job,' Tom says as he looks around the garden. Then he gives Shaun a knowing smirk. 'Although the job did have its perks.'

'Oh yeah. What was that then?' Shaun asks. He's intrigued.

'Sally, the woman that owned the garage, was a right filthy sort,' Tom says, chortling. 'She liked it when I sat and watched while her and her husband, Terry, used to go at it.'

Shaun frowns. *That sounds very weird to me.*

'You'd sit and watch them shagging?' Shaun asks carefully.

'Yeah.' Tom snorts with a booming laugh. Then he mimes masturbation. 'Meanwhile, I'm knocking one out in the corner. Hilarious.'

Yeah, that doesn't sound hilarious. Just creepy, fella.

'Had a bit of falling-out though,' Tom admits. 'I roughed Sally up one night. I thought that's what she wanted. Terry wasn't best pleased so I had to leave the job.'

Tom grins, teeth flashing, waiting for Shaun to share the joke. The silence stretches. Shaun's throat goes dry. Maybe he needs to keep his eye on him going forward.

'You said on the email that you've got a spare road bike?' Tom asks nonchalantly.

'Yeah, that's right,' Shaun nods, welcoming the change of subject, though his neck prickles with unease. 'You a cyclist?'

'Bit, when I was younger,' Tom replies. 'More mountain bike trails and that. But Mont Ventoux is legendary.'

'Aye, it certainly is.'

'Yeah, I've seen it when I was watching the Tour de France on the telly. Half the reason I took this job.'

'Well, if you fancy a ride out tomorrow morning, we can take one of the Tour de France routes up?'

'Tour de France route? Fuck me,' Tom chortles. 'That don't sound easy.'

'Actually, it's not too bad,' Shaun reassures him. 'We'll do about twenty kilometres and then come back.'

'Sounds good to me,' Tom says as he leans over and clinks Shaun's bottle of beer with his. 'Twenty k ain't that far.' Tom gestures with his hand held at an angle. 'It is when the feckin' gradient is like that.'

'Hello?' calls a woman's voice. Her accent is very posh. 'Anyone there? Hellooo?'

Shaun recognises the voice. It's the stuck-up woman from across the way.

Darcie, wasn't it? Like that ballet dancer woman.

Tom gives Shaun an amused look and raises his eyebrow.

Shaun gets up from where he's sitting and sees Darcie tottering down the side of the cottage, glass of red wine in hand.

'Ah, there you are,' Darcie says in a slurred voice. 'Hiding out the back, were you?'

Bloody hell, she's hammered.

'Everything okay?' Shaun asks with a frown.

Darcie peers at Tom who is now standing. 'Oh, hello. I don't know you, do I?'

'This is Tom,' Shaun explains. 'He's just arrived. He's here for a few weeks to help me with the renovation.'

Tom nods a hello.

'Well, hello, Tom,' Darcie says with a drunken grin and then gestures back towards the farmhouse. 'We're having a bit of a party over there. And I wondered if you boys fancied joining us for a bit?'

Shaun gives Tom an amused smile and then shrugs. 'Yeah, sounds grand.'

Tom nods with a wry expression. 'Why not, eh?'

They follow Darcie back down the side of the cottage.

'You'll have to excuse us. We're all a bit past it and drunk,' Darcie says. 'But we still know how to have fun.'

Tom gives Shaun a knowing smirk.

As they step out onto the road, the moon shines full and the farmhouse is lit up. It's a clear night except for a ribbon of cloud behind which the stars have disappeared, as if a shroud has been pulled over them.

Darcie's silk dress catches the moonlight as Shaun's gaze lingers on her figure.

'Well, Darcie, you certainly don't look past it from where I'm standing,' he says in his well-rehearsed flirty voice.

'Oh,' Darcie giggles. 'My mother always warned me about handsome Irishmen with the gift of the blarney.'

Shaun smiles to himself. Darcie seems very different to the uptight snotty woman he met this afternoon. The drink seems to have loosened her up a lot. And she's definitely attractive. If she wants to flirt with him, that's fine. And, in fact, if she wants to take it further than that, why not? Shaun has no ties so casual sex with a MILF would round off the night quite nicely, thank you very much.

Darcie looks back with an inviting smirk. 'I'm going to have to keep my eye on you, aren't I, Shaunie?'

Tom shakes his head, lets out a little laugh and then swigs from his beer as they walk.

As they cut through the farmhouse garden, the sound of nineties dance music fills the air – 'Show Me Love' by Robin S.

The other four women are sitting around the table drinking,

vaping, talking loudly and laughing. There are candles and lanterns dotted around the low walls and patio.

'I found Shaunie,' Darcie announces. 'And, everyone, this is Tom.'

There are lots of hellos and little waves.

'Come and sit down, boys,' Darcie says, pointing at two empty chairs.

Shaun watches Tom as he grins and takes a seat. His first impressions of him have changed. There is something not quite right about him.

It's gone midnight and the booze has been flowing. Shaun has switched to red wine and his head is definitely nicely fuzzy. Darcie has continued to catch his eye, giving him flirty little smiles or coming over and whispering something witty into his ear. Her lips have brushed against his ear. He's enjoying the attention.

The women are now all drunk and their laughter raucous. 'Club Tropicana' by Wham! starts to play and Abi, Katie and Darcie get up to dance on the patio, singing at the top of their voices.

'I love Wham!' Abi shouts as she twirls around.

Shaun finishes his glass of wine and pours himself another.

Over on a small stone wall near the pool, Steph and Tom are deep in conversation. They're sitting very close, and whatever they are talking about, it seems intense. It looks like Steph is pouring her heart out to him.

Oi, oi, Shaun thinks. *What's going on over there?*

He has no idea if Steph is married, but she's definitely attractive for someone who has just turned fifty. Less obvious than Darcie, but she has lovely eyes.

Out of the corner of his eye, Shaun sees Darcie dancing

over to him. She reaches out her hands, takes his and pulls him up. 'Stop being boring and come and dance with us,' she yells.

Shaun looks at Ruby who rolls her eyes at him.

Getting up, Shaun starts to dance with Darcie as they move away from the table.

'Need You Tonight' by INXS starts to play and Darcie uses it as an excuse to dance provocatively in front of Shaun. She backs up into him as her hips gyrate. He puts his arm gently around her waist. She pushes so that she is against him, grinding into his crotch.

Something catches Shaun's eye. A shadow over the box hedge on the far side of the pool. For a moment, it looks like someone is standing behind the hedge, watching them.

What the hell is that?

He peers into the darkness again. The clouds move across the moon above and the light in the garden fades. And so does the figure. It's gone.

Must be a trick of the light or too much red wine, Shaun concludes.

Then Darcie turns, leans close and whispers into Shaun's ear, 'I've got a beautiful view of the night sky from the balcony in my room.' She gives him a knowing look.

Shaun gives her a nod.

She reaches out for his hand and pulls him towards the villa.

Shaun takes another look across the pool. There's definitely no one there.

FOURTEEN
STEPH

1 August 2022

I roll over and wince at the daylight. My head is pounding. Like someone is tightening a vice around my skull.

Grade A hangover.

Then I'm piecing together the night before. The dinner, the drinks, the dancing... and Tom. It's a bit of a blur. *Did we kiss? Did we sleep together? I can't remember.*

I look down and realise that I'm wearing Tom's shirt.

I get a horrible sinking feeling deep in the pit of my stomach. *Fuck.*

My train of thought is interrupted as the door handle turns slowly. Tom appears. He's holding a tray. There's coffee, orange juice and pastries on it.

He's wearing a T-shirt that shows off his muscular physique.

Jesus, why did you have to drink so much, Steph! You idiot!

'Morning, morning,' Tom says in his chirpy Cockney accent and with a little twinkle in his eye.

I squint at him, desperately trying to work out from his face what happened between us. If anything.

'Don't worry,' he laughs as he sets the tray down. 'We didn't sleep together.'

'Really?' I'm relieved. 'What about this?' I ask suspiciously as I look down at his shirt.

'You guys all jumped in the pool,' Tom explains. 'Remember?'

I pull an embarrassed face. 'I don't. Sorry. Oh no.'

Tom hands me an orange juice. 'Here you go.'

'Thanks,' I gasp. My mouth is so dry it feels like sandpaper.

'Then you dragged me in here "to talk",' Tom says with a smirk. 'And you took off your wet dress. But you did keep your underwear on.'

'Oh no!' I'm so embarrassed I bury my face in my hands.

'Hey, you're only fifty once,' Tom says. 'And you guys all really went for it, to be fair. Impressive stuff.'

'Okay,' I groan. 'So then what happened?'

'You tried to kiss me, asked me to sleep with you, and then fell onto the bed,' Tom continues. 'You then took off your bra!'

I give a little squeal of utter humiliation. 'NO!'

'Yes,' Tom laughs. 'So I took off my shirt and made you put it on. And then you pretty much passed out.'

'Where did you sleep?' I ask him.

Tom points to the other side of the bed. 'Just there. You were pretty hammered so I wanted to make sure you weren't sick in your sleep.'

Aw, he's sweet.

'Right,' I mumble, wanting the earth to open up and swallow me. I don't think I've done anything like this since my early thirties. And it strikes me that I haven't really waxed as much as I should have. The thought that I might end up in a bed with a man just hadn't crossed my mind.

'For the record, you snore,' Tom jokes as he sits down on the bed and grabs a coffee and croissant.

'And that was it?' I ask. I want to believe that Tom didn't take advantage of me while I was passed out. My instinct is that he's telling me the truth.

'Scout's honour,' Tom says with a three-fingered salute. 'Actually, I was in the Boy's Brigade.'

'Oh Jesus,' I sigh. 'Sorry.'

'You don't need to be sorry. You guys all seemed to have a great time,' Tom reassures me. 'Sore head?'

'Banging,' I admit.

Tom reaches into his pocket and hands me a blister pack of pills. 'Take two of these. Paracetamol and codeine. It'll get rid of your headache and smooth the edges off your hangover.'

'Thanks,' I say as I pop two out and swallow them with my orange juice.

'Big climb this morning,' he says with a grin.

I give a loud groan. 'Don't remind me.'

Looking at his Apple Watch, he taps it. 'It's 7.30 a.m. Shaun said you guys need to get going before nine at the latest.'

'I just want to stay in bed,' I admit. 'What about Shaun and Darcie?'

'I haven't seen either of them yet.' Tom shrugs and then pulls a face. 'But I'm not a fan of that Darcie. I know she's your mate and everything, but what a snooty bitch. She walks about like her shit don't stink, excuse my language. If she'd spoken to me like she spoke to you lot last night, I'd have given her a slap.'

I bristle. 'I don't slap my friends.'

'Well, maybe you should,' Tom snorts.

That's such a weird thing to say, I think, feeling uncomfortable.

Tom then leans over and gently pushes a strand of my hair from my face. 'Sorry,' he says quietly. 'I shouldn't have said that. I apologise.' He sounds like he means it.

'It's fine,' I reassure him. I don't want there to be an awkward atmosphere in the room.

Then Tom leans in, kisses me softly on the mouth and his words are forgotten.

FIFTEEN

The morning light creeps under her eyelids, and her stomach clenches. Shaun's still breathing deeply beside her, and just the sound of him makes her skin crawl.

Get out, get out, get out.

Her head pounds with the familiar morning-after chorus.

She'd been magnificent last night, though, hadn't she? The way his eyes had followed her across the patio, how his breath had caught when she'd leaned in close. That moment when she'd known – *known* – she had him hooked. Better than any line of coke, that feeling. After that, she's not particularly interested in the actual sex. Not really.

But now... Her therapist's voice echoes: *Let's explore why you need this validation, Darcie. Your fear of true intimacy.* Stupid cow. She'd fired her the next day. What's wrong with wanting to be wanted?

The feeling is addictive, but it's not like she's shooting up in some crack den. She's just... playing the game. Always winning, never letting anyone else set the rules.

The sheet rustles as Shaun shifts in his sleep. She's repulsed by the idea of him. She needs him gone. Now.

'Morning,' Shaun says with a croaky voice as he rolls over onto his back.

Oh God.

Darcie doesn't respond. She just needs him out of there as quickly as possible. His very presence is making her feel anxious. She hopes that he doesn't try to take her in his arms or give her a cuddle.

Keeping her back to him, she sits up on the edge of the bed. Then she reaches for a white cotton bath towel, wraps it around herself and stands. It's so strange that last night, while she was drunk and in the shadows of the bedroom, she was more than happy to be naked with him. Now she can't bear for him to see her naked in the daylight. He feels like a stranger to her.

Please just go away.

'You okay?' Shaun asks as he sits up in the bed.

She hasn't even turned to look at him yet.

'Fine,' she says dismissively. She can't bear to see him. She just wants to click her fingers and for him to disappear.

Go away.

'It wasn't that bad, was it?' Shaun says in a jokey tone.

An awkward silence.

Eventually, she turns her head and meets his confused frown with a detached expression. She wants there to be no misunderstanding about how she feels this morning. 'I'm tired and hungover. But I'm fine.'

'You don't seem fine,' he says as he pushes his fingers through his black unkempt hair. He now has dark stubble on his chin and jawline. 'I thought we had a good time last night. I know I did.'

Oh great, we're going to have some sort of discussion about this. Why can't he just put his clothes on and leave?

Darcie shrugs. 'I just need to have a shower.'

'Great,' Shaun says with a cheeky grin that makes her heart sink. 'Mind if I join you?'

Yuck. I can't think of anything worse.

'No, I don't want you to join me.' She gives a withering sigh. 'I just need you to get dressed and leave. Okay?'

Shaun narrows his eyes. 'Wow. That's pretty cold.'

'We just had sex, Shaun. That's all. We don't have to make a big thing of it, do we?' she says in a condescending tone.

'Yeah, and you seemed to really enjoy it,' Shaun says in bewilderment. And then he gestures to the room as he becomes annoyed. 'And can I just remind you that it was you who gyrated your arse into my crotch and then dragged me up here? So, I don't know why you're acting like such a cold bitch.'

Darcie fixes him with a cool stare. 'What do you want me to do? Roll into your arms this morning, tell you that you were the best shag I've ever had and ask if we can have some beautiful holiday fling this weekend? You weren't that good. Believe me.'

'Jaysus!' Shaun looks angry. 'That's not what you said last night. You seemed to be enjoying yourself all right.'

'I just faked it,' she sneers. 'And I'm sorry if I've damaged your fragile little male ego, but I want you to get dressed and leave right now.'

Shaun's nostrils flare as he goes over to his clothes and begins to pull them on. 'You are a seriously fecked-up lady, you know that?' He taps his forefinger to his temple. He's clearly furious.

Now dressed, Shaun goes to the door but glances back at her angrily. 'I think it's probably best that we don't speak the rest of this weekend.'

Darcie gives him a sarcastic smile. 'Although I will be crushed by that, I had no intention of giving you another thought.'

Shaun goes out of the door and slams it behind him.

Now that he's gone, Darcie is suddenly flooded by self-loathing and emptiness. She has to take a deep breath to steady herself.

Oh God. Why am I so fucked up?

Heading for the en suite, she tries to look at herself in the mirror, but she can't.

She cranks the rainfall shower to its highest setting and steps in, tilting her face up into the scalding spray, letting it sting.

Then everything just feels too much. She slaps the palm of her hand against the tiles of the shower, over and over again, sobbing uncontrollably. *Why do I feel so utterly fucking wretched all the time?*

Darcie lets the hot water flow over her for the next few minutes as she tries to settle the uncomfortable knot in her stomach.

She reminds herself that Brennan is probably dead. She should be pleased by that news. As she turns off the shower, she shakes her head in disbelief. She's completely forgotten what the world feels like without Patrick Brennan in it. A world where there isn't a continual nagging threat of danger. She has wished and prayed for this day for so long, but she had convinced herself that it would never come.

Drying herself, Darcie lets her dark imagination play out Brennan's final moments. The terrible pain of burning to death. The agony he must have felt. *Good. No less than he deserves.*

Darcie laces up her designer trainers. She's clean now. She's managed to wash the smell of that man and last night off her. She stands and looks at herself in the mirror. The terrible emptiness and self-loathing have subsided. The mask of Darcie, the uber successful influencer, is back on. *Phew. Time for a photo and a post.* The middle-aged mummies of London love a post about something like a hike up a mountain. Something a bit outdoorsy. It makes her seem a little more relatable. It's not all posts about fashion, food and exotic locations with an occasional reference to her daughter and hubby.

Checking her DMs on her Instagram account, she sees that

there's a message from someone that follows her. A woman called Jemima.

Hi there. Are you aware that your husband has a terrible reputation for inappropriate behaviour and sexual harassment? My sister just told me she was a runner on a TV show that he was in and said he was a nightmare. Female crew members weren't allowed to be on their own with him!! Don't see you posting about that on here?

Darcie's heart sinks, but this isn't new. There have been rumours about Hugo for the past twenty-five years. He's assured her it was just idiotic behaviour when he was in his twenties, and ancient history. But she's always had her suspicions those rumours are true. And no matter how many years have passed, she knows that kind of predatory behaviour simply can't be buried in the past.

Darcie ignores the message and moves on. She lifts her phone, adjusting the angle: pink Sweaty Betty vest top, black shorts, black Gucci cap, Celine sunglasses. Ruby's voice echoes in her head: *Darcie, there are only three people who could ever pull off wearing sunglasses indoors. Elvis, George Michael and Bono. And you're none of them!* The memory of them both laughing about it makes her chest tight. When did they stop being able to tease each other without drawing blood?

Abi knocks and pokes her head in. 'I just wanted to see how you were doing after the news about Patrick Brennan. How are you feeling?'

'I know I should be happy,' Darcie admits, 'but I don't know how to process it. I feel numb.'

Abi frowns. 'Why?'

'I think I'm just scared that it isn't true.'

'What happened?' Abi asks.

'He set fire to himself in the garden shed.'

'Bloody hell,' Abi says, pulling a horrified face.

'I know. Frankly, I don't care how he died,' Darcie says. 'He left a suicide note. They have to identify the body through DNA, but apparently it's just a formality.' She can feel her eyes filling with tears.

'Hey.' Abi gives her a hug and whispers, 'It's over. This horrible nightmare is now over and you're finally rid of him.'

Darcie grits her teeth with growing anger. 'Do you know how many nights I've been awake fantasising about killing him? I'm glad he died a painful death. I know that sounds horrible, but it makes me happy to think about it. Fuck him. I'll dance on his grave.'

SIXTEEN

'Come on, guys!' Ruby yells from the ground floor of the villa. 'We need to get going. Chop-chop.'

They are meant to be leaving at 9 a.m. for their hike up Mont Ventoux. It's a four-hour walk to the summit and back, so if they're going to avoid the hottest part of the day, which is apparently 2 p.m. onwards, they need to go right now. She is looking forward to seeing the Chapelle Sainte Croix, the small chapel at the summit of the mountain. There has been a chapel on that site since the fifteen hundreds.

Ruby had actually suggested that they leave at 6 a.m. as the sun came up and hike as the sun rose. But the others – well, Darcie and Abi – thought that was way too early.

Ruby walks out onto the patio, sits down on a reclining chair and pops on her sunglasses. She's feeling unsettled about the events of last night. On the surface, the little voice in her head is being all judgemental about Darcie and Steph's behaviour. She just isn't sure how to process watching her sister actively seduce another man in front of her and all her friends last night. She knows that Darcie has never managed to be faithful to Hugo. Deep down, she can't blame her. It's not like

Hugo has ever been faithful to Darcie. In fact, he's been a complete shit to her sister.

She's always been like this. Memories flash: Darcie at seventeen, sneaking back through their bedroom window smelling of cheap vodka and someone else's cologne. At twenty-five, explaining away another 'meaningless fling' with that brittle smile. Now, at fifty, still chasing that high of being wanted, needed, chosen.

'Life's too short to overthink everything, Rubes,' she'd always say, but Ruby remembers the morning-after shadows under her eyes, the way she'd check her phone obsessively, waiting for calls that never came. Their mother's pursed lips, their father's thunderous silences – they'd left marks that no amount of conquest could erase.

And as for Steph! Ruby knows that Tom isn't much younger than Shaun, but Tom is so boyish in comparison to Shaun's manliness. And the whole thing smacks of desperation on Steph's part. Of course, Steph is a bit desperate. She's never had a meaningful relationship. As far as Ruby can remember, she's only ever lived with two men. Jason, who was a pompous prick who moved to New York to be with another woman. And Raheem, who was a total drip. Or as some witty television comic actor once said, 'Wetter than a haddock's bathing suit.' Plus there's something a bit 'off' about Tom. Maybe it's because he's young and not comfortable in his skin. She can't put her finger on it, but there's definitely something phony about the way he acts.

Ruby wonders why either of them would bother hooking up with these men for a night. A nasty little fling when the purpose of this weekend was to spend time with old friends. Not only is it a bit pathetic, it's also rude.

Taking her La Roche-Posay suntan lotion – SPF 50 because she's not vain enough these days to sacrifice getting a tan for skin cancer – Ruby looks out across the neat garden and pool.

Then she tilts her head back to gaze at the azure sky. It's cloudless. Perfect. The sun is beating down on her so Ruby shifts into the shade, too aware of how her clothes dig into places that used to be firm.

Twenty-five years ago, she would have been stretched out in a bikini, soaking up every ounce of sun to get a golden tan. A smattering of freckles on her face and arms. Suddenly she's back there with Ashley, her boyfriend at the time – the late nineties – a talented production designer for television dramas and commercials. Ashley was mixed race and lived in Stockwell, which Ruby thought made both him, and therefore her by proxy, cool and edgy. It makes her cringe to think of that now. And in those summers, they would lie in bed and Ashley would trace his forefinger over her freckles, telling her they were cute, like a constellation of stars. They'd hang out in the Notting Hill Arts Club or go to sweaty club nights in south London. She kept Ashley a secret from her parents. They just wouldn't have approved. They didn't spend all that money on her private education for her to 'shack up' with a mixed race guy with short dreadlocks who smoked marijuana. But that inability to truly rebel against her parents' aspirations for her meant that she and Ashley would never work. So Ruby actively allowed their relationship to fizzle out.

It was soon after that that Ruby met her husband, Nigel. He was the perfect fit. She remembered her parents' faces when she first took him home to meet them. Relief and joy that she'd met a public schoolboy who had been to Oxford and was now a Crown Court barrister. Older than her, mature and well-connected. Ruby's father's expression when Nigel revealed at dinner that his grandfather had been a Conservative peer. Bingo. Ticked every aspirational box for her parents. But Ruby still wonders what her life would have been like had she had the courage to follow her heart and stay with Ashley. Her life would have been completely different. When she looks back, it feels like a 'sliding doors' moment. And it's tinged with regret. Ruby begins to rub the suntan lotion on her arms and legs. She takes a long, deep breath. Nostalgic thoughts have transported her away from the present for a few minutes. Deep down, her disapproval is a defence mechanism against the uncomfortable truth that she is jealous that her friend and sister spent the night having wild sex with two younger men. It's painful for her to accept that neither Shaun nor Tom gave her a second glance. It is as if she was invisible. And that makes her want to cry.

Ruby takes out her phone to check for work emails. There's a relief and comfort in the mundanity of going into work mode. It's a safe space. There would be some people who would scoff at her doing this. She's away for the weekend. Leave it until next week. But she's a partner and that means that the company effectively owns her arse. There are just a few boring emails from her PA reminding her to check a draft contract. Switching to social media, she immediately sees one of Darcie's posts from about ten minutes ago. She ignores it, turns off her phone and looks up at the morning sunshine again.

Hearing raised voices, Ruby's eyes are drawn up to the open shutters on the first floor. Someone's rowing.

'Just fuck off, will you?' shouts a voice. It was Darcie.

Then Ruby sees Steph storming out of a room and slamming the door shut behind her.

It's Darcie's room, she thinks.

Oh, Jesus. What now?

Ruby is surprised to see Steph losing her temper. It almost never happens. That's what makes Steph such an incredibly good lawyer. She's never flustered and never loses her cool. Steph is the glue that holds their group of friends together. And even though she despises the way that Darcie had talked to Steph the night before, Ruby knows that there's an element of truth to what she had said. This friendship group means more to Steph than anyone else. This group is like family to Steph and Ruby knows that her friend is desperately lonely. It's why she wanted to treat her to the NYC getaway. Steph's the one that organised the last three trips abroad.

Out of the corner of her eye, Ruby sees that someone is coming out onto the patio.

It's Steph. She looks upset.

'You okay?' Ruby asks with concern as she sits forward on the reclining chair and takes off her sunglasses.

Steph nods, but her puffy eyes show she's been crying.

'Is my sister being a bitch again?' Ruby sighs.

'Something like that,' Steph mutters. 'I tried to hurry her up and she told me to fuck off. I'm sure she's just tired and hungover. I'm just going to fill my water bottle and grab some snacks for everyone.'

Ruby watches as Steph walks off with slightly drooped shoulders. Even though Darcie was a cow, Steph does sometimes have a bit of a martyr complex about her.

'Morning, morning,' Abi says brightly as she comes out of the farmhouse. 'Have you spoken to Darcie yet?'

'I did knock earlier to speak to her, but there was no reply. I heard the shower on.' Ruby explains. 'I just assumed that she was shacked up with that Shaun.'

'Oh no. She kicked him out a while ago. He didn't look very happy when he left.' Abi pulls a face. 'Darcie is still a bit rattled by the phone call from the police.'

Ruby's pulse quickens. After two years of this nightmare...

'Not surprising. That's why I went to check on her.'

'She's trying to get her head around the fact that he's dead,' Abi says. 'Apparently he set fire to himself in a garden shed so they do have to officially identify the body. Not the way I'd choose to leave this planet, but hey. He's a total psychopath.'

'I know this is horrible, but I'm glad he's dead,' Ruby admits. 'He's made her life a misery for two years.'

'No, I agree. It's not horrible. It's good bloody riddance,' Abi says as she puts on some suncream.

There is a little lull in their conversation. Ruby tilts her head back as a breeze blows across the pool and over the garden. It makes a lovely rippling noise on the water.

'Has Darcie mentioned Hugo at all?' Abi asks.

'Not really.' Ruby shakes her head. 'Just the usual comments about him being a prick and an alcoholic. Why?' She was aware that Steph had already asked her a similar question.

'I had a phone call from a journalist asking me about him,' Abi says.

Ruby raises a quizzical eyebrow, although she suspects that she already knows the answer. 'Asking you what about him?'

'Had he ever been sexually inappropriate towards me or anyone I knew. Or had he made any inappropriate comments,' Abi says.

This was exactly what Steph had told her. It sounded as if this journalist was contacting everyone in Darcie's life to see what dirt he could dig up on Hugo.

'Steph had a very similar conversation with what I'm assuming was the same journalist. What did you tell him?'

Abi shrugs. 'I told him to sod off.'

'Good. Hugo is an arsehole and a bit lechy,' Ruby admits. 'But the last thing Darcie needs is to see her husband and her personal life splashed all over the papers and social media. It would ruin everything she's built up.'

Ruby suddenly feels very protective towards her sister. It's strange how her feelings can fluctuate so much. Siblings might fight and quarrel, but God help anyone who plans to hurt them.

'Oh yes.' Abi pulls a face. 'I hadn't even thought of that. But she'd get cancelled.'

'Definitely,' Ruby agrees, now feeling a little uneasy.

Abi takes her sunglasses off and puts them on the table. 'The thing is, this journalist claimed that he already had someone on record saying that Hugo had shown her his cock and tried to push her into a cupboard at a party at his house.'

Ruby shakes her head. 'Oh shit. Any idea who it is?'

Abi shook her head. 'No idea. But if they run the story, there might be others who come out of the woodwork. Hugo had a bit of a reputation back in the day.'

SEVENTEEN
STEPH

The Mercedes rental's tailgate feels heavier than it should as I hoist my rucksack inside. My hands are still shaking slightly – leftover adrenaline from Darcie's outburst upstairs. *Just breathe. Don't let her get to you.*

Through the front windscreen, I spot her weaving down the path, sunglasses already on despite the early hour.

I busy myself adjusting the straps of my rucksack, making each side perfectly even. It's what I always do when things feel out of control – straighten, organise, align. While Darcie... I flinch at the memory of her voice upstairs, that familiar sharp edge that always comes the morning after she's made another mistake she can't face.

Then I see a small white Fiat 500 parked up outside the cottage. Even though I can't see clearly, I get the distinct impression that the person sitting in the car is looking over in my direction. It might be my imagination, but it feels a little creepy.

I turn back and check that I've packed the bright green first aid box that I found inside the farmhouse. Inside there are lots of plasters, a bandage and some antiseptic cream. I have no intention of taking all of it on my hike, but I thought I'd better put it in just in case any of us have got blisters or cuts when we return to the car. I smile as I realise that I'm yet again acting as the mother of our group. I don't even realise that I'm doing it half the time!

'Hey!' shouts a voice.

I glance over and see Tom and Shaun wheeling their road bikes out onto the road from the cottage. Then I notice that the Fiat which was parked outside has now gone. I reassure myself that it was probably just a tourist who was lost or something equally innocuous.

Shaun is dressed in tight yellow-and-blue cycling gear and wraparound Oakley sunglasses. Tom is in less lycra, thank God. He's got a good body, but there is something unpleasant about any man in too much lycra. Maybe I'm just a bit old-fashioned, but I like to leave something to the imagination. Now I sound like my mother, I realise.

Tom is wearing a navy bandana, sunglasses, tight grey T-shirt and shorts. He looks very cool and *very* fit. I can see his muscular arms, chest and slim waist. I get a flash of us in bed a few hours ago. Tom over me, his hands running through my hair as his body pressed into mine.

Shaun then glances down at the Apple Watch on his wrist. 'You guys need to get going.'

'I know,' I sigh, feeling a little flushed, even embarrassed, by the image I've just conjured in my mind. 'I've tried to hurry them up, but girls will be girls.'

'Well, if you manage to lose Darcie up there, that wouldn't be a bad thing,' Shaun jokes sardonically. But I can tell that he's not joking at all.

'Oh dear.' I pull a face. 'Do I take it that it wasn't all sunshine and roses this morning?' I ask, but I know the answer. I've seen that puzzled, irritated look on Darcie's 'cast-offs' many times before.

'Your friend is a piece of work all right,' Shaun says in a tone that makes me feel a little uneasy. Whatever Darcie said to him, it has made him angry.

'How far are you guys going?' I ask, keen to change the subject. I don't want to try and defend Darcie. In fact, I don't want to talk about Darcie at all, thank you very much. I get irritated that everywhere we go, she becomes the immediate topic of conversation. I might be being childish, but this is *my* birthday celebration weekend.

'It's about twenty klicks from here to the top if we take the classic Tour de France route,' Shaun replies. 'But it's a hell of a climb.'

Tom looks at me. 'Yeah, I'm not looking forward to it. I think my sweat is about 90 per cent proof.'

I laugh – a little too much.

Tom gives me a sexy wink that makes me blush a little. *Wow, a holiday romance. I definitely didn't see that coming.*

Darcie comes out with her rucksack.

'Oh great,' she mutters under her breath when she sees Shaun.

Shaun gives me a sarcastic smile. 'Well, good luck. And remember what I said about your "lovely friend" there.'

Tom laughs, but Shaun's words are laced with menace.

'I'll see you later,' Tom says to me quietly. 'Unless I end up in an ambulance needing oxygen.'

I watch as they swing their legs over their bikes and cycle away. I admire Tom's thick calves as he stands up on his pedals as they go. And of course, his cute arse in those shorts.

'Close your mouth, Steph,' Darcie jokes. 'I can see your tonsils.'

I ignore her. 'I hear that you and Shaun didn't hit it off this morning,' I say.

Darcie's wearing her black baseball cap and big Celine sunglasses so I can't really see much of her face.

'Oh, that.' She snorts dismissively. 'He was just being a bit clingy. I think he was expecting a shag fest this weekend so I put him straight. I don't think he liked it. You know what men are like, especially at that age. All ego.'

I look up and see Ruby, Abi and Katie coming out of the front door.

'Hey hey, let's go!' Katie says with enthusiasm.

Katie is wearing a very similar outfit to Darcie – pink top and black shorts. She spots Darcie and looks down at her clothes. 'Oh God, we're matching, Darce.' She laughs and shakes her head.

'Copycat,' Darcie jokes and opens the passenger seat. 'Right. I call shotgun. Otherwise I think I'm going to be sick.'

'No complaints here,' Katie says in a tone that sounds a bit caustic.

Ruby comes over and waves the front door keys. 'I've locked up.'

Abi opens one of the back doors. 'You okay driving again, Steph?'

'You know me. Bit of a control freak,' I joke. I can't think of anything worse than sitting in the back with someone else driving.

The others get into the back and pull on their seat belts.

'Oh God, I think I'm going to die,' Darcie groans. 'Can I just stay here and lay by the pool?'

'NO!' we all say loudly in unison.

Abi frowns and leans forward to talk to Darcie. 'You need to tell everyone what you told me earlier, Darce,' she says quietly. 'About Brennan.'

Katie looks confused. 'Yes. I've been so worried about you. What happened?'

'He set fire to himself in his garden shed,' Darcie explains.

'And he left a suicide note,' Abi adds.

'Wow. What a freak,' says Ruby.

'I'm sorry to say it, but bloody good riddance,' I say with a tinge of anger. 'He's ruined your life for the past two years, Darce.'

'I know. I know.' Darcie holds her hands up. 'But until they check the DNA, I don't want to let myself believe that he's dead.'

'I hope he is,' Ruby growls.

'I don't want to talk about it any more, please,' Darcie snaps.

There is silence as I start the engine, snap on the air-conditioning and look at my phone. Then I tap the postcode I've got for the car park at Mont Ventoux into the car's satnav.

'How far is it?' Katie asks as I slip the car into reverse and start to manoeuvre back out of the shaded car parking space.

'It's about twenty klicks to where we're going to park for our hike,' I explain with wry smile.

'Klicks?' Ruby snorts. 'We're not in a Vietnam movie, platoon leader!'

Everyone laughs.

I turn the car around, pull out of the farmhouse drive and turn right onto the main road.

'Darcie looks like she's done two tours of Vietnam,' Katie jokes, but it feels like there's some malice to her quip. I can't work out what's going on between them, but something is definitely up.

I look in the rear-view mirror. A stony silence falls in the car. We're all a bit hungover so it's not surprising.

After about twenty seconds, I see a white Fiat 500 coming towards us. It slows down to let us pass as the road is narrow. The driver is a man in his forties with a shaved head and sunglasses. I give him a slight wave of thanks, but he doesn't reciprocate. In fact, it's as if he deliberately looks the other way as he drives past. I can't work out if it's the same car that I saw parked outside the cottage earlier.

'That was rude,' Abi says from the back.

'What do you expect?' Ruby jokes. 'We're in France.'

'Hey,' Katie says with a grin. 'Why do French people hate remote controls?'

'We don't know, Katie,' Ruby says raising an eyebrow.

'Because they're easy Tou-louse,' Katie replies.

We all groan, but there's a nicer atmosphere in the car.

As we drive through Bédoin and head for the main road to Mont Ventoux, I glance down at my phone and click my eighties easy playlist on Spotify.

'Save a Prayer' by Duran Duran comes onto the car stereo.

'God, Darce,' Ruby says. 'We went to see Duran Duran at Wembley Arena. When the hell was that?'

'Yeah.' Darcie nods. 'I was about fifteen. So, 1987.'

'I lost the hearing in my right ear from you screaming "Simon, Simon, I love you! I want your babies!" in my ear,' Ruby chortles.

I glance out of my window. There's a little restaurant to our right that has palm trees outside. It has an olive green awning outside and the words *Cuisine de Famille... et galéjades* are printed in white.

'What's galéjade?' Abi asks from the back.

I shake my head. 'Beats me.'

Ruby taps on her phone and then frowns. 'It means "tall stories".'

We all look confused.

'Family cooking and tall stories?' Katie snorts. 'Doesn't really roll off the tongue, does it?'

I turn right down a tree-lined avenue that is now bathed in sunshine. There are cafés and restaurants with outdoor tables all the way down. Their awnings are an array of different colours as we pass – taupe, burned orange and deep navy. It couldn't look more quintessentially Provençal if it tried.

'We'll have to come here tomorrow,' Ruby says. 'It's beautiful.'

'Even though last night's food was incredible, Steph,' Katie says. 'This is your birthday celebration so you're officially banned from cooking.'

It's nice to hear someone putting the focus back on me and the reason for our weekend away.

'Absolutely,' Ruby agrees.

Darcie shoots me a concerned look. 'Can you pull over? I think I'm going to be sick.'

I push up the indicator and pull over to the side of the road outside a café.

Darcie opens the door, jumps out and vomits into the gutter.

'Classy,' Ruby says in the withering tone.

'I can hear you!' Darcie snaps as she takes a few deep breaths.

'You're not twenty-five any more, Darce,' Abi says mockingly.

Katie leans forward. 'I think you might be putting the customers off their *petit déjeuner.*'

They all laugh in the back. It feels like they're ganging up on her for some reason.

'Are you okay?' I ask, ignoring them.

'I guess so.' Darcie takes off her sunglasses and blows out her cheeks. 'What I really want to do now is a four hour hike in the blazing heat,' she groans sardonically.

She closes the passenger door and starts to pull on her seat belt.

I look in the rear-view mirror and notice that the little white Fiat 500 that I saw earlier is now one car behind us in the traffic.

EIGHTEEN

RUBY

'It's about five minutes from here, guys,' Steph says from the front of the car as they drive slowly up a steep road.

Mont Ventoux looms above them ominously. The idea that they're about to hike to the top makes Ruby feel uneasy.

How high did Steph say it was again? Nineteen hundred metres. It doesn't sound that high, does it?

Ruby knows that she's not that fit so she's worried that she's going to be shown up on the hike. What if she just can't keep going? Maybe she can wait for the others or make her way back to the car if the going gets too tough. But then she remembers Shaun warning that they should stick together as solo travellers have been robbed in the past. She could always fake a twisted ankle to slow the pace down. Is that too duplicitous? The racing thoughts are making her anxious.

'Hold Me Now' drifts from the car speakers, and Ruby's anxiety shifts into something else. The scent of Darcie's expensive perfume mingles with leather seats, but suddenly Ruby's catching whiffs of Toby Shackleton's cheap aftershave in his white Capri, that bloody furry dice swaying as they raced through Chandler's Ford. Her mother's lips pursed in that familiar way: *'Really, Ruby, a comprehensive school boy?'* The disapproval that had made him taste sweeter.

The song changes, but Ruby's mind is still time-travelling – Toby's bleach-blond hair, Fila tracksuit and Tacchini jacket, everything her parents had taught her to look down on. Her classmates sneering Gary and Sharon like curse words. She'd loved the danger of it then, until Toby dumped her for Lisa Baker. She then threw herself into her exams and secured a place to read Law at Trinity College, Oxford.

Now she watches Darcie stare out the passenger window, morning sunlight catching the shadows under her eyes. The same lost look she'd had at fifteen, after their father's lectures. Even angry as she is about yesterday's row, Ruby's chest tightens at the sight. The news about Patrick Brennan has clearly thrown her.

Watching her last night drink too much and then take a random young man to bed just made her feel uncomfortable, even protective. Darcie's behaviour has always seemed like attention-seeking and a cry for help. Ruby has lost count of how many times Darcie has acted out, only to be wracked with self-loathing and hopelessness the next morning. Why did she do that to herself?

'Here we go, guys,' Steph says brightly as she pulls the rental car into a space on the far side of the car park at Sault-en-Provence, a tiny village that many use as the access point for visitors wanting to hike or cycle up Mont Ventoux.

Ruby looks out. The car park is full of hardcore cyclists tightening parts of their bikes with spanners, chatting to others or looking at maps. There were also very serious-looking walkers with professional walking sticks and Berghaus clothing and hiking boots.

'Right, everyone, time to tackle the Beast of Provence,' Steph says.

Ruby takes a little breath. Steph's words have made her

anxious again as she doubts her capacity to complete the walk. 'I feel a bit ill-prepared, looking at all these guys. Are we going to be all right doing this walk?' She's wearing expensive, waterproof, grey hiking shoes with a pink trim, but she feel faintly ridiculous as she gets out of the car.

'Don't be a pussy, Ruby,' Darcie hisses from the front as she gets out. 'I'm hungover and I'm okay to do it.'

All Ruby's concern for her sister goes out of the window. It's always one-way traffic with her. Me, myself and I. Not for one moment would Darcie think to reassure her, realising that she's feeling a bit nervous about the hike.

She's so selfish.

They all go to the boot to take their rucksacks, retie their laces and make sure that they're prepared for the hike. Blister plasters, water and energy bars.

Outside of the air-conditioning of the Mercedes, the air is now thick with heat even though it's only mid-morning. The sun seems to be pulsating it's so hot. Nothing stirring. Ruby looks around. A cabbage white butterfly flutters silently from a nearby hedgerow. Beyond that, pale Limousin cattle are sheltering under the parasol of an oak tree. The grass around them is dry and caramel in colour.

Abi puts a comforting hand on Ruby's arm, bringing her back into the moment. 'We're going to be fine. We'll take it nice and slow.' She points up to the mountain. 'A lot of the lower parts are completely in the shade because of the forest and all the trees. It'll be cooler as we go higher with the breeze.'

Ruby gives Abi a grateful smile. Her words were just what she needed to hear. That's what she loves about Abi. She's so kind and thoughtful.

Steph closes the boot of the car and clicks the automatic lock so the indicators flash.

'Right, have we got everything, troops?' she asks, sounding like an officious sergeant major.

'Sir, yes, sir.' Katie laughs, giving her a salute. 'Anyway, this is just the warm-up for when we climb Kilimanjaro.'

'Are you still serious about that?' Steph asks. Katie often mentions her ambition to climb Kilimanjaro. She has done for years.

'Deadly,' Katie replies. 'It's number one on my bucket list.'

But then Steph frowns as she looks across the car park.

'Everything all right?' Ruby asks, sensing that Steph has seen something that's unsettled her.

'That car.' Steph points over to the small, white Fiat 500.

'What about it?' Katie asks as she pulls the rucksack onto her back.

'It was parked outside our farmhouse earlier,' Steph explains. 'Then it drove past us when we left, it was behind us for a bit of the journey and now it's here.'

Ruby narrows her eyes. It definitely sounds strange. 'You think someone's following us?'

'I don't know.' Steph gives a little laugh. 'Sorry, I'm sure I've got it wrong because that sounds completely ridiculous, doesn't it?'

There's an awkward silence amongst them.

Ruby peers over at the car, trying to see who is sitting inside, and then says, 'Wasn't that the rude French bloke that didn't wave earlier when you let him go?'

Steph nods. 'That's right.'

'Except we don't know he's French, do we?' Darcie points out.

'Is it the same number plate?' Katie asks.

'Yes.' Steph nods. 'Unless I've misremembered it.'

Darcie doesn't say anything. She's definitely spooked.

The door to the car opens and a tall man gets out. He's wearing a black patterned bandana, big Aviator-style sunglasses and a tight black T-shirt.

'Maybe we should go and talk to him?' Ruby suggests. In

fact, she's quite happy to go and confront him if he has indeed followed them for some reason.

'And say what?' Darcie snorts. 'Excuse me, are you following us?'

They watch as the man goes to the boot of the car and pulls out an expensive-looking camera with a long lens which he tucks away into his rucksack.

'And now we're all staring at him,' Katie whispers.

Trying not to stare, Ruby sees the man lock the car and strides across the car park. He's going to have to walk straight past them to get to the entrance to the pathway.

'He's coming this way,' Abi hisses under his breath.

Ruby freezes as they all attempt to act as naturally as they can. As the man marches past, she can see that he's probably in his late thirties and has tattoos of Roman numerals on the underside of both forearms.

'Have a nice walk, Darcie.' The man smirks without breaking stride.

There's a moment of silence as they process what's just happened.

A chill runs up Ruby's spine. *What the hell did he just say?*

'Oh my God,' Steph gasps as they all look at each other, aghast.

'Did he just say "*Darcie*"?' Katie asks in bewilderment.

'Yes, he fucking did. Hey! You!' Darcie shouts as she turns and jogs off after him. 'Come back here. Hey!'

'Darce!' Abi says as she trots off after her.

The man is walking very fast and he soon disappears out of sight.

Darcie and Abi come back to where the others are standing.

'Do you know him?' Katie asks.

'No, of course I don't know him,' Darcie pants.

Steph shakes her head. 'Then who the hell is he?'

Darcie's struggling to get her breath. 'I can't breathe,' she gasps as she leans forward.

Ruby goes to her. 'You're having a panic attack. Look at me, Darce.' Her sister has suffered from panic attacks ever since Brennan held the knife to her throat.

Darcie is now bent double, trying to breathe.

Ruby crouches down. 'Look at me. Remember, breathe in for ten, hold for ten and then breathe out for ten. Nice and steady.' Ruby has used this breathing technique to help her sister's panic attacks several times before.

Darcie nods as she follows Ruby's instructions, taking long deep breaths.

After a minute, Darcie straightens but continues to concentrate on her breath.

'Okay?' Ruby asks.

Darcie nods.

Katie comes over and puts a reassuring hand on her arm. 'Do you want to sit down somewhere?'

Darcie shakes her head.

'Right, well we're definitely not going up there after that,' Ruby says assertively. 'We can't.'

'No way. I'm fine. Honestly. We're going up the mountain,' Darcie says firmly.

'What about that creepy bloke?' Steph asks.

'Well, it's not Brennan, because he's lying dead in London,' Darcie says as her breathing returns to normal. 'That creep could have been anyone. Well, not anyone... we know it's not... Brennan...' Darcie trails off but then continues. 'Maybe the bloke's wife follows me on social media? Or maybe he does or he's read my book? I know I moaned about it earlier, but we've come all this way. We can't just turn around and go back without hiking up the mountain just because some bloke says hello to me. I might have known him, but he was wearing sunglasses and a bandana.'

Ruby isn't wholly convinced by her sister's blasé, casual manner.

'I agree with Ruby,' Steph says. 'I still think it's very weird. I don't think we should go.'

Darcie shrugs. 'Well, I'm going up there, even if I have to go on my own. I've got photos to take.'

Abi looks at Ruby and rolls her eyes.

'And anyway, I've come tooled up.' Darcie snorts as she reaches into her rucksack and pulls out a six-inch kitchen knife. 'I took this from the farmhouse. Any fucker tries anything, I'm going to shank them.'

'Jesus Christ, Darcie,' Ruby hisses.

Katie laughs. 'You really are mental.'

'Shank?' Abi says, shaking her head. 'You are aware that you're not in a south London drug gang?'

'Look, I'm going up there,' Darcie says, pointing to Mont Ventoux. 'You can go back, stay here or come with me.'

NINETEEN
DARCIE

They've been walking up the mountain now for fifteen minutes. Darcie has managed to put the strange incident with the man in the car park out of her mind. *Brennan is dead.* What other explanation is there? He left a note. And she knows that Brennan has threatened suicide before. He's dead and Darcie is looking forward to living her life without the spectre of him hanging over her.

There is a gust of wind that rattles the leaves in a nearby tree. The air is fresh and a little cooler than down at the farmhouse which is a relief. And the views across the landscape are incredible. To her right, a huge gate is manacled to a post with a rusty length of chain. Behind that a solitary farm building and a scattering of goats. And beyond that, a steep, empty landscape of scrubs, trees and a sky that is impossibly blue and cloudless. It's so wonderfully Provençal and rustic. It will make for some great photos with a bit of fiddling around on her photo app.

Darcie walks with Steph while the others are in front. Steph has been her usual bossy self, reminding everyone to stick together. Mother Hen.

Darcie notices that Steph is looking out to their right and frowning.

'You okay?' she asks.

Steph gestures to something she's looking at within the forested area at the foot of the mountain. Then Darcie sees what she's referring to. A white misty haze has now concealed the tops of the trees.

'What's that down there?' Steph asks.

Darcie can't work out what it is. 'That can't be fog, can it?'

Steph shakes her head. 'No, that doesn't make any sense. It looks like smoke to me.'

Darcie shrugs. 'Maybe they're burning something in the forest. I'm sure it's nothing to worry about.'

'I wonder where Shaun and Tom are,' Steph says, now looking out to their left. There had been some mention of them going on a bike ride, but Darcie really doesn't care.

'You and Tom,' Darcie says, furrowing her brow. 'That's not a thing, is it?'

'A thing? God no,' Steph snorts but Darcie senses that Steph isn't being entirely honest.

'I mean you're old enough to be his mother, for starters,' Darcie says dismissively.

'Hey,' Steph laughs. 'Only just. And I'd like to point out that you slept with Shaun last night and he's not much older.'

'Yeah, well, I'm bloody regretting that.' Darcie sighs. 'He was so weird and clingy this morning. I hope he doesn't lurk around later thinking that anything is going to happen.'

Steph gives Darcie a bemused and knowing look as she raises an eyebrow.

'What?' Darcie says with a defensive tone, but she knows exactly what Steph is referring to.

'How many times have we been in this situation before?' Steph says with a grin. 'Remember that time we went to stay in that apartment in Majorca in our twenties? The one that Abi's friend owned. Jason.'

'Don't remind me,' Darcie groans.

'We drew straws for who was going to have to sleep on the sofa bed in Jason's bedroom. You lost so you had to go in there. You shagged him on the first night and then spent the next six days trying to avoid him,' Steph says. 'He kept pestering us, asking if you liked him. Abi had to explain that you shagging him was only a sign that you'd drunk too much and had no control when a member of the opposite sex showed the slightest bit of interest in you.'

'Oh, that's a bit harsh,' Darcie tries to protest meekly.

'Is it? He was really unattractive. He had weird buck teeth and wore a trilby when we went out.'

Abi turns and laughs. 'Oh God, you're talking about *that* Jason.'

'All right, all right,' Darcie sighs. 'That was twenty-five years ago. Ancient history, guys.'

Katie turns to look at them. She's squinting at the sun. 'Anyone got any spare sunglasses?' she asks, putting her hand up to shade her face. 'I've managed to leave mine by the pool.'

'Nope,' Abi replies as everyone shakes their head.

'Bugger,' Katie sighs. Then she looks at Darcie. 'Can I borrow your cap, Darce? As you've got sunglasses. Otherwise I'm going to be squinting all the way up.'

Darcie doesn't like the idea. The baseball cap is part of her look, her image.

'Please, please, pretty please,' Katie says in a silly voice.

Darcie nods reluctantly. She doesn't want to appear to be petty in front of the others. She takes it off and hands it to Katie. 'Okay. As long as I can have it back to put on in any photos that I want to take at the summit.'

Abi visibly bristles. Darcie knows it's because she asked to borrow the cap earlier. *Jesus, Abi can be such a baby!*

'Bloody hell,' Ruby mutters under her breath.

Darcie can feel her anger rise immediately. Her sister is definitely judging her for something. She knows it from the withering tone of her voice. 'If you've got something to say, Ruby, just say it.'

'You're a fifty-year-old woman, for fuck's sake,' Ruby snaps. 'You want to borrow back your baseball cap to wear in photos that you're going to post on Instagram! What are you, fourteen?'

'Well, clearly no one would pay you to endorse products in photos,' Darcie sniped.

'Get over yourself, Darcie,' Ruby growled.

They walk in an awkward silence for a few seconds.

Steph points over to the thick forest below them. 'That smoke is definitely getting worse down there.'

TWENTY

SHAUN

Shaun unclips his feet from the cycling shoes attached to his road bike and takes a deep breath. He glances back, but there's no sign of Tom yet. *Feckin' amateur*, Shaun chortles to himself. He'll have to wait for Tom to catch up. He's about a kilometre from the summit and all the vegetation has disappeared. It's been replaced by white, gleaming limestone. At first glance, it looks like there's been a huge of snowstorm. Except it's baking hot. It's why Mont Ventoux is often referred to as 'the bald mountain'. The mistral winds up this high are incredibly strong which makes cycling even more difficult, especially if you're cycling against them. Shaun has known the wind to hit 150 mph. The last time he was up here, he saw two cyclists blown over and wiped out due to a sudden, violent gust of wind.

Looking down, he can see the vast sprawl of Provence like a patchwork quilt of varying colours and shades. It's a view that's uninterrupted by any other mountains surging up. Mont Ventoux stands out on its own. Majestic.

To his left, Shaun looks at the Tom Simpson Memorial. He likes to stop here every time he cycles up the Bédoin Tour de France route. The memorial honours the British cyclist Tom

Simpson who tragically died on this spot from heat exhaustion during the 1967 Tour de France. It's a huge piece of granite with the silhouette of a cyclist on it. There is also a plaque with the following inscription:

*A La Mémoire de Tom Simpson
No mountain is too high*

Shaun knows that this memorial is a shrine and a place of pilgrimage for many Tour de France enthusiasts. He's seen many cyclists stop here and lay down small items of memorial – a water bottle, a medal, or just a scribbled note.

As Shaun wipes the sweat from his face and eyes, he gets a waft of something in the air. The distinct smell of burning. As he looks out to the east, he can see that smoke is now covering the lower parts of the mountain. *Wildfires.*

The whole of Europe is experiencing a heatwave. He'd heard on the news in the past week about wildfires in Spain, Italy and Croatia.

His thoughts then turn to 'the girls' from the farmhouse who are attempting to trek up the mountain this morning. The smoke has started to envelop the road and pathways lower down. He hopes they're okay. Taking out his phone, he sees that he has two bars of signal. He knows that due to the media and fans that flock to the mountain during the Tour de France, the mountain has its own mobile phone mast.

He searches for Steph's number that he's saved onto his phone – *Stephanie O'Brien*. He still hasn't managed to ask her if her name is Irish or if she has Irish relatives. Maybe later. After the way Darcie spoke to him earlier, he's probably not going to go anywhere near the farmhouse again until they leave. *Feckin' stuck-up bitch.* He only gave her a ride because he was drunk and she was clearly gagging for it. Then she had the cheek to act as if she'd done him a huge favour. *The neck of that woman!*

Feck her. Maybe he'll go back over and see if any of her wee friends are interested in hooking up. That will serve her right. See how she likes him going off to bed with one of her mates. Shaun chortles to himself at the very thought of it.

Shaun finds Steph's number and rings her. It goes straight to voicemail.

'Hey, Steph. It's Shaun,' he says. 'I can see smoke coming from further down the mountain. I just wanted to check that you guys were okay. It looks like it's getting worse.'

Hanging up his phone, Shaun scours the road for Tom.

Where the hell has he gone?

Shaun glances at his watch. It's been over forty-five minutes since he last saw Tom.

He can't be that unfit, can he?

His instinct is that he shouldn't trust Tom. Or he should at least be wary of him. Shaun can't quite put his finger on it. It's just the odd comment or look that feels a bit off.

There is a deep rumbling noise. At first it sounds like a thunderstorm, except the sky above is a translucent blue. Hardly a cloud to be seen.

The noise is getting louder. It sounds mechanical and rhythmic. It's coming from above.

Shielding his eyes from the sun with his hand, Shaun gazes up and sees something approaching.

It's a French police helicopter. A Eurocopter AS332 Super Puma with a powerful 1A1 turboshaft engine. It's a deep royal blue colour, with white trim and the letter *POLICE* in blue on the door.

The helicopter hovers above where the smoke is coming from. They are clearly assessing how dangerous the wildfires are. It strikes Shaun that maybe he needs to start to make his way back down. It might be too risky to push on to the summit if there are fires on the mountains.

TWENTY-ONE
STEPH

I glance at my sports watch which is recording our hike on its digital readout. We've been going for about thirty-five minutes and clocked up 2.65 kilometres which I reckon to be pretty good going. My heart rate is 134 bpm which is good too. I know I'm slightly obsessive about keeping a regular check on all this, but it's hard-wired into my DNA.

Of course, Mont Ventoux is used for skiing in the winter months. Over to our right are the high lines of the ski lift. A red metallic chair dangles and moves in the wind, making a slightly eerie creaking sound. The slopes are now overgrown with heather and grass which have browned in the heat of the summer. It gives off that lovely smell that is so redolent of the carefree days of childhood. And in the distance, there are the wooden ski chalets glistening in the sun. With mountains around us, it feels as if we are hiking in somewhere more like Austria or Switzerland than Provence.

Mont Ventoux towers above us as we go, but the views are just stunning. Hills that are covered with vineyards. Fields that are awash with the purple of lavender that look like great blankets. We pass a narrow river to our right and I see a father and what I assume are his two sons fishing.

There are evergreen shrubs and fauna. I recognise an oak tree and a cedar tree. But as we get higher and the road gets steeper, we begin to enter the forest. Beech and fir trees, Scots pines, moors and scree. Underneath, the floor is populated by an explosion of colour. Pink, blue and yellow. I've read that there is a very rare pale pink orchid that is unique to the forest.

Looking up ahead, I see that I'm on my own at the back. I think that I naturally gravitate to this position. So, walking at the back means that I can keep on eye on everyone.

Abi and Katie are about fifteen yards ahead of me. For a moment, I had thought Katie was Darcie – they're wearing the same coloured shorts and top – but I can see Darcie is now up ahead walking with Ruby.

We seem to have put the strange incident with the man in the car park behind us. However, I can't help but feel a bit jumpy when I sense a hiker coming past us up the road. That is until I turn to look and realise it's not the man we saw getting out of the Fiat 500.

I join Abi and Katie on the left so we're walking as a three.

'I'm so glad we're doing this,' Abi says. 'We haven't all been together for so long.'

'New Year's Eve,' I say. We'd hired a cottage in Wales and saw the New Year in together.

'Oh yeah,' Katie remembers. 'Hugo got hammered and fell down the stairs. We used to laugh at stuff like that in our twenties. But I thought there was something pitiful about a man in his fifties getting that drunk.'

'I felt sorry for him,' I admits.

'Really?' Katie pulls a face. 'He's a total prick. And he's ruining Darcie's life. I told her to kick him out of the house.'

'I don't think she will,' I say. There seems to be some weird toxic bond between Darcie and Hugo that I'll never understand.

'She deserves better,' Katie snaps, getting angry. 'Darcie would have a whole new lease of life if he was out of the picture.'

'He's definitely more creepy the older he's gets,' I admit.

Abi pulls a face. 'I've noticed that. He gets so lechy when he's drunk. Until Darcie shouts at him.'

Katie suddenly grabs at my arm. 'Is that a snake?' she squeals, pointing at something in a tree.

We all stop walking.

Abi freezes in horror. 'Where?' she asks looking terrified.

I spot what Katie is looking at and roll my eyes. 'It's a vine curled around that branch, you dimwit.'

'Are you sure?' Katie asks.

'Yes,' I laugh.

'Oh yes. I can see that now,' Katie sighs with relief.

Abi looks at me. 'Oh God. Are there snakes on this mountain? I hadn't even thought about that.'

I love the fact that because I booked this trip, everyone thinks that somehow that makes me the fountain of all knowledge when it comes to Bédoin, Mont Ventoux or Provence in general.

'There are vipers,' I say, waiting for their reaction.

'Vipers?' Katie asks in horror. 'They're really dangerous, aren't they?'

'Not really,' I reassure her. 'Anyway, if you're going to climb Kilimanjaro, Katie, then you're going to need to be a bit braver than that.'

'Right. Good point.' Katie nods, but I'm not sure she's convinced. 'Anyway, I thought we were all going to climb Kilimanjaro together?'

'I'll come with you. Definitely,' I reply.

Abi pulls a face. 'Maybe.'

We all start walking again. The vegetation is starting to change. It's still colourful and fragrant – irises, thyme, honeysuckle. But the trees are starting to thin out as we get higher.

'You know what, if it wasn't for Steph,' Katie says going back to our conversation from before, 'I wouldn't see you guys at all. Well, not as much at least. I don't know why the rest of us are so crap at organising stuff like this.'

'Hey, I like doing it,' I say, shrugging.

Abi grins. 'And we all know why.'

'Don't you dare call me a control freak,' I protest with a laugh.

'If the cap fits,' Katie says.

'I was going to be kinder and say you've got OCD,' Abi says.

'We're not allowed to bandy around neurodivergent terms like OCD willy-nilly,' I say, raising my eyebrow in a ticking-off way.

'I'm not bandying it around. I'm sure you do have actual OCD,' Abi explains. 'I remember we all went out clubbing one night and crashed at yours and Ruby's flat in Clapham. I think we got in at 4 a.m. I woke up to you hoovering by my head at 8 a.m. You'd cleaned the flat top to bottom.'

'It makes me less anxious,' I protest with a self-effacing laugh. 'I used to drive my parents mad. Every time we went out, I'd be obsessed about whether we'd turned the cooker off. My dad would have to go back into the house every time.'

'Well, we love you just the way you are,' Katie says with a warm smile.

'Thanks, Katie,' I say drily. 'You sound like I'm care in the community.'

We all laugh.

The trees now form an arched canopy over the dusty path and it's a relief to be out of the sun's direct rays. To our right, I spot a lime tree. *Le tilleul.* I recognise its fronds and leaves which are heart-shaped. I remember reading that in a book when I was a teenager. A boy giving a girl the heart-shaped leaf of a lime tree and thinking it was the most romantic thing I'd ever read. In France, the lime tree is also a symbol of liberty and they were planted to commemorate victories in battles.

Abi gives me a knowing look. 'So... I'm guessing that a night with Tom will help get François out of your system?'

'Yeah, you haven't even told us what happened with you and Tom,' Katie giggles.

'Is he better or bigger than François?' Abi snorts, using her hands to demonstrate her question about Tom's manhood.

'Abi!' I laugh.

The very sound of his name makes me cringe. I catch myself absently rubbing the spot on my neck where François always kisses me hello – right below my ear, very French, very practised. Fifteen years of those kisses, stolen in hotel rooms or my flat when his wife thinks he's at late meetings. His Clapham house with its Georgian windows haunts my Google Maps – I've lost count of the times I've walked past, imagining a life where I belong there.

'Je t'aime, ma chérie,' he whispers every time, and I pretend not to notice how easily those words fall from his lips, how his wedding ring catches the light as he dresses to leave. Five, six times a year I let myself believe him when he says 'soon'. Soon, when the children are older. Soon, when the timing is right. Soon.

Seven months I'd managed to stay away. Seven months of deleting his texts unread, of walking the long way around Clapham to avoid his street. My head was clearer. My self-esteem restored.

Then three weeks ago, his shadow on my doorstep, those theatrical tears I used to find charming. 'I cannot live without you, Steph.'

Katie looks at me. 'I'm assuming that François is still "happily married" with two children?' she asks sardonically, using her fingers as inverted commas.

I nod but feel a little embarrassed.

'He is such a cock,' Abi sneers.

'I know,' I sigh.

'We did all tell you that he was never going to leave her,' Katie says.

'I know that too,' I say.

'You seem so much happier since you decided never to see him again,' Abi stated.

I'm feeling incredibly guilty.

I know that I should have slammed the door in his face. But I let him in, we made love and he stayed the night. And now I'm right back in that cycle of self-loathing.

Katie grins. 'So dish the dirt on Tom.'

'Not much to tell,' I say with a shrug, trying to push thoughts of François from my head.

'Fuck off,' Katie laughs. 'You're not getting away with it that easily.'

'Must be nice to have a much younger man in bed?' Abi asks with a raised eyebrow. 'How many times?'

'We didn't have sex last night,' I say. 'After we jumped in the pool, I dragged him into the bedroom and then passed out apparently.'

'And nothing happened?' Abi asked incredulously.

'That's what Tom said.' I shrug.

Katie frowns. 'What about this morning when you woke up?'

I make an expression and then smile.

'Oh, but this morning, you did,' Katie says victoriously.

'How many times?' Abi asks excitedly.

I pull a face and hold up four fingers.

'Four times!' Abi exclaims. 'You lucky bitch.'

'Thing is, I haven't had a wax for while,' I admitted. 'I wasn't expecting anyone to be down there this weekend.'

They all laugh.

Katie asks, 'Oh, so he was down there, was he?'

I give them a knowing smile.

'I went for a wax just opposite Battersea Park last week,' Abi explains. 'And I think the woman was Spanish. And she was looking directly at my fanny and said, "It's such a lovely area." I didn't say anything, but I was thinking it's been a while since I had a compliment like that. And then she says, "It's beautiful." So, I'm starting to worry about what her intentions are. I say, "Really?" And then she says, "Yes. You've got the park with that Japanese pagoda, the little zoo. And you're on the river. Lots of bars and restaurants." She was talking about Battersea!'

We all howl with laughter. It's moments like these that remind me why I love this group of women.

The wind picks up and it's refreshingly cool on my face. I glance to our right and see a sea of purple lavender, their heads bowing with the weight of insects. And the smell from them is glorious.

Katie looks at me intently. 'And how long has it been since you saw that French prick?' She's obviously referring to François.

'I don't know,' I say with an uncomfortable shrug.

But they know me too well.

'You've seen him, haven't you?' Abi groans angrily.

Katie looks at me with such disappointment. 'Tell me you haven't, Steph. Why?'

'But he makes you ill and completely insane,' Abi sighs.

'I know, I know.' I shake my head with embarrassment. 'It's the last time, I promise.'

'Jesus! It's the last time until he comes over and waves le penis in your face,' Katie jokes.

I frown. 'I'm pretty sure it's not le penis.'

'Le cock?' Abi suggests as we all laugh. 'That definitely sounds more French.'

'And did you take a nibble of le cock?' Katie chortles.

'Maybe,' I giggle. 'He did put it right in my face.'

'Well, just whack it away with the palm of your hand if you don't want to,' Abi says with a grin. 'I've pretty much stopped doing that now anyway. Too much effort for no reward. And I think that ever since I had that C-section, I've lost feeling down there. I think they must have cut my fanny nerve endings.'

I shake my head. 'I'm pretty sure that's not the correct medical term for them.'

'Well, ladies, le cock is not something I have to worry about ever again,' Katie says and then gives me a stern look. 'Promise me that's the last time.'

I hold my hand up defensively. 'I promise.'

Katie and Abi share a sceptical look.

'I don't believe her,' Katie sighs.

Abi shakes her head. 'Nope. Neither do I.'

TWENTY-TWO

The trees have started to thin out as we're getting higher up. The views are even more breathtaking, but the smoke below us seems to be getting thicker. It's now midday and oven hot. I'm squinting in the white sunlight and the air is filled with the rhythmic chant of cicadas. Apparently they only start this chant when the temperature hits twenty-seven degrees. My forehead and the back of my neck are damp from sweat. I've made the mistake of wearing hiking socks and now my feet feel like they're on fire. I wish I'd worn thinner socks. The air feels thick with heat. This is why the French stay indoors with their impossibly beautiful shutters closed for this part of the day. Only a madman or woman would walk up a mountain.

'I thought it got cooler the higher up we go,' Abi sighs, blowing out her cheeks. Her face is a little ruddy.

'Not quite yet,' I say. 'But the winds do get very strong further up which will be nice. Apparently there's a local saying that sometimes the mistral can be powerful enough to blow the ears off a donkey.'

Katie laughs. 'I'll definitely video that for YouTube.'

I check my sports watch again. 'Hey, we're over the five kilometre mark, guys. Five point one three, to be precise. One point nine klicks to go.'

'Oh, Steph.' Abi laughs at me. 'It's not a race. Let's just enjoy the hike at our pace.'

When I think about not looking at my watch and ignoring how far we've come or how far we've got to go, I instantly feel anxious.

I smile at my eccentricity, reach for my water bottle and take a sip. It's a horrible feeling having to ration my water intake, although I know there are several places to get water on the way.

Abi swigs from her bottle too and then we stop for a few seconds.

'Did you say we can get water up at the summit?' Katie asks. She must have read my mind.

I nod. 'There's a shop that sells water. And there's some toilets and a water fountain about two kilometres from here,' I explain.

'Isn't that two klicks?' Abi teases me.

'Yes, two klicks,' I laugh.

We start to walk again.

Abi takes out her phone and starts to take some photos.

Katie drops back a little so that she's walking at my side. She gives me a little smile to show that she's contented.

We walk in a comfortable silence for a few minutes.

Katie reaches up to move a strand of hair from her face. She has that delicate bracelet on her left wrist. I noticed it first when she arrived at the airport.

'I love your bracelet,' I say.

Katie lifts up her wrist to show me. 'It's Soru.'

'I've been meaning to have a look at their stuff,' I say. 'It's really beautiful.'

'Thank you,' Katie says. 'Sophie bought it for me for Christmas.' Sophie is Katie's daughter. 'I wear it every day now. Never take it off, even when I take a shower.'

'How's Sophie doing at RADA?' I ask her.

Katie smiles. 'She's absolutely loving it. I went to see the end of year production. *The Seagull* by Chekhov.' She pulls a face. 'I didn't understand a word. Everyone just seemed miserable. But Sophie was fantastic.'

'You must be so proud,' I say.

'I am. I just sat there beaming,' Katie admits. 'And she introduced me to her friends as "my gay mum". I guess it's far more interesting and cooler to have a gay mum than a straight mum these days?'

'It is in Gen Z land,' I snort.

'Justin went on a different night,' Katie says uncertainly. Then she gives me a meaningful look. 'I think he might have met someone.'

'Oh, right… How does that make you feel?' I ask.

'A bit weird.' Katie gives an uncertain shrug. 'But I'm the one who decided the marriage was over so I can't say anything. And he's been so incredibly supportive of me.'

Her words sound hollow or distracted. There's something else going on. Something that she's not telling me.

I give her a questioning glance. 'I feel like there's a "but" coming?'

'I don't know. It's just that he was being very weird about it when I asked him if he'd met someone,' Katie admitted. 'Justin has always been the worst liar in the world. He goes red and fidgets with his hands.'

'Maybe he just feels uncomfortable talking to you about it?' I suggest as we start to walk around a long bend heading left.

The wind swirls up for a few seconds and it's cool against the sweat on my face, bringing momentary relief from the heat – and something else. Smoke. Thicker now, with an acrid edge that catches in my throat. That can't be someone's bonfire or a controlled burn. My eyes track to where dark clouds are building above the treeline, too low and too grey to be weather. That's not woodsmoke drifting up from the valley – it's sharper, wilder. Could it be a wildfire?

'I thought Justin was hiding something from me. He had that look he gets when he's got something uncomfortable to say but can't bring himself to tell me. I wondered if he was seeing someone I knew. There are a couple of divorced women at his office that are our age,' Katie explains.

'Would that be a problem?' I ask.

I'm aware that the smoke below us is looking ominous. But Katie is pouring out her heart so I don't want to interrupt her or change the subject.

'No,' Katie says a little too quickly. 'I'd just need a little bit of time to get my head around it. But I really do want him to be happy. And there's part of me that feels terribly guilty at having hidden my sexuality from him for so long.'

'I think you've been incredibly brave,' I say supportively.

'Thank you.' Katie takes a breath. 'Even though I've been surrounded by open-minded, tolerant people most of my life, my view of the world is a bit tainted.' She looks over at me. 'I can still see my father's screwed-up face when we'd go shopping in Liverpool and see a gay woman.' Katie mimics her father's thick Scouse accent. '"Big fat fucking dyke. Look at the state of it."'

'Oh God,' I groan and shake my head.

I admire Katie's honesty. She's always been an open book.

I point over to the smoke above the trees. It's definitely getting worse. 'Do you think we should be getting worried about that?'

Katie peers at where I'm pointing. 'Isn't it some forestry thing? Where they burn the ground before planting new trees?'

'I'm not sure. Maybe it's nothing.' I'm wondering if I'm just being melodramatic.

'And what about you?' I ask.

She frowns. 'Me?'

'Have you met anyone?'

'I have.' Then Katie squints as she takes a moment.

'That's good, isn't it?' I ask, but I sense there's some kind of issue.

'Yes. Sort of. I don't know.' She gives a frustrated sigh. 'But it's so complicated. I think I'm in love with her.' Then Katie thinks. 'No. I *am* in love with her. But she's married. And so it's all a bit of a mess at the moment. We just need to sit down and talk it out, but I get the feeling she's avoiding doing that. If I'm honest, she's leading me a merry dance which is really pissing me off now. It's not fair.'

'Sounds stressful,' I say.

'Yeah, it is. I need to have it out with her,' Katie admits.

Slightly ahead of us are Darcie and Ruby who are deep in conversation. I'm about to say to myself that it's nice to see them getting along so well when I hear the sound of raised voices.

Oh great. Here we go.

Their argument gets so heated that they stop.

The crack of palm against cheek splits the air. For a moment, everything freezes: Ruby's hand still raised, Darcie's head snapped sideways, a strand of blonde hair caught across her reddening cheek. Even the birds seem to stop singing.

'Whoa!' I lunge between them, but Darcie's already backing away, her hand pressed to her face. Something breaks in her expression – not just anger, but a deeper wound. She turns and runs up the path, tears already falling. Abi races after her.

'What the hell was that about?'

Ruby is clearly shaken that she's lost control and struck her sister. 'Stuff with our father,' she says bitterly, her voice cracking with tears. 'She's persuaded him to change his will, but she won't tell me the details. I don't know what's wrong with her.'

'Right,' I say. 'Walk with me while you two cool off, okay?'

Ruby nods. 'Sorry...' I can see she looks ashamed now that she slapped Darcie.

'It's all right,' Katie says quietly and then in an attempt to lighten the tone, 'I love Darcie. But sometimes she annoys the shit out of me so much that I want to give her a good slap too.'

The gradient is getting steeper. I can feel it on my thighs and calves. I'm having to work harder to keep at the same speed.

'Is it me, or is the air thinner the higher we go?' Ruby panted.

'No, it is,' I say brightly. 'The air is 20 per cent thinner at the top of the mountain than the bottom.'

Darcie and Abi are walking about twenty-five yards ahead of us now.

There seems to be a ghostly haze of smoke across the trees on the slopes right beside us. The sunlight is creating strange shadows in it. But the others don't seem worried about it so I'm not going to say anything. They already think that I'm Mrs Serious Killjoy, but I walk over to the edge of the path. To my horror, I can see that the thick forest below is on fire. Huge orange flames are visible and dark plumes of smoke are swirling up into the air.

'Jesus Christ!' I say loudly. I can't help myself.

Katie rushes over to my side. 'What is it?'

'Oh shit,' Ruby gasps as she looks down.

Katie furrows her brow. 'Fuck. That doesn't look good. We were walking down there earlier, weren't we?'

'I think so,' I say quietly.

The wind picks up and I can see that a haze of smoke has started to envelop where we're walking. It's not thick, but it's enough to obscure my view of Darcie and Abi who are still marching along.

A young couple in their late twenties – sunglasses, walking sticks, expensive hiking boots and clothing – are striding down the mountain towards us.

The man can see the confused look on my face and slows his pace to come over to where we're standing and looking.

'Hi, guys,' he says in an accent that I think is Dutch. 'They're closing the mountain.' Then he points to the forest that's ablaze. 'Wildfires.'

'What?' I say. I so wanted to hike to the top today.

The young woman nods and then points to the road behind us. 'Yes. They've closed the access roads. They're not letting anyone else come up here. And they're sending everyone down. It's too dangerous.'

I can see that there's no one behind us. I just hadn't noticed.

'Thank you,' Katie says with an anxious smile.

'No problem,' the young woman replies.

The couple walk away, heading down the mountain.

I look at Ruby and Katie. 'I suppose we'd better tell the others and head back.'

But as I look uphill, not only has the smoke thickened, there's no sign of Darcie or Abi anywhere.

They've vanished.

TWENTY-THREE
DARCIE

Darcie's fingers brush her cheek, still burning from Ruby's slap. The same spot where their father used to pat her patronisingly, telling her to be more like her sister. And now here's Ruby, jumping to conclusions about the will, about everything – always so quick to think the worst. Always the good daughter passing judgement. Darcie swallows against the familiar tightness in her throat. Funny how a slap from your sister can make you feel fifteen again, standing in that kitchen while Ruby got another perfect report card, another pat on the head, another 'why can't your sister be more like you.'

Darcie puts her hand to her face.

Fuck, that really hurts.

'I can't believe she actually hit you like that,' Abi says, shaking her head in disbelief.

Darcie knows that Abi will have her back. She always does. It's nice to have a friend that doesn't judge or challenge her all the time.

'She's such a bitch,' Darcie huffs angrily as they march on. 'Well, that's it. I won't be saying another word to her for the rest of this weekend. She just pecks away at me until I get upset. But slapping me like that is the final straw.'

'I know,' Abi agrees.

For a few seconds, they stride on at a good pace. Darcie knows how unfit Ruby is. She doesn't even go to the gym or have a personal trainer. At her age, it's madness. You only have to read any paper or magazine to know that after the age of fifty, being fit, lifting weights and keeping active is the key to avoiding major disease and therefore attaining longevity. Darcie aims to be as fit and healthy as she possibly can be now so that she can enjoy a long retirement. Of course, she has no idea who she is going to spend that retirement with. It certainly won't be Hugo. The doctor has told him that unless he stops or cuts down his alcohol intake, he'll be dead within five years. His brother, Oscar, has suggested Hugo have a stint in the Priory in Roehampton. Hugo told him that was absurd as he wasn't 'a fucking alcoholic'. She thinks about the message she received on Instagram. What would happen if Hugo's past ever caught up with him? Not only would his career be finished, so would hers. It doesn't bear thinking about.

Darcie tries to put all this out of her mind as she glances back. The others are out of sight. She doesn't care. She wants to put distance between them and show her sister up. She hopes that Ruby starts to moan, groan, puff, pant and generally piss Steph and Katie off.

Abi looks back. 'Shouldn't we wait for the others?'

'No,' Darcie snorts. She doesn't want to be anywhere near Ruby at the moment. 'They need to keep up with us.'

'It's getting quite smoky up here, isn't it?' Abi remarks, pointing to the blackening clouds of smoke that seem to be rising towards them.

'I suppose so,' Darcie replies, but the bitter smell of burning is definitely getting stronger. 'I'm sure it'll clear when we get a bit higher.'

'You haven't even told me anything about last night,' Abi says with a knowing look.

Darcie shrugs. 'Nothing much to tell. It was all over in a second. Very disappointing.' This was a complete lie. The sex had been good actually. And Shaun had been very attentive to her needs. But the whole thing had left her cold and feeling empty.

'Really?' Abi pulls an awkward face. 'There was quite a lot of noise. I thought you guys were having a whale of a time.'

Even though Darcie knows this is almost certainly true, she gives Abi a withering look. 'Are you saying I'm lying, Abs?'

'No. No, of course not,' Abi replies.

'And he was very needy and weird this morning. He really gave me the creeps.'

'And what about this mystery person you told me about on the plane?' Abi says conspiratorially. 'You haven't even given me the juicy gossip about.'

Darcie thinks of the affair. She gets a flash of them together. Tender, loving, easy. It feels so right. Not just another meaningless fling. What they have is important, vital and dazzling. But she just doesn't want to talk about it. Not yet.

'I'll tell you about it later. I promise.'

'Such a tease,' Abi sighs. 'I take it you won't be going back for seconds with Shaun then?'

'God no,' Darcie groans. 'There's no chance of that.'

'Doesn't Hugo get suspicious that you're seeing people behind his back?' Abi asks.

'No. Actually, I'm pretty sure he doesn't really care,' Darcie says. 'Remember that film producer that I was seeing a while back?'

Abi nods. 'The one that looked like George Clooney?'

'Yes. Last Christmas I bought him this beautiful Paul Smith overcoat. Velvet collar,' Darcie explains. 'And I left it in the boot of my car. But Hugo found it. He knew that it wasn't for him. It was the wrong size. And Hugo already had a designer coat that was similar.'

'What did he say?'

'He just looked a bit sad and said, "You've bought him a nice coat for Christmas. Lucky bloke."'

'And that was it?'

'Yep. Then he just walked away.'

'He didn't say anything else?'

'No. But we don't talk about anything. We don't have sex. And he's emotionally unavailable,' Darcie explains. 'Life's just too short to be with someone like that.'

'Why don't you just get divorced?' Abi suggests. 'Bella's down in Bristol now.'

'I've asked if we can talk about a divorce, but he just refuses,' Darcie explains. 'So we just plod on in silent misery.'

Abi stops for a second. 'Darce, the smoke really is getting thicker.'

'It's fine. Probably doing some forest clearing thing where they burn the tree stumps,' Darcie suggests. She'd seen it once on a documentary. But something flutters in her stomach as another wave of smoke rolls in, thick and acrid.

'I really think we should wait,' Abi says, pointing back to the others. 'And I could do with a breather.'

'I can't be around her,' Darcie insists. 'Come on, pussy. We'll stop in ten minutes, okay?'

Abi gives a sigh as they start again and walk on. Darcie can feel that the walk is getting harder and steeper the longer they go on.

'What about that creepy bloke down at the car park?' Abi pants.

'I'm sure he just recognised me from one of the magazine articles or profiles that came out when I launched my book. Or his wife is a social media fan and follows me. Who knows. He looked pretty harmless to me.' Darcie shrugs, knowing that some of this is bravado. However, with Brennan dead, she is definitely starting to feel safer and calmer. 'I've been recognised a couple of times. Remember that woman came up to me in Harvey Nic's and wanted a selfie?'

'But that bloke was just creepy.'

'Come on, Abs.' Darcie gestures to their surroundings. 'Look at this. We're not going to get attacked here in broad daylight. We're not in London now.' She laughs. 'I've got that big kitchen knife if any fucker dares come near us.'

'Okay, Darce,' Abi chortles. 'You're officially mental.'

Darcie feels that familiar warmth spread through her chest – the same fizzy thrill she got at fifteen, watching her father's face purple at her first tattoo. *Mental. Dangerous. Wild.* Each word a tiny rebellion against Sunday school hymns and pressed white dresses, against everything good Christian girls were supposed to be.

In front of them, the route splits two ways. The main path and a road going to the left which has a big sign that reads *Sommet du Mont Ventoux 2 km*. It also has a cartoon drawing of a mountain and its peak. The smaller footpath that bears to her right has a sign saying *Gorges du Toulourenc 2.7 km*. The sign has a similar cartoon picture of a waterfall and some caves.

Abi takes her phone and holds it up. 'Come on. Let's take a selfie here.'

Darcie is wary of Abi's suggestion. 'Okay, but you can't post it.'

Abi narrows her eyes. 'What? Why the hell not?'

'I'm going to take some photos when we get to the top,' Darcie explains calmly. 'I don't want photos of me on this mountain going out on your social media first. They might get reposted.'

Abi takes a visible breath. She looks annoyed. 'Oh, fuck off, Darcie. You're not bloody Beyoncé. Do you want us all to sign NDAs before we travel back home?'

'That's not fair!' Darcie is hurt by Abi's words.
What the hell has got into her?

'Really?' Abi continues. 'You told me you'd help me launch an Instagram profile. Then you told me you were "a brand".' Abi uses her fingers to signal the speech marks. 'You swan around like you're fucking Victoria Beckham. But you just post stuff on Instagram and write the odd blog. That's it. Oh, and now you've written a book. Big wows.'

Darcie can't believe Abi is acting like this. She's so ungrateful.

'Abi?' Darcie says quietly. The wind has been taken out of her sails. 'Don't be like that.'

Abi turns and starts to walk back the way they've come.

'Abs?' Darcie calls after her.

'Get over yourself, Darcie,' Abi shouts without looking back.

Glancing around, Darcie sees that they've gone around a long bend. And a thick haze of smoke now hangs over the whole area. There's no one around. She's on her own.

Darcie's phone vibrates with a phone call. She's surprised there's a signal up here. She assumes it's going to be Steph nagging her to wait.

'Abi, wait there for me!' Darcie shouts at the top of her voice but Abi has vanished.

The caller ID reads, *Notting Hill police station.*

'Hello?' Darcie says answering her phone.

Silence.

Darcie panics. *Why hasn't he answered me?*

'I've got some bad news, I'm afraid, Darcie,' Darren says very quietly.

Darcie's stomach tenses with dread. *What is it?* 'The person's remains we found at the property are not Patrick Brennan.'

Darcie takes a sharp intake of breath. The nightmare isn't over.

Are you fucking joking?

'Darcie?' Darren says after a few seconds.

'I'm here. I just can't believe it,' she growls angrily.

'I'm sorry,' Darren says. 'Brennan murdered his flatmate but framed it so that it appeared that he had died in the fire. Officers found Brennan's clothes, his phone and his jewellery at the scene. He'd even left a suicide note.'

'Jesus,' Darcie whispers as her mind races. 'Someone spoke to me a couple of hours ago. A total stranger. He was British and he used my name.'

Silence. Her head is spinning as she tries to process what she's been told.

'Okay. I need you to keep calm,' Darren says. 'Someone looking like Brennan was spotted on CCTV in Dover a few days ago. But we can't be sure it's him.'

'Are you bloody kidding me?'

'Okay. Where are you now?'

'I'm up a fucking mountain in France,' Darcie snaps, but her voice is shaky. 'Has anyone seen him since Dover?'

'Yes. Interpol and the French police then spotted someone that looked like him at the Gare de Lyon in Paris four days ago,' Darren explained.

Paris?

Darcie is overwhelmed by a surge of panic. Her heart is now thumping so hard it feels like it's going to explode in her chest.

'Oh my God. He's definitely in France then?'

'Yes, I'm afraid so.'

Darcie's pulse is racing as she gasps for breath. 'Where did he go from there?'

'We don't know,' Darren admits. 'We lost him.'

'For fuck's sake,' Darcie hisses in terror. 'Was he coming here?'

'We don't know, but...'

'But what?'

'There are trains from Gare de Lyon to Avignon,' Darren says. 'It's a two-and-half-hour journey on a high speed train from Paris. And there are trains from Avignon to Bédoin.'

He's coming to kill me. I know he is!

'So he could have been here for days watching me?'

'It's possible,' Darren concedes. 'But we just don't know where he was going.'

'Bit of a huge bloody coincidence though, isn't it?' Darcie says, feeling herself getting angry. 'I go off to France for the weekend and Brennan heads to France too.'

'I really think you should fly home today, Darcie,' Darren says.

'No. I refuse to!' Darcie shouts. 'He's not going to ruin my life anymore. And if he comes anywhere near me, I've got a knife and I'm going to stab and kill him. And that will be all your fault for not putting him in prison when you had the chance. And I'm happy to explain that all to the media too. This is what you've driven me to.'

'Darcie?' Darren says, sounding concerned.

Darcie hangs up as her eyes fill with tears. She doesn't want Darren to hear her cry. *Fuck him!*

She wipes away her tears and then looks up the mountain road.

The smoke has got significantly thicker. It catches on the back of her throat and she coughs. She can barely see a few feet in front of her.

'Abi?' she shouts at the top of her voice. 'Abi?'

But Abi doesn't respond.

TWENTY-FOUR
STEPH

The smoke is now thick and acrid. My eyes are starting to sting a little from it. And Darcie and Abi are nowhere to be seen.

The logical part of my brain is telling me that they'll appear any second now and we can just make our way back to the car park like everyone else. But the paranoid voice is suggesting something terrible has happened.

'For fuck's sake!' Ruby groans, holding her phone. 'No bloody answer! We told them not to go too far. Idiots.'

Katie shakes her head. 'Why haven't they stopped so we can catch them up?'

'Or come back?' I suggest.

The visibility along the road is no more than thirty metres. Maybe less. I'm starting to panic. The mountain has been closed because it's dangerous and we've lost two of our group who've gone wandering off.

Two male cyclists appear out of the smoke, whizzing towards us. They're both decked out in bright orange-and-black cycling gear.

Katie walks across and begins to wave them down. 'Hello? Hi there,' she says loudly as the older man slows his bike to stop.

He gives her a curious look as the young man, who I guess is his son, stops beside him.

'You need to get off the mountain,' he says in a patronising tone. He has a thick French accent.

'You must go now. It is dangerous,' the son says with a very serious expression.

I nod. 'Yes, we know. But we've lost two of our friends further up that way,' I explain, but the smoke is now prickling my nostrils. 'Did you see them?'

The man furrows his brow and then shakes his head. 'No.' Then he looks to his son for confirmation.

The son peers at me. 'Your friends, they were cycling?' he asks.

'No,' Ruby replies. 'They were walking. Like us.'

'They both have blonde hair,' Katie explains. 'Same age as us.'

The man looks confused. 'I am sorry, but we didn't see anyone like that. There are a few cyclists coming down. But the smoke is getting worse, so maybe we just didn't see them.'

I don't like the sound of that one bit. *They can't have just vanished. Where the hell are they?*

'Okay, thank you,' I say with a concerned expression.

The man nods. 'I hope you find your friends. Bonne chance.'

And with that, the man and his son cycle away at speed.

'For God's sake,' Ruby hisses angrily as she grabs her phone and tries to call Abi.

I stare up the road, but visibility is getting worse with every minute that goes past. And the winds keep blowing the smoke uphill so that it swirls and turns.

'Still no bloody answer,' Ruby says gesturing to her phone. 'I'm going to kill them when I find them.'

I do think that it's partly Ruby's fault. If she hadn't lost her temper with Darcie and slapped her, then she wouldn't have stormed off.

'Come on,' I urge them.

We start to walk again, picking up the pace so we are somewhere between a fast walk and a slow jog.

'We can't keep going indefinitely,' Ruby points out. She's out of breath.

I glance at my watch. 'We'll go for fifteen minutes. If we don't find them, we'll think about heading back and calling the emergency services.'

'They're so fucking reckless,' Katie mutters angrily under her breath.

Suddenly Ruby goes over on her ankle and falls to the ground.

'Ow, ow, Jesus,' she groans with a grimace, clutching her left ankle. 'Fucking hell, that hurts!'

Katie and I race over to help.

'Are you all right?' I ask as I crouch down to check on her.

'Yeah, I'm sure I'll be okay,' Ruby reassures me as she puts her hands up. 'My ankle just went over.'

Katie and I take one hand each and pull her up so that she's back on her feet.

'Ow, ow,' Ruby says as she hops, trying to put some weight on it. 'I'm sure I'll be fine in a minute. I can walk it off.'

Katie and I look at each other as Ruby hobbles.

This is not good.

'Bollocks!' Ruby grits her teeth, trying to walk, but she has to hobble again. 'Sorry.'

Katie puts up her hand. 'Listen. Steph, you stay here with Ruby. Just don't move from here. I'll speed up there, grab those two twats and come down again.'

'You can't do that. You'll be on your own,' I protest.

'I'm so sorry, guys. I'm such a clumsy cow,' Ruby says apologetically.

'It's fine,' Katie reassures me. 'Seriously. I do those mental spin classes most days. I'll be up and down before you know it.'

I'm not happy about Katie walking off and leaving us. But I can't see any other solution.

'Keep your phone on,' I tell her. 'And don't move from the main path.'

'And if you can't see them after fifteen minutes, turn back,' Ruby says. 'Seriously.'

Katie nods. 'It'll be fine. I'm sure they're probably just sitting up on a rock, drinking water and waiting for us to catch them up.'

I'm not sure that I share Katie's confidence. The mountain is covered in smoke, for starters.

Just as Katie is about to start walking, a figure appears out of the smoke.

It's Abi.

Thank God.

I watch as she marches towards us. She's seething.

I look beyond Abi, fully expecting to see Darcie emerging from the smoke behind her.

But she doesn't.

And the longer I don't see Darcie walking behind Abi, the more I panic.

'Where the hell is Darcie?' Katie asks, sounding confused.

There is a horrible silence as Abi gets closer.

I'm feeling very uneasy about what Abi is going to tell us. My pulse is starting to race.

'Where's my sister?' Ruby calls out as Abi gets closer.

'She was on the phone to someone. And she was being a major pain in the arse,' Abi says loudly as she finally gets to us.

'What are you talking about?' Ruby asks.

'She wanted to get some decent photos of herself at the top of the mountain,' Abi explains as she tries to get her breath. 'She's waiting for the smoke to clear so she's staying put. I told her that I was coming to find you guys and she just shrugged. And then her phone rang so I left her to it. She was doing my head in. You know what she's like.'

'For fuck's sake!' Ruby groans.

'She's so selfish,' Katie says angrily.

I look wide-eyed at Abi. 'But the mountain's closed because of the fires and smoke. They're closing all the roads and sending everyone down.'

'What?' Abi pulls a face. 'We didn't know that. But I did wonder why there were so many cyclists coming past us.'

Katie points back the way that Abi has walked. 'How far up there is she?'

'Not far. Ten minutes, if that,' Abi replies.

'Right, I'm going to get her. And I'll drag her down here by her bloody extensions if I have to,' Katie says with a huff as she storms off up the road.

I shake my head. This was meant to be a lovely hike with my best friends for my fiftieth birthday. It's turning into a shit show.

'And Ruby's twisted her ankle,' I say, rolling my eyes. 'I put a bandage in my rucksack. I'll strap it up for you.'

'Thank you,' Ruby says as she sits down on the grassy verge.

'Christ, can anything else go wrong?' Abi sighs as she slumps down next to Ruby.

As I take off my rucksack, I look up, expecting to see Katie.

But she's vanished into the smoke.

TWENTY-FIVE

SHAUN

Shaun is now sitting down on a stone step at the Tom Simpson Memorial. He takes a long swig of water. He checks his watch again.

Where the hell is Tom? he wonders. *He can't be that unfit.*

Sticking out his right leg, Shaun leans forward, trying to stretch out his right hamstring. It feels tight. He's had problems with it before when he used to play football back in Dublin. Hooking his fingers under the toes of his right foot, he can feel the hamstring pulling. It's a bit sore, but it's been worse.

Then he sees something out of the corner of his eye.

Glancing around, Shaun is becoming aware that there are more cyclists here than normal. There also seem to be various animated conversations going on. Raised, concerned voices.

There's definitely something wrong. He can feel it in the air.

Two men in their forties are walking over to their bikes which are propped up against the stone wall of the monument nearby. They have small Union Jack badges on the sleeves of their cycling jerseys.

'Everything all right?' Shaun asks them.

The taller cyclist looks over at him as he puts on his helmet. 'Not really, mate,' he replies. 'They're closing the mountain for the day because of the fires.' The cyclist gestures to where Shaun had seen the smoke below about ten minutes earlier. 'We've travelled all the way from Kent to cycle up here. Hope it's open tomorrow, or we'll be gutted.'

'Oh yeah. Right. That is a pity.' Shaun nods. 'Thanks for letting me know.'

Standing up, he's now starting to worry that something has happened to Tom. Has he had a fall or is there a mechanical fault with the bike?

Then he sees a cyclist coming around the bend.

It's Tom.

He cycles over to where Shaun is sitting.

'About friggin' time,' Shaun groans, tapping his watch as Tom gets to him gasping for breath. 'Where the feck did you get to?'

'Sorry,' Tom pants as he stops the bike. 'Jesus, that's seriously steep, isn't it?' He takes his water bottle from the side of his small rucksack and drinks for a few seconds and tries to get his breath back.

'It averages 7.5 per cent,' Shaun explains. 'But that last bit is 12 per cent.'

'Twelve!' Tom exclaims. 'No wonder I think I'm gonna have a bloody heart attack.'

Shaun notices that there are thin red marks and scratches on Tom's neck, his jawbone and the back of his right hand.

'Jaysus, what the hell happened to you?' Shaun asks, pointing to his injuries.

'Came off the sodding bike,' Tom says, shaking his head. 'Ended falling down through the undergrowth. Arse over a tit.'

'Looks nasty.'

'It's a bit sore.'

'You were lucky you didn't break anything,' Shaun says,

then he gestures to the growing haze of smoke that's coming up the mountain. 'We can't go any further today, mate. They're closing the mountain. Wildfires.'

'Oh, right.' Tom nods and then gives a wry smile. 'I'm not gonna complain. More than happy to coast down and take it easy for a bit, bruv. Otherwise I think I'm gonna puke.'

As Tom turns, Shaun sees there's a cut at the back of Tom's neck and blood has trickled down to the top of his T-shirt.

'You've got a pretty nasty cut on the back of your neck as well,' Shaun says, pointing. 'Get some antiseptic on that when we get back.'

'Will do, mate.'

TWENTY-SIX

DARCIE

It's been ten minutes since Abi waltzed off and left while she was on the phone to Darren at Notting Hill police station. Darcie can't believe that Abi left her on her own. Especially after all they'd said about sticking together to stay safe. And now Darcie knows that not only is Brennan alive, but he might well be travelling to Provence, the situation is far more dangerous. In fact, Brennan could already be there on Mont Ventoux. She thinks of the man that followed them in the Fiat. The man who told her to have a good walk. That thought sends a shiver down Darcie's spine. She glances around frantically. With all the smoke, it's hard to tell if someone is out there hiding and watching her every move.

Darcie has no idea what she's meant to do now.

Over to her right, there is a small outcrop of rocks where the footpath and road split two ways.

Darcie's eyes move down the footpath and beyond. There is a small range of mountains in the background. Even though there is smoke, it looks very dramatic, even spooky down there. It'll be a good distraction. The perfect place for a few selfies. Or is that a stupid idea? Maybe if she just keeps her wits about her.

She takes a few steps along the footpath, trying to waft the smoke away from her face. Her eyes are stinging. What if they can't actually get up to the summit? That would never do. She's been posting about hiking to the top of Mont Ventoux for days now. She can't very well tell her followers that she didn't make it. It would seem like a failure.

Darcie gets the distinct impression that someone is watching her. And now the smoke has covered the mountain, it's hard to see more than twenty yards in any direction.

She stops for a moment to unlock her phone and notices three missed calls from Hugo and two from Steph. She had put her phone on silent for the hike.

There is also a very dramatic text from Hugo.

HUGO:

You need to CALL ME NOW! It's very URGENT.

Darcie immediately panics.

Bella? It must be Bella.

She finds Hugo's number and dials it immediately. Her hand is a little shaky.

'About time,' Hugo says answering his phone.

'Is it Bella? Is she okay?' Darcie asks feeling flustered.

'What?' Hugo splutters. 'Why are you asking about Bella?'

'You told me it was urgent. And to call you now,' Darcie replies, relieved that whatever it is, it isn't anything to do with their daughter. 'What the hell is going on?'

'I've had Duncan on the phone,' Hugo explains, sounding very agitated. 'The papers are running stories all next week.'

Duncan is Hugo's agent from a high-profile central London talent agency. They seem to have a love-hate relationship. Hugo blames Duncan for the decline of his career. But that is Hugo. Everything is someone else's fault. He never takes responsibility for his own actions, ever.

'Stories? What stories?' Darcie asks, already feeling exasperated at the sound of his voice. 'I'm up a fucking mountain in France, Hugo. What are you talking about?'

But she knows already. Of course. The journalist has been sniffing around her friends, digging for dirt.

'Usual bullshit,' Hugo groans. 'Sexual harassment, groping, inappropriate behaviour.'

Darcie has seen it with her own eyes. Lechy men with whom she'd worked in the past had now toned down or stopped inappropriate comments or behaviour for fear of being reported to HR. It was a relief. 'Pull yourself together,' she snaps. 'Haven't we been here before? The papers are always looking for stories like this.'

'This time it's happening,' Hugo explains.

The seriousness of his tone worries her.

'How can they go to print unless they have people going on the record?' Darcie says as she gets a sinking feeling in the pit of her stomach. 'Is there any basis to what they're saying?'

There was a deafening silence at the end of the phone that gives Darcie her answer.

'Hugo?' Darcie barks down the phone.

'I don't know, do I?' Hugo says. She can hear that his voice is slurry.

'Have you been drinking?' Darcie groans as she glances at the clock on her phone. 'It's not even midday in the UK.'

'Of course I've been fucking drinking,' Hugo thunders. 'This is serious. They've asked Duncan if I want to comment on the allegations that they've put forward.'

Darcie's mind is now racing ahead. She doesn't care that much if Hugo gets cancelled and loses what's left of his career. But the repercussions for her and Bella will be vast.

'I'll ask you again, Hugo,' Darcie says in an icy tone. 'Is there any truth in the allegations that they're making? Duncan must have told you what they're alleging that you've done.'

Another painful silence.

Darcie looks down at her phone, composes a quick text to Bella to warn her there might be a newspaper story about her father and sends it.

Then Darcie hears a sound from some undergrowth over to her right. A sort of rustling or fluttering noise. Maybe it's just a bird. She tries to put it out of her mind.

She focuses on what Hugo has told her. If the national papers run a series of stories exposing Hugo as a sex pest, molester and generally a vile, predatory man, it's going to ruin her career. The carefully crafted image of a happily married couple with a beautiful daughter and seemingly perfect aspirational, metropolitan lifestyle. It will all go in the blink of an eye.

Darcie's pulse is now racing with anxiety. She'll lose everything.

'Can't Duncan negotiate with them? He represents some really big hitters. Give them a different story so they drop the one on you?' Darcie says, trying to think on her feet. 'You know how this works. Offer a trade-off.'

'Duncan has already tried that. Apparently they're not interested,' Hugo says, sounding broken. 'I don't know what to do, Darcie.'

'Oh, fucking grow up, Hugo, and grow a pair,' Darcie sneers.

'I'm going to fly out to where you're staying in France,' Hugo says.

Darcie is incensed. She can hardly believe her ears. 'No you're fucking not!'

'I need to get out of the country for a few days, Darcie,' Hugo explains as if he's already made the decision. 'I need somewhere to hide out.'

'Don't you bloody dare fly out here, Hugo. You hear me?' she shouts angrily. 'I absolutely forbid you to do it. It's Steph's birthday. You're not going to spoil that by turning up with all this shit.'

'Please, Darcie. Where else can I go?' Hugo pleads.

'You should have thought of that before you acted like a predatory prick for all those years. And the papers will follow you out here and then we'll have journalists or paps outside our farmhouse. This is your fault. You and your fragile little ego. Well, you're going to get fucking cancelled. And in the process, so am I.'

Silence.

'And there it is,' Hugo says sarcastically. 'You're only worried about how this all affects you. That little bullshit fake world you've created online. Happy fucking families. A lovely photograph of us three sitting on the beach in the South of France with the fucking nanny tucked out of the way. It was you that wanted a divorce! Well, we're both going to be exposed for what we really are.'

'Don't you dare try and blame me!' Darcie shouts. 'This is all your fault.'

'Actually, it's not. The story has come from someone you know,' Hugo says.

'What? What are you talking about?' Darcie hisses.

'One of your friends has gone on record,' Hugo says in a supercilious voice. 'So you've got one of them to thank.'

'How do you know that?' Darcie asks, but she has a horrible feeling that he's telling the truth. It doesn't sound like something that Hugo would make up. Why would he?

'The editor told Duncan,' Hugo says. 'A close friend of my wife has gone on the record and made allegations about my behaviour. She's not the only one, of course. But she was the coup de grâce that meant that the story is running. Of course, I wondered if it's actually your sister?'

'My sister wouldn't throw me under the bus, Hugo,' Darcie snaps.

'Well, someone has,' he says.

TWENTY-SEVEN
RUBY

Ruby sits on the kerb massaging her sore ankle. She feels so guilty about twisting it. Even though the smoke and mountain closure is going to stop them getting to the summit of Mont Ventoux, coming down off the slopes is going to be more difficult and slow for everyone.

Abi sits beside her, drinking water from her bottle after a coughing fit from the smoke. Steph is standing with her hands on her hips, gazing up the mountain into the thick smoke. It's been ten minutes since Katie left them to go up to find Darcie and bring her back down. Her sister is such a drama queen. It's always about her. And it always has been.

Ruby uses her hands to try and stand up to see if the pain when she stands has been temporary.

For a moment, she thinks it's okay. Then as she puts her full weight onto it, there's a sharp pain that makes her wince.

'For fuck's sake!' she growls. 'Why am I so clumsy?'

'It's not your fault,' Abi says. 'These things happen.' Then she pats the ground. 'Just sit down until Darcie and Katie come back.'

'Yeah.' Ruby is resigned to hobbling for the rest of the day.

The whole thing has made her feel stupid. Ruby has always lacked coordination. She was terrible at PE and was always the last one to be picked when they played netball or hockey. She can remember the groans of whichever team ended up with her on their side. She can also remember the withering look of their officious PE teacher, Mrs Wilson, who seemed to be continually perplexed by Ruby's inability to do anything properly. And her lack of confidence just made it a self-fulfilling prophecy. It didn't help that Darcie and Abi, who were two years below her at Milton Hall School, were captain and vice captain of the school hockey team. Abi even played hockey for Hampshire all over the country for a while. Darcie used to tease Ruby, asking how they could be sisters when Ruby was so dreadful at anything sporty.

And things didn't change as Ruby got older. Three years ago, after a bad back and neck, Darcie had persuaded Ruby to join her hot-yoga class in Notting Hill. Not only was Ruby as supple as a wardrobe, she also had no balance. When it came to standing on one foot with her hands pressed together in a prayer-like pose, Ruby could keep that going for a whole five or six seconds. The other West London mummies seemed to be able to balance for minutes with utter grace. That was the last time that Ruby did hot bloody yoga. She would have preferred to spend the night at Guantanamo Bay!

Her train of thought is broken by a strange rumbling sound. A deep and rhythmic noise that sounds like it's coming from above. Glancing up, Ruby sees that there is a white-and-blue police helicopter hovering high above them. They must be monitoring the fires.

'What if we're stuck on this mountain?' Ruby says, thinking out loud.

Abi shakes her head. 'We're not,' she says confidently as she points to the slopes and ridge behind us. 'The fires and smoke are coming from down there. That's the north side of the mountain.' Then she points across the road on the opposite direction. 'We parked down that way which is the south side of the mountain. There aren't any fires down there.'

'How do you know that?' Ruby asks.

'When Darcie and I got up there, you can see down both sides. We'll be fine.' Abi grins. 'Once we find you a stretcher.'

Ruby narrows her eyes with a smirk. 'I hope you're joking?'

'Of course,' Abi laughs. 'We're not in a war zone. You've just sprained your ankle, that's all.'

'Darcie wouldn't help carry me down anyway,' Ruby snorts.

'No, not at the moment.' Abi then sings, 'She ain't heavy, she's my sister.'

Ruby laughs and rolls her eyes.

'I can't see them anywhere!' Steph shouts over to us.

'Well, staring into the smoke isn't going to make them come down any faster,' Ruby says. 'Come and sit down.'

Steph nods and wanders over to where they're sitting. 'I can't relax until I know they're both okay.'

Abi then points. 'There. I can see someone coming down now.'

All three of them squint.

Out of the smoke comes the figure of a man who is jogging. He has a rucksack on his back.

Ruby's eyes focus.

Bloody hell!

It's the man who had been driving the Fiat 500 that had followed them from Bédoin and had said hello to Darcie.

'What the fuck!' Abi says angrily.

Ruby watches him intently. 'What the hell is he doing?'

'Shit!' Steph looks anxiously up the mountain towards where they know Darcie and Katie are.

They all look at each other.

'Excuse me?' Steph shouts after the man at the top of her voice. 'Hello? Excuse me?'

The man doesn't slow and turn. It's as if he hasn't heard Steph shouting at him. But he must have done. Why didn't he stop?

Ruby gets a horrible sinking feeling deep in the pit of her stomach.

'He must have passed them on his way down,' Abi says quietly. 'What if he's done something to them?'

There's a horrible silence.

Steph frowns. 'I thought the police rang from London and said that her stalker had killed himself.' Then she grabs her phone and starts to dial.

'It's not confirmed,' Abi says. 'What if the police got it wrong and it's not him? And what if that was him who just ran past us?'

'I think we're jumping to conclusions at the moment,' Ruby says. 'And we're being paranoid.' This is what Ruby would like to believe but she's actually scared that something is terribly wrong.

Abi gets to her feet. 'Right, I'm not going to just sit here and wait for them to come back.'

'This is getting ridiculous,' Steph huffs, getting frustrated. 'We just need to all be together and go back to the car right now!'

Ruby can see Steph's annoyance. It's so unusual for her to lose her shit. But she also knows that they're all getting increasingly scared with every minute that goes by.

'Here we go,' Steph says with a sigh of relief.

Ruby looks up and sees a figure marching out of the smoke.

It's Darcie. She looks annoyed.

Thank God.

'What are you all doing sitting here?' Darcie yells angrily as she approaches.

'Where's Katie?' Steph asks.

Darcie shrugs as she gets closer. 'She's with you. What are you talking about?'

'She left about fifteen minutes ago to come and find you,' Ruby says, getting to her feet and starting to worry again.

Darcie looks confused as she arrives at where they're all now standing. 'I didn't see her.'

'What?' Steph asks. 'I just watched her walk up that road to go and find you and bring you back down here.'

'Well, I didn't see her,' Darcie snaps. 'I'm not lying to you, am I?'

'No one is suggesting that you're lying, Darcie,' Ruby says, trying to placate her.

'I don't understand how you could have missed her,' Abi says, shaking her head anxiously.

Darcie looks upset. 'Neither do I. Now I'm really worried.'

'It's just one pathway up there, isn't it?' Steph asks.

Darcie takes a moment then shakes her head. 'Where me and Abi stopped, the pathway split two ways.'

Abi nods. 'The one that went left was signed for the summit. The one to the right was signed for Gorges du Toul... Toul-ler-something.'

'Toulourenc?' Steph suggests. 'Gorges du Toulourenc?'

'That's it,' Darcie says.

'That path takes you down the mountain to a waterfall and some caves,' Steph explains.

Ruby looks at her sister. 'Where were you standing?'

Darcie looks a bit sheepish. 'About fifty yards along the footpath to the waterfall. I was trying to get some photos with the other mountains in the background.'

'For fuck's sake, Darcie!' Ruby thunders. 'Katie has walked straight past there and continued up towards the summit. She must be wondering where the hell you are.'

'I didn't ask her to come up there and find me,' Darcie snarls.

'Well, if you weren't acting like such a prima donna, we'd all be walking back down the mountain to the car,' Abi says.

'Oh, fuck off, Abi,' Darcie sneers.

'Jesus. None of this is helping us, is it?' Steph says holding up her hands to try and pacify everyone.

'You must have seen that creepy man jogging down the mountain about two minutes before you arrived?' Abi asks. 'He would have run past you?'

Darcie nods. 'I saw the back of him,' she admits. 'I didn't know it was that creep from the car park.'

'I was worried about your stalker,' Steph says. 'But I'm assuming that he's dead?'

Darcie's face falls.

Ruby looks at her. *Now what?*

'It's not him,' Darcie says very quietly.

'What do you mean?' Ruby asks with concern.

Darcie looks at them all. 'It wasn't Brennan's body in that burned out shed. It was his flatmate. Brennan killed him and made it look like it was him.'

Ruby feels her stomach clench with the news.

Abi is horrified. 'Where the hell is he now?'

'He's somewhere in France,' Darcie says and then pulls a face. 'He might have got a train from Paris to Avignon.'

Steph's eyes widen. 'Avignon? Jesus Christ, Darcie! Avignon is about an hour from here.'

Ruby watches her sister's breathing becoming increasingly shallow. She looks like she might be having another panic attack.

'I know.' Darcie nods. 'There's... there's a train from Avignon to Bédoin...'

Ruby goes to her. 'Take deep long breaths, Darce. Nice and steady.'

Then they all look up the mountain.

Steph takes out her phone. 'I'm ringing Shaun and Tom.

We need to get up there and find Katie as soon as we can. And we need their help.'

Ruby nods. 'And we need to split up and check both those paths just in case.'

'Shaun, it's Steph,' she says as she walks away to talk on the phone.

Darcie has a dark look on her face as she breathes deeply, hands on her thighs. 'I've thought of something else.'

'What's that?' Ruby asks.

'Katie is wearing my baseball cap and she's wearing very similar clothes to these,' Darcie says, gesturing to what she's wearing. 'I posted this morning with my cap on. And if Brennan is monitoring my Instagram account...'

Darcie didn't need to finish her sentence.

TWENTY-EIGHT
STEPH

My eyes are stinging from the smoke. I take a few tentative steps down the footpath, keeping close to Shaun.

We've been searching for twenty minutes. Where the hell is Katie?

I glance at my watch. We agreed to meet back at where Ruby is sitting at 2.15 p.m.

The logical part of my brain is telling me that Katie got to the fork in the road and took the main path up to the summit. Why wouldn't she? In fact, why would she take this much smaller footpath leading down to the Gorges du Toulourenc waterfall and caves? It's well signposted. Isn't it?

Then the other part of my brain counters. What if the smoke was too thick and Katie missed the signs? What if she took this footpath instead? It's narrow and dangerous. What if she lost her footing and fell down a ravine? What if she's just lying there injured and we can't see her because of the smoke?

My whole body is riddled with anxiety. I've convinced myself that one false step and I'm going to plummet down a vast canyon to my excruciating death.

Visibility is probably down to ten yards now. I've heard helicopters circling overhead.

'Where the hell is Tom?' I ask.

'No idea. He's making a habit of disappearing today,' Shaun groans.

I'm not sure what he means by this.

As I think about it, I lose my concentration on what I'm actually meant to be doing.

As a result, I suddenly lose my footing on some loose rocks. My balance goes and I'm about to tumble.

Shaun reaches out and I grab hold of his hand.

'Thanks,' I say with relief.

'Tom?' Shaun shouts.

Shaun then stops, turns and looks at me.

'I want you to wait here,' he says and points to a small fallen tree trunk to the side of the path. 'Sit on that. I'm going to find that bloody idiot. Don't worry. I won't be long.'

I wait for nearly ten minutes on the fallen tree.

Finally a shadowy figure emerges slowly from a bank of acrid smoke. It looks otherworldly. Ethereal. I can't see who it is yet.

I cough as the smoke catches on my throat. My eyes are stinging and raw. I don't care.

I'm praying that they've found her.

What the hell happened? How could she just vanish? I ask myself. It just doesn't feel real.

The figure is now only ten yards away. I can see it's Shaun.

'What is it?' I ask anxiously.

'Tom's found her,' he replies.

My whole body reacts with relief.

But then I can see that there's something wrong. He has a grim expression on his face.

Why does he look so serious? It's good that they've found her, isn't it?

'Is she all right?' I ask nervously.

Shaun gestures to the ridge. 'Tom's trying to get down to her now,' he explains sounding a little flustered.

'Show me,' I say, my pulse racing. I get up and follow Shaun to see what's going on.

TWENTY-NINE

I watch in horror as two men in black boiler suits and boots carefully lift my friend and place her into a black body bag at the side of the road. Tears fill my eyes and my bottom lip quivers.

No, no, this can't be happening.

I swallow, trying to fight back the tears. I need to keep it together.

Two French police officers are unravelling yellow tape that has *Police Technique Et Scientific – Zone Interdite* written in black letters. I don't know exactly what it means. I can't think straight. It's like I'm trapped in some terrible anxiety dream that I can't wake myself up from.

Two police cars have been pulled across the road to block it off from traffic. Their blue lights are flashing silently but I can hear the odd crackle of a police radio and people speaking in French. There's an ambulance nearby too but the French paramedics quickly confirmed what we already knew. She is dead.

Officers in white forensic suits and blue latex gloves examined her body for about an hour. Now officers are being lowered down to where we found her, presumably to look for forensic evidence. It's like I'm watching some crime thriller or cop drama on the television. It isn't real. It can't be.

The two men in front of me then zip the body bag up. The sound tears through the air – that horrible, final zip – and suddenly I can't breathe. I want to stop them, to tell them they've made a mistake. That's not a body in there. That's my friend.

It thumps me in the gut. She's gone. I'm never going to see her again.

And I picture her face laughing. Of us chatting and her telling me all about her life. Joking about the past. That was only about an hour ago. She was walking beside me.

Then the men lift her up off the ground and move her gently towards a blacked-out van.

'Oh God,' cries out a voice behind me.

I turn to see Ruby as she puts her hands to her face and dissolves into tears.

Taking a step towards her, I pull her into my arms.

I feel Ruby's whole body tremble with her sobbing.

I look around and everything feels surreal. I'm numb. I'm disassociating myself from the trauma of what's happened. It's my body's natural defensive mechanism. The distress of what's taken place is too much for my brain to bear so I no longer feel connected to my body.

My eyes move and meet Tom's. He gives me an empathetic look. Shaun stands next to him, giving a tiny shake of his head as if he can't believe what we're all witnessing.

A woman is walking towards me – she hands me her card.

Détective Marie Jobert
Officier de Police Judiciaire
Commissariat de Police d'Avignon.

I feel Ruby continue to hug me tightly.

'What are we going to do?' she whispers in between her sobs.

'I don't know,' I say gently. 'But we'll all be here to support each other.'

Ruby nods.

I'm aware that Detective Jobert is now standing right by me.

I let Ruby go and look directly at her. 'It's okay. We're going to get through this.' I'm not sure if I actually believe this, but I want to reassure Ruby and take away her pain. I don't believe a word of what I've just said.

Ruby looks bewildered. Her eyes are puffy and wet.

'Stephanie?' Detective Jobert says gently.

'Yes. It's Steph,' I say, turning to meet her gaze. But my voice doesn't feel like my own. As if the sound has come from somewhere else. It's disorientating.

'I am sorry.' Detective Jobert gestures towards the black mortuary van. 'I know this is very difficult for you and your friends. But there are questions that I would like to ask you about what happened this morning and what you saw. And my colleagues from Forensique, they must come to where you are staying. They will need to take DNA samples and fingerprints from everyone.'

'Of course,' I say with an understanding nod, but I'm finding it difficult to listen and process what she's saying.

One of the forensic team comes over with a clear plastic bag and hands it to her. She holds it up. Inside is Darcie's black Gucci baseball cap.

'Do you recognise this?' she asks me.

'Yes,' I reply. It's so disturbing to see that cap now in a police evidence bag.

Detective Jobert raises an eyebrow. 'Your friend was wearing this when you found her?'

'Yes. Sorry. I took it off her when we were giving her CPR,' I explain. I'm worried that I shouldn't have done that for some reason. Have I somehow tampered with the evidence? I panic.

'It is fine,' she reassures me and then she pulls out her notebook. 'Let me check we have the correct address for where you are staying.' She peers at her writing. 'Château Cardou. And that is in Bédoin, yes?'

The noise of the van doors slamming distracts me. I glance over at the black van.

'Sorry, yes. That's correct,' I reply but my voice catches in my throat. She's in there. In that van. All alone. My heart shatters again.

'And there were five of you staying there. You flew in from London yesterday?' Detective Jobert confirms from her notes. 'And you were due to leave on Monday morning?'

Due to leave. Her use of the word 'due' strikes me. What are we going to do? We can't go home. We need to contact her family. I organised this trip so it should be me that does all that, shouldn't it?

Abi appears by my side. Her face is also red and puffy from where she has been crying. She reaches for my hand and takes it. I smell the familiar scent of her shampoo and it brings me a fleeting moment of comfort.

'Where are they taking her?' Abi asks me as the van's engine starts. The sudden noise of the diesel engine startles me. My nerves are frayed.

'She will be taken to Avignon Hospital Centre,' Detective Jobert explains to us both. 'Please, don't worry. They will take very good care of her there.'

Her words sound comforting but also so incredibly strange. How can they take care of her? She's gone.

'Can we see her when she's there?' Ruby asks.

Detective Jobert thinks for a moment and then nods. 'Yes, I can make arrangements for you to do that.'

'Thank you,' Ruby says.

I don't know if I want to see her. Do I? Walk into a mortuary and see her lying there? I'm not sure that I could bear that. Is that what I'm meant to do? What if I don't want to see her? What if I just want to remember her as she was? Does that make me look bad or uncaring?

Abi bites at her nails and tears roll down her face as we watch the van drive away. I put my arm around her shoulders to comfort her. We're all silent and motionless until the van is out of sight.

And she's gone.

And then there is a terrible silence. An emptiness.

The smoke has started to thin and slowly disappear.

A noisy flapping of wings from a nearby tree fractures the peace.

I turn and watch as a large bird of prey – maybe a falcon – uses its mighty wings to climb into the air before they are still and it bobs and glides on the air currents.

'I think it would be best for you all to go back to where you are staying in Bédoin,' Detective Jobert explains. 'This has been very shocking for you all. You'll be more comfortable there. And I can send officers to you.'

Tom comes over warily. 'Anything I can do?' he asks, but he looks jittery.

I meet his eyes, but I'm not sure what to say.

Detective Jobert looks to me as if expecting an explanation for who Tom is.

'Tom and Shaun.' I gesture to where Shaun is standing. 'They're staying across the road in a cottage. We met them yesterday.'

Detective Jobert raises her eyebrow as if this is of some interest to her. 'And you are English?'

'Yeah,' Tom replies, looking uncomfortable.

Detective Jobert looks Tom up and down. 'And you were walking with this party from the farmhouse?'

'No.' Tom shakes his head. He's clearly in shock too. 'Shaun and I were out cycling.'

Shaun joins at the sound of his name.

'I called them to help us with the search,' I explain to Detective Jobert.

Her pen hovers over her notepad. 'Together the whole time?'

'Sort of,' Shaun says, just as Tom adds, 'He's fitter than me – I had trouble keeping up.'

'And you knew the deceased?' Her pen scratches against paper.

The deceased. My hands curl into fists.

'Not really,' Shaun says.

'A little bit,' Tom murmurs under his breath.

'I stopped a man in a pickup truck by the access road. He had a rope. We attached it to the back. Then he helped us pull her out,' Shaun says.

I can hear the thunderous bark of a couple of dogs in the distance.

Detective Jobert's questions sharpen. 'This pickup truck that helped with the body – where is the driver now? You didn't get his name? His licence plate?'

We all look around, the absence suddenly glaring. No one remembers seeing him leave.

It strikes me that her question is absurd, given everything that was going on.

'Sorry, no.' Shaun pulls a face. 'We were all just so worried that I guess we didn't notice that he'd left.'

Detective Jobert narrows her eyes. 'And you two live in a cottage across from the farmhouse?'

There is more barking and it sounds as if it's getting closer.

'That's right.' Shaun nods. 'We're renovating the place for the owners who live in London.'

'And how long have you been here in Provence?' she asks.

'I've been here for nearly three months,' Shaun replies.

Tom looks at her. 'I arrived yesterday.'

She frowns. Tom's statement seems significant to her. 'Yesterday?' she asks.

'Yeah,' Tom says, sounding a little bit defensive. I don't blame him. Everything Detective Jobert says or asks seems to be laced with suspicion. I guess it's just her way. She's a detective, after all.

'Sorry,' Abi says, sounding stressed. 'I don't mean to tell you how to do your job, but shouldn't we be focusing on who attacked our friend? I mean, they're here somewhere on the mountain. Shouldn't you be looking for them and stopping anyone from leaving?'

Detective Jobert gives Abi a slightly patronising smile. 'Thank you for your concern...' She searches for her name.

'Abi.'

'Abi,' Detective Jobert says. 'But I have officers down at all the access roads to the mountain. They are stopping every vehicle, cyclist and walker as they leave and interviewing them.' She then points to the area below us. 'I also have our dog unit out trying to get a scent near to where your friend was found.'

'Oh, right,' Abi says a little apologetically. 'Of course.'

'Please, we will do everything we can to find out who murdered your friend and bring them to justice,' Detective Jobert assures us.

Her use of the word 'murdered' hits me hard. No one has used that word yet. It feels so alien to even hear it being said.

But it's true. That's what's happened.

Someone has murdered our friend.

THIRTY

I stop at the junction along the road that leads through Sault-en-Provence. It's about ten minutes from here to the main route that's going to take us back to Bédoin and our farmhouse. But I'm driving on some kind of strange autopilot. Not able to concentrate. Driving on the subconscious memory of our arrival here. Distracted and numb. There are only four of us in the rental car now. When we arrived here, we were five. I feel sick at the thought of it.

My mind is fogged. I take my foot off the brake, pull forward, when suddenly a van comes flying past.

'Shit!' I gasp as I slam my foot on the brake which throws everyone forward.

Silence.

'I'm really sorry,' I apologise very quietly. 'I just didn't see it.'

No one says anything for a few seconds.

'It's all right,' Ruby reassures me gently. 'Do you want me to drive?'

'No. I'll be fine.' I hear my voice and words. Will I be fine? How can I be fine?

Looking both ways, I make a conscious effort to concentrate. The road is now clear so I pull out very slowly and turn left.

For the next few minutes, we drive along in a horrible silence.

No one knows what to say. What can we say? We don't want to talk about what's happened. It's too raw. Too painful. But talking about anything else will feel insensitive and wrong. I look into the rear-view mirror and see that everyone is sitting gazing out of the windows, lost in their own thoughts and grief.

The village of Sault-en-Provence comes into view in front of us. The sun beats off the buildings that are cream-coloured in this light. A small sea of rust-coloured terracotta roofs. Beautiful wooden shutters painted delightful colours – turquoise, soft pink, olive, sky blue – that are closed against the heat of the late afternoon. A few people shuffling along the pavement with a bag of shopping. Houses that are tight to the cobblestoned roads. Three old men sitting in the shade, smoking and playing cards. And beyond this, fields of sunflowers and vineyards in a shallow valley below us. Low hills with areas of limestone and shrubs for as far as the eye can see. Everything looks the same as before. But it also looks different.

I see a woman in here thirties walking along. She has two children – a boy and girl – in tow. They are both holding their mother's hand, with a large ice cream in the other. The boy's ice cream has run down his chin and onto his dark T-shirt. The mother stops, crouches and then takes a tissue to clean him up. They are all smiling. Of course they are. Not a care in the world. A mother with two beautiful children in the glorious sunshine of the late afternoon, in a place that looks like this.

Before I really notice, we're heading north on the D974. It's a single lane main road. On our left, a small bank of dark shrubs and rocks leads up to an endless bank of tall trees – umbrella and Aleppo pines, evergreen oak and cypresses. To our right, the landscape sweeps away into the distance. Great plains and low hills of limestone that look like they belong to a different planet. In different circumstances I would point this out. Make a comment about the lunar-esque scenery.

But I feel utterly detached, as if this can't be reality. I get fleeting seconds where I am distracted by a thought. I remember that I'm having a new front door fitted to my flat in Clapham. And then my mind is taken away with thoughts of new keys for the new locks on the door.

And then I notice that I'm driving along a road in Provence. And I'm jolted back into the present.

The incessant silence in the car is starting to feel overwhelming. It's making my anxiety worse. I reach over to the car stereo and turn it onto a very low volume. At first, all I can hear is some French voices chattering on what I assume is a local news radio channel. I hit the search button and some French pop music comes on, but it's too upbeat and happy. I turn the stereo off. I'll just have to bear the silence instead.

I see a police car pass us coming the other way and wonder if it's headed up to the mountain.

Then my mind suddenly finds focus as I realise something.

'We didn't tell that detective about the car,' I say with a frown. 'The Fiat that followed us. That we saw that man get out of. The one who spoke to Darcie.'

For a few seconds, no one says anything.

'No,' Ruby agrees quietly. 'We do need to tell her.'

My mind is now whirring. 'In fact, she should have that information now so they can put out some kind of alert. APB or whatever they call it.'

Abi shrugs. 'How are we going to do that? We can't drive back there.'

'No,' I agree. 'But you've got the registration, haven't you?' It's a relief to be having some form of conversation. A way of returning to a recognisable reality.

'I got a photograph.' Ruby nods. 'I'll take a look and note it down for her.'

Then I remember I have the card that Detective Jobert gave me. I fish it out of the pocket of my shorts. 'Actually, I've got that detective's card. I think it's got her phone number on it.'

I hand it back and Ruby takes it from me.

'I'll send the photo to...' Ruby peers at the card. 'Detective Jobert. Then I can ring her to make sure she's got it.'

'Good idea,' Abi agrees.

And now my mind turns to a darker question. Where is Brennan now? He knows where we're staying.

In half an hour, we're going to be back at the farmhouse and I have no idea if we're going to be safe there. What if he's driven to Bédoin and he's there waiting for us?

THIRTY-ONE

My whole body feels prickly with anxiety. I've made endless cups of tea for everyone. It's the English solution to any trauma or crisis. It feels strange to be sitting outside in this Provençal idyll nursing hot tea in a mug. Abi declined the tea and poured herself an enormous vodka and tonic. I don't blame her. My hand hovers over the bottle, but I pull back. Not today. Today I need every nerve ending sharp, every thought crystal-clear. Today I need to feel everything, even the pain.

My hands shake as I make another cup of tea I won't drink. The familiar ritual reminds me of Gran, how she'd wrap my trembling fingers around a warm mug after each nightmare, each teenage heartbreak. 'Everything looks clearer after tea, love.' But she was wrong about this one. Nothing's clear. Not why my friend wandered off alone, not why someone would hurt her, not why I'm standing in her bedroom watching strangers bag up pieces of her life.

I was fifteen when Gran died – my first real loss. I'd spent every weekend in her kitchen, learning her recipes, soaking in her stories, while my parents chased their careers and my older brother, Chris, chased his dreams to Australia. Now, watching the others break down in waves of grief, I remember how Gran's death felt: like drowning while everyone else could still breathe. But this is different.

At the moment, the farmhouse is crawling with forensic officers. They're going through her bedroom with a fine-tooth comb. They are dressed in white forensic suits, white rubber boots and blue nitrile gloves. Every so often I see one of them coming down the stairs holding a see-through bag with something inside. Something that I assume is relevant evidence.

One of my closest friends on the planet has been attacked and murdered.

I'm never going to see her again. How is that possible? This can't be happening. My eyes fill with tears and I bite my lip. I try to hold it back but it's no use.

'Oh God,' I whisper as my shoulders shudder and my whole body is crushed by pain, loss and grief.

I feel a comforting hand on my shoulder.

'Hey,' says a voice.

It's Abi.

I try to smile at her through my teary eyes, but my face crumples as I stand. We cling to each other and this makes me cry more. We're both experiencing the same thing. And only we know how painful this is.

'It's okay,' Abi whispers.

I nod. But it's not okay. And as the tears subside, I feel a little twinge of anger.

'Who the fuck did this to her?' I ask, shaking my head.

'I don't know. I just don't understand,' Abi admits very quietly.

Detective Jobert approaches, sunglasses nested in her dark hair. I catch myself studying her features, a habit I'm trying to break, and force my attention to what matters: her expression, the notepad in her hand, whatever news she might be bringing.

'Steph,' she says and gestures to where I've been sitting. 'I'd like to get a detailed statement from you now. If you're feeling up it?'

She says 'If you're feeling up to it' in a tone that implies that she's already made the assumption that I am. And, however unnatural and chilling it is to think about, she is now running a murder investigation.

I nod. 'Of course,' I reply as I go back to where I was sitting at a long, wrought-iron table. There are six iron chairs with patterned turquoise cushions that have been tied on. There's an exquisite wooden gazebo. The wooden beams have small white flowers hanging from them. I don't know what they are.

'I'll go,' Abi says to me, touching me on the arm.

'I will need to speak to everyone,' Detective Jobert says to her in a serious tone that reminds me once again of the enormity of what's actually happened. I get a sinking feeling in the pit of my stomach as Abi walks away.

Detective Jobert's dark eyes hold mine, steady and searching. My skin prickles under her gaze. Maybe she's looking for signs that my grief isn't genuine. Or am I just being paranoid? She can't possibly think that one of us is responsible for her death. That would be ridiculous. We were best friends. I can't even entertain the thought that one of us would hurt her. In fact, I don't know why that is whirling around my head. Maybe it's just human nature in a situation like this to feel guilty. It's certainly my default setting. If I see a police car behind me in the traffic in London, I immediately feel a pang of guilt. As if I've done something wrong. Is that normal? Doesn't everyone think like that?

'So, Steph,' Detective Jobert says as she takes out her black notebook and clicks the end of her pen. 'I have your full name and address in London. I have the flight number that all of you were on. But I will need your passport number before I leave today.'

I've already anticipated this and I have put my passport into the side pocket of my cream shorts. I take it out and hand it to her. 'Here you go.'

'Ah, thank you.' She takes it and notes down the passport number and other details. Then she hands it back to me. I spot an engagement and wedding ring on her left hand. She also has a tiny tattoo of some musical notes on the underside of her left wrist. She sits forward and fixes me with a stare. 'I'm going to need you to walk me through what happened this morning, step-by-step. What time did you leave here?'

'It was just after ten,' I reply. 'I wanted to go earlier but, you know.'

She gives me a look as if she doesn't really know what I'm talking about.

'And everyone was okay? No arguments between anyone?' she asks, searching my face as if looking for my reaction.

'Not really,' I say. 'I mean no.'

But she seizes on my hesitation. 'Not really or no? They are two different things.'

'I'd had a little tiff with Darcie before we left,' I explain, but I can feel my pulse quicken a little, as if this is somehow significant.

Detective Jobert gives me a quizzical look. 'A little tiff?' She clearly doesn't understand this.

'Sorry. I mean argument or quarrel,' I clarify, but both of those words sound far worse than 'tiff'. It makes it sound more serious than it actually was.

'You had an argument,' Detective Jobert says as she writes it down.

'Yes,' I reply, but I'm puzzled. 'Sorry, but can I ask you why you need all these details? We are a group of friends on holiday. What happened this morning has nothing to do with any of us. This man, Patrick Brennan, who stalked Darcie in London. The police in London think he's in France.'

'Yes, I know that,' she replies. 'I have spoken to the police in

London and Paris. The only thing that I know is that Patrick Brennan was at a train station in Paris. And that is seven hundred kilometres away from here.'

And then she says something that sends a chill up my spine.

'So we don't know who is responsible, do we?' she says with a nonchalant shrug.

What? Oh God, how can she think that any of us had something to do with her death? That's insane.

'Sorry, but that's ridiculous,' I say hesitantly. I don't want to get her back up, but what she's suggesting is absurd.

She narrows her eyes. 'Is it? Most homicides are committed by people known to the victim. In fact, it's very rare for a homicide to be committed by a total stranger.'

My breathing is getting shallow. I take a nervous swallow and rub my nose.

'But that's what happened,' I protest. 'I know my friends. I know what they're like.'

'Yes.' She nods. 'That is true. But your friend was strangled. And we've had no reports of any attacks like that.' She holds my gaze. 'In my experience, it usually means the victim knew their killer. Or the killer knew them.'

THIRTY-TWO

SHAUN

Shaun comes out of the back of the cottage and over to where Detective Marie Jobert is sitting. He hands her his Irish passport. 'Here you go.'

'Thank you,' she says quietly as she takes it, flicks through it and begins to note down his passport number and other details in her notebook.

Shaun sits forward nervously. Then he looks over at the young uniformed police officer who is taking a look around the garden. He's so young that he doesn't look like he even shaves yet. He's dressed in a black uniform, with a baseball cap and *POLICE MUNICIPALE* printed on the back of his jacket. The young police officer gives him a look. Police officers make Shaun feel nervous. They always have done. Where he grew up in Dublin, the Garda were the enemy. His da was always in trouble with the Peelers. Petty theft, drunken fighting but nothing major.

'Sure you don't want a drink?' Shaun asks. 'There's cold water in the fridge.'

She shakes her head. 'I am fine really,' she says as she hands his passport back. 'Until we find a suspect, I am going to have to ask you and Tom not to leave Bédoin.'

'Of course,' Shaun says with an understanding look.

'You and Tom were cycling on the mountain when Steph called you for help? Is that right?' Detective Jobert asks.

'Aye, that's right,' Shaun says. 'We were cycling the route from Bédoin. The Tour de France route.'

'Yes. And how far had you got when you received the call?'

'I'd stopped up by the Tom Simpson memorial,' Shaun explains. 'It's only just over a kilometre from there to the summit.'

She nods. 'Yes, I know. My husband is a keen cyclist.' Then she taps her pen against the page of the notebook with a quizzical look. 'You said that *you* had stopped at the memorial? Was Tom not cycling with you?'

Shaun pauses for a moment. If he tells her that Tom wasn't there, does that put Tom in an awkward position? Shaun can't see how it would. It's not as if Tom is a murderer. And Detective Jobert has insisted that she interviews them both separately. Shaun can see the logic in that. He's seen enough television cop shows to know that detectives interview people individually to see if their version of events are the same. Shaun has no idea what Tom will tell her about their cycle that morning so he just needs to stick to telling the truth.

'No,' Shaun replies, shaking his head. 'We were having a wee bit of a competition to see who would get to the summit first. I've been riding the mountain nearly every day for the past three months so I left him behind.'

The young police officer answers his mobile phone and walks away down the garden.

Detective Jobert looks up from her notebook. 'Tom wasn't with you?'

'No,' Shaun says. 'He caught me up eventually.'

'How long were you and Tom not cycling together? Roughly?' she asks.

Shaun thinks for a second. 'Forty-five minutes. It might have been longer.'

'Was it longer?'

'I guess so. An hour?'

'But then he caught you up at the memorial?' she clarified.

'Yeah.' Shaun nods. 'That's right.'

'I noticed that Tom had scratches on his neck and his hands,' Detective Jobert says, using her pen to point to her own neck and hands.

Shaun nods but wonders why she is asking about them. 'He told me he'd fallen off his bike and into the undergrowth. Clumsy eejit.'

She fixes Shaun with a stare which makes him feel uncomfortable. 'Did you believe him?'

'Yeah.' He shrugs. He's not sure he likes the way that her questions are developing. 'I don't know why he'd lie about it.'

'No,' she says unconvincingly. Then she frowns. 'I'm a little confused. You don't know Steph or any of the others staying in the farmhouse.'

Shaun raised an eyebrow. 'How do you mean?'

'You don't know them from the UK, do you?'

'No. But the owners pay me to look after the farmhouse and the guests. I do shopping, test the pool, stuff like that,' Shaun explains but he doesn't quite know what she's getting at.

'Why did Steph call you? She's not a friend. You don't know her,' she asks suspiciously.

Before Shaun can explain, the young police officer, who has now finished his call, comes over to Detective Jobert. He leans close and starts to speak to her in a low tone. He is speaking fast and Shaun can't make out what they are talking about. But at one point, they both look over at him.

Oh shit. This is not good.

Shaun fears that his past is about to catch up with him. And there is no way that he's going back to Dublin.

Luckily she gave me my passport back, he thinks.

Detective Jobert fixes him with a quizzical stare. 'There is a warrant out for your arrest in Ireland. It was issued after you arrived in France.'

'No.' Shaun shakes his head. 'That must be a mistake.'

She shakes her head. 'I've just seen your passport. It is not a mistake.'

'What is the arrest warrant for?' Shaun asks, but he knows full well what it's for. His heart is now beating hard in his chest and his mouth is dry.

Detective Jobert looks at the young police officer. 'We don't know. We don't have those details yet. But you might be required to come to Avignon at some point for further questioning. Until then I'd like you to stay in Bédoin.'

THIRTY-THREE
DARCIE

Darcie throws her washbag and toiletries into her Louis Vuitton bag, shuts and zips it up. She quickly checks around the room to ensure she hasn't left anything behind. Her stomach is knotted with an overwhelming anxiety. All she knows is that she has to leave the farmhouse and fly home right now.

As she wheels her bag along the polished wooden landing, she spots an open door to her right. There is yellow police tape in a crisscross over the opening.

It's Katie's room.

Darcie peers in.

She sees Katie's open suitcase on the floor. Her tiny sandals and trainers in a line. Two dresses and other clothes hanging in the wardrobe. And the crumpled marks on the pillow where she slept. Then she gets a waft of the perfume that Katie had worn the night before. When they'd all sat around the pool, laughing and dancing. When everything had been normal.

Then Darcie is gripped by guilt. She has a flashback of dancing with Shaun on the patio. And then dragging him away to her bedroom. Why? Why hadn't she just stayed with her oldest friends rather than drag a random man to her bed? *What the hell is wrong with you? Why didn't you spend that time talking to Katie?*

The idea of never seeing or talking to Katie hits Darcie like a train. It's too much. Her eyes fill with tears and she starts to weep uncontrollably.

'Hey, hey,' says a comforting voice.

It's Abi.

'I'm sorry,' Darcie sobs. 'I ruined everything last night. I'm so selfish. And that was the last time we'll all be together. The last time we'll be with her. I'm such a selfish wanker.'

'No. We all drank too much,' Abi says, hugging her tight. 'Katie had a lovely time last night.'

'But it's my fault she's dead,' Darcie whispers.

'No. No it's not,' Abi reassures her.

Then Abi moves back and looks down at her suitcase.

'Where are you going, Darce?' she asks with a confused frown.

'I need to go. I need to get home,' Darcie says as she rubs the tears from her face. 'I'm not safe here.'

'The police won't let you leave,' Abi says.

'I'm not staying,' Darcie snaps anxiously. 'That man... he killed Katie.'

'We don't know that yet,' Abi says.

But Darcie's need to get out and away is overwhelming. She pushes past Abi on the landing and heads for the stairs. 'Sorry, Abs, but I've got to go.'

Darcie wheels her suitcase down the hallway, through the living area where there are police officers and out to the patio where Steph and Ruby are sitting.

'Steph, can you take me to the airport?' Darcie says hurriedly.

Steph narrows her eyes. 'What?'

Ruby gets up. 'You can't go to the airport.'

'I can,' Darcie replies. 'There's a flight to Stanstead in two hours. I got a standby ticket online.'

Ruby approaches and points over to Detective Jobert. 'They're not going to just let you leave the country while all this is going on.'

'Why not?' Darcie is getting angry. 'I didn't kill anyone. I'm not a bloody suspect. She was one of my best friends. And I want to go home. Steph?'

Detective Jobert turns to look over. She has clearly spotted Darcie and her suitcase.

Oh, great, here we go.

'Where are you going?' Detective Jobert asks, looking confused.

'The airport,' Darcie says as if it's a silly question. 'I need to go home.'

'I'm afraid that's not possible. You must stay here.' Detective Jobert is shaking her head.

'I'm not safe here,' Darcie says in a frustrated voice. 'There is a man out there who has been stalking me back in London. He's here. And he killed Katie because he thought she was me.'

Detective Jobert gives her a frown. 'Why would you think that?'

'Katie had borrowed my baseball cap. We were wearing very similar clothes. We have blonde hair. About the same height. There was smoke everywhere. Don't you get it? I was the target, but he killed her by accident.'

'Yes, one of your friends mentioned this.' Detective Jobert nodded calmly. 'But we don't know that. And I haven't even taken a statement from you yet.'

'I don't need to give you a statement,' Darcie huffs. 'We went for a hike up that mountain. There were fires which caused a lot of smoke. Someone attacked our friend Katie, believing it was me, and killed her.'

Darcie is suddenly overwhelmed by the enormity of what's

happened. 'Oh God,' she says as she closes her eyes and more tears come. She begins to cry uncontrollably.

Steph comes over and puts a reassuring hand on her arm. 'Come on. Why don't you come and sit down inside and I'll make you a cup of tea.'

Darcie glares at Steph angrily. 'I don't want a fucking cup of tea, Steph! That's not going to fix this. It's your bloody fault we were up that mountain in the first place. Why didn't we just stay here by the pool for the day? Then Katie would be alive, wouldn't she?'

'Darcie!' Ruby barks. 'That's not fair, and you know it.'

Darcie looks at Detective Jobert with pleading eyes. 'Please, I just need to go. I can write a statement on the plane and email it to you.'

'I'm very sorry, Darcie,' Detective Jobert says gently. 'But I'm going to need you all to stay for at least a couple of days. I'm going to take your passports just in case anyone has any silly ideas.' She looks at Darcie. 'And if anyone does try to leave, I'll have to arrest you.'

'You can't do that,' Darcie hisses.

'I'm a police officer running a murder enquiry,' Detective Jobert says sternly. 'I can do whatever I feel is right.'

Abi goes over to her. 'Come on, Darce. Let's just go inside.'

'I really do need to take your statement, Darcie,' Detective Jobert says, gesturing to the inside of the farmhouse. 'Are you up to talking to me now?'

Darcie gives her a withering look. 'Well, as I'm now under fucking house arrest, I might as well.'

She waltzes into the living area and slumps down onto the sofa.

Detective Jobert follows her. She sits down on a stylish leather armchair opposite the sofa. Then she takes out her black notebook and pen.

'Can I just check a few things? You were with the others on

the plane that flew into Marseille yesterday morning, is that correct?'

'Yes,' Darcie sighs. She doesn't want to have to go through all the details. Every ounce of her being wants to be somewhere else. At home.

'And then you all got into a rental car and Steph drove you here?'

'Yes.'

'How did Katie seem on the flight and on the journey here?' she asks.

'Fine. She was fine,' Darcie says dismissively.

'And you all came here. And can you tell me what happened then?' Detective Jobert asks.

'I don't understand why you're asking me all this.' Darcie frowns at her. 'The man who killed her is called Patrick Brennan. He's been stalking me in London for over two years. He came into my house and held a knife to my throat. He's threatened to kill me. And now he's travelled to France. He's here in Bédoin. I know he is. And he followed me up the mountain and then killed Katie by mistake.' Darcie gives a sigh of frustration. 'So what bloody difference does it make what we did at this farmhouse yesterday afternoon? Why aren't you out there looking for this psycho?'

'I do have officers out on the mountain and the surrounding areas searching for whoever attacked your friend,' she explains very calmly.

'Why aren't you with them? What are you doing here?' Darcie asks rather pointedly.

'Because I have no proof that this man you're talking about is the person who murdered Katie,' she explains. 'There is no evidence of that. Only what you've told me.'

'Well, what other explanation is there?' Darcie says, shaking her head.

'I would like to continue to question you, Darcie. And then

I'd like you to write a statement too,' Detective Jobert says in a quiet voice. 'We can do that here. Or we can go to the police station in Avignon if you'd prefer that?'

'Are you threatening me?' Darcie snaps indignantly.

'No, I'm not. As I said, I'm trying to run a murder investigation,' she says. 'So, shall we start again?'

THIRTY-FOUR
STEPH

It's now early evening and most of the police and forensic officers have left the farmhouse. It seems as if they have photographed every inch of the interior. It felt surreal watching as they dusted for prints on the doors, windows and door handles. It's now eerily quiet after all the chaos and upheaval.

Detective Jobert has arranged for two uniformed officers to park up outside our farmhouse for our protection. It doesn't bear thinking about. The pit of my stomach is tight and uncomfortable. We've been instructed to keep the doors and windows locked, as well as try to limit our time outside. I'm scared. I wish we could just go somewhere else, but Detective Jobert told us to stay put as she would be back early in the morning. She also promised to keep us up-to-date with any developments, as well as letting us know when we could visit Katie at the morgue in Avignon. But it feels that we're sitting ducks in the villa.

Ruby has taken charge of phoning and liaising with the British Consulate. We've been told that the nearest one is in Marseille. We have to inform them of Katie's death and that there is a murder investigation going on. The consulate will liaise with the French police on our behalf as UK citizens. And eventually they will arrange for the repatriation of Katie's body. Abi has the unenviable task of phoning Katie's elderly parents in Liverpool to tell them what's happened. Abi has already phoned and spoken to Justin, and he's going to tell their children, Max and Sophie. My heart breaks when I think of what they're going to go through in the next few days, weeks and months. They're going to be devastated. It's hard enough that Katie has died. But the way in which she has died makes the whole thing so much worse. It's going to be on the news and in the papers. It's going to be hard for any of us to get away from it.

As I sit in the living area, I realise that some of us have left our rucksacks in the boot of the hire car. I get up and head for the front door.

'Where are you going?' Ruby asks anxiously.

I gesture. 'Just to get some stuff out of the car.'

'Be careful,' she says quietly.

I glance up the stairs to Darcie's closed door. Ruby has been checking in on her to fetch water or tea that returns untouched. The last time she came down for tea, her eyes were red-rimmed. 'She keeps saying it should have been her,' Ruby whispered, hands shaking as she filled the kettle. Darcie is a shell of her former self – nothing like the polished influencer who arrived yesterday with her matching luggage and camera-ready smile. Each time someone mentions Katie's name, a muffled sob echoes down the stairs.

The solid oak door is incredibly heavy as I unlock it and pull it towards me. The handle and door furniture are all made from ornate wrought iron.

I take a step outside into the warmth of the evening. It's lovely after the chill of the AC in the farmhouse. Like getting slowly into a warm bath. If only I didn't have a terrible, taut feeling continually in my gut. I tried to do some deep breathing exercises earlier, but nothing seems to be working.

The air is filled with the sound of cicadas and the smell of lavender, honeysuckle and baked earth. Someone is having a barbecue nearby and there is that lovely waft of char-grilled food. A dog barks in the distance and another returns the bark.

I pull the front door behind me so that it's nearly closed and pad down the stone pathway that snakes through the neat front garden and to the shaded car parking space. The sun is starting to descend in the perfect blue sky, but it's still baking hot.

The car keys settle between my knuckles without thought – muscle memory from a thousand late-night walks home from Clapham South. My fingers curl around the metal, finding their usual grip. A lifetime of learned vigilance, even here in this French garden.

My sandals crunch on the dry dirt of the ground as I make my way over to the Mercedes, click the automatic locking system and pull up the automatic tailgate.

Then I hear a noise.

I stop and look around.

Nothing.

Maybe I should just scuttle back into the farmhouse and be safe.

I tell myself that I'm being ridiculous. Paranoid.

I start to reach in to take my rucksack, along with Abi's and Darcie's. I think Ruby must have kept hers with her in the car.

I get the feeling that someone is watching me. My anxiety grows as my stomach tenses.

There's another noise which sounds like a person's footstep.

I freeze, listening intently as I scan the garden behind me and the small driveway that leads down to the road.

You're just being paranoid, Steph, I tell myself. It's not surprising given the day we've had.

Turning back to the car, I take the other two little rucksacks and throw them over my right shoulder.

I spot something in the corner of the boot. A small plastic bag. Reaching over, I take it out and see what's inside. It's

Katie's sandals. She brought them so she could change into them when she got back to the car. She said that her feet would be boiled and swollen. I can feel myself getting upset as I take the bag.

Reaching up, I pull the tailgate down and close it.

Suddenly I get the feeling that someone is standing behind me.

I move the keys slowly so I can use them as a weapon.

My heart is banging against my chest like a drum. I try to get my breath, but I'm terrified.

Then I turn sharply to confront whoever it is, bracing myself in case I'm attacked.

'Just thought I'd see how you guys are getting on,' says a soft Cockney voice.

It's Tom.

'Jesus Christ!' I exclaim in both relief and shock. 'You scared the life out of me, you silly bugger!'

'Sorry,' he says apologetically as he takes a couple of steps towards me. Then he reaches out and puts a comforting hand on my arm. 'I can't imagine what you're all going through.'

I nod. 'Thank you.'

'If there's anything that Shaun or I can do,' Tom says. 'Just let us know.'

'That's very kind,' I say.

What I want to say is that I want to share my bed with him tonight. I don't want to be alone. And I want to feel protected.

'Look, I don't know how you're feeling,' he says gently. 'But if you want someone to talk to later. Or just sit with. Let me know, okay?'

Our eyes meet and I smile at him shyly. 'Actually, I would like that.'

'Good. Great.' He smiles back at me and his eyes twinkle. 'I'll see you later then.' He turns to head back down the driveway to the cottage.

As I watch him walk down to the road, I spot a car drive slowly past.

It's the white Fiat 500.

Jesus, I think to myself as my pulse starts to race.

'Tom?' I call, trying to sound calm.

He turns back to look at me with a quizzical expression.

My head is already whirring with the implications of seeing that car again.

I jog down to where Tom is standing on the edge of the road.

'Everything all right?' he asks with concern.

The Fiat is now parked on the right, a little further down the road. I can't believe that he's got the balls to come here and just sit there. Part of me is very scared. But part of me is also incredibly angry.

Tom sees me looking and follows my gaze towards the parked car.

'What's wrong?' he asks.

'That car,' I explain. 'It followed us to the mountain. Then the man who was driving it parked in the same car park as us.'

Tom narrows his eyes. 'What? Are you kidding?'

'No. It gets weirder,' I say. 'As he came past us in the car park, he said, "Have a nice walk, Darcie." It freaked us all out.'

'You think he had something to do with what happened to Katie?'

'Maybe,' I reply. 'Darcie's had a stalker in London for two years. He held a knife to her throat one night. There's a possibility he's out here in France.'

'That's terrible,' he says, his eyes wide in disbelief. 'I heard you guys talking to that detective about it.'

'The police in London think that he might have followed her out here,' I say, then explain. 'Katie and Darcie were wearing similar clothes. Katie was wearing Darcie's black baseball cap that she wears on lots of social media posts. They're both blonde.'

Tom runs his hands through his hair and shakes his head. 'Jesus, you think this guy mistook Katie for Darcie.'

'Maybe. We don't know,' I say, but my eyes are locked on the car.

'What does this stalker look like?'

'That's the thing,' I say. 'Darcie just doesn't know. He wore a mask when he broke in.'

'Haven't the police got a photo?' Tom asks.

'Darcie said that in the CCTV images they showed her of Brennan, he was very scruffy-looking, with long hair and a beard,' I say. 'But they were such bad quality that they were completely useless.'

Tom stares down the road at the car. Then he looks at me. 'You think he's come back here because he realised that he didn't kill Darcie and he knows that she's here, don't you?'

I nodded. 'Is that mad or paranoid?'

'Neither.' Tom shakes his head.

I point the other way to the marked police car where two officers are sitting. 'Do you think I should tell them?'

Tom nods. 'I'll go over, but my French isn't great.'

'Yeah, neither is mine,' I admit.

Tom jogs to the police car, gesturing frantically at the Fiat. The officers' blank faces tell me everything – they don't understand a word. When he returns, his expression is grim.

'No English,' he says. 'Not a bloody word.'

My fingers fumble for Detective Jobert's card. Voicemail. Of course. 'Detective Jobert,' I say, trying to keep my voice steady. 'The Fiat from the mountain is here, outside our house. Your officers don't understand us. Please call.'

The message feels pathetically inadequate. Somewhere down that road, Katie's possible killer sits waiting.

Tom comes marching out of the cottage holding what looks like a rifle.

What the fuck?

'What are you doing?' I ask, eyes widening in astonishment.

Tom gestures with the rifle to the car. 'I think we should go and have a little chat with the driver of that car.'

'With a rifle?' I ask, furrowing my brow.

'I'm not going to shoot him,' Tom says. 'But if the man really is who you think he is and he's come back to attack Darcie, don't you think it's a good idea to let him know that you've got a man who's armed with a rifle about the place?' Then he nods over at the police car. 'And those two clowns don't seem to be doing anything.'

'What are we going to say?' I ask as my breathing starts to become shallow at the very thought of confronting the driver.

'I'll think of something,' Tom says calmly. Then I remember he told me this morning that he was in the army and served in Afghanistan. He probably knows what he's doing and can handle himself.

I take a deep breath. 'Okay,' I say quietly.

Just as we start to take a few steps down the road, I hear the Fiat's engine start.

Tom glances at me. 'Bollocks. Have you got your car keys?'

I nod, reach into my pocket and pull them out.

Tom nods back towards the farmhouse. 'Come on. We're going to follow him.'

'We're going to do what?' I ask incredulously.

'We can't let him just drive away without confronting him,' Tom explains. 'He's just going to come back later.'

My fingers tighten on the key fob. This is insane. But Tom holds that rifle with the easy confidence of someone who's done this before, who knows exactly what he's capable of. The soldier in him shows in every precise movement, every calculated decision. And right now, that military certainty feels like the only solid thing in this nightmare.

Tom breaks into a run so I follow him. Part of my brain is telling me not to be so stupid. But the other part is telling me that I have to do something.

We get to the Mercedes. I jump into the driver's seat and start the ignition.

Tom pulls his seat belt across with his right hand as he holds the rifle with his left.

I slam the car into reverse as I turn the steering wheel.

THIRTY-FIVE

I hit the accelerator so hard that we lurch forward, out of the entrance to the farmhouse and turn left onto the road. I can see a huge cloud of dust behind me where the tyres have spun on the dry ground.

I glance up.

The white Fiat is about fifty yards ahead of us.

'There he is,' Tom says pointing.

'Is that thing loaded?' I ask.

Tom frowns. 'You don't think I'd come out here with a unloaded rifle, do you?' he snorts.

'No, I suppose not,' I say, catching myself thinking that just when I thought this day couldn't get any more hideous, strange or surreal…

I push my foot against the accelerator to pick up our speed a bit. I want to narrow the gap between us and the Fiat.

Within seconds, we are up to 70 km/h as we hurtle along the main road through Bédoin.

There are small trees and hedgerows to our left, houses and driveways to our right.

Spotting a bend, I slow a little, but Tom still needs to grip the door handle to steady himself.

We're now going 90 km/h.

'Sorry,' I mutter.

'Don't apologise,' Tom says. 'I'm impressed.'

'I still don't know what we're going to say if we do manage to stop him,' I say.

'Let me deal with that.'

We hit a tight bend going left.

Tom pushes his hand against the dashboard.

I can hear the tyres squealing beneath the car. I'm gripping the steering wheel for dear life. The muscles in my hands are sore from the effort.

'Shit,' I gasp. I feel like I nearly lost the back of the car.

We hammer up a long hill.

The Fiat is now less than twenty yards in front of us and darts out to overtake a dawdling tractor.

I have to do the same or I'll smash into the back of it.

I see the old farmer glance at us as we speed past.

I look at the dashboard. We've hit 100 km/h. I try to regulate my breathing.

'Fuck this,' I say out loud. 'We haven't come this far to let this fucker get away.'

I can't quite believe those words came out of my mouth as we hurtle through a tiny village.

The houses and the hedgerows blur past us.

Up ahead, I spot a silage truck with a silver tank on its back. It's waiting to pull out onto the main road.

The driver must have miscalculated how fast we're going because he pulls out.

'Jesus!' I say, putting my foot on the brake hard.

The Fiat swerves to avoid the truck.

'Fuck,' Tom growls.

I've now stamped on the brakes. I feel like everything inside my body is contracting as we skid along the road towards the tanker.

The Fiat clips the side of the lorry and flips onto its roof. It then skids along the road upside down.

The steel back of the tanker is coming towards us.

I wince and hold my breath.

I think I'm going to die.

I manage to bring our car to a halt.

I unclip my seat belt, open the door and get out.

The lorry driver is climbing down from his cab, gesticulating and shouting in French. He shakes his fist at me.

Oh, fuck off. It was your bloody mistake, I think angrily.

Moving around the lorry, I see that the Fiat is about thirty yards down the road on its roof.

Tom and I break into a slow jog.

I notice that he's got his rifle with him. 'What have you got that thing with you for?' I ask. 'He might be dead in there.'

'And he might be alive and armed,' Tom points out. 'I'm not taking any chances for either of us.'

Just as we approach the Fiat, the driver's door opens and the man who was driving it crawls out onto the road.

He looks up at us in bewilderment. His face is covered with blood and he is shaking like a leaf.

'What the fuck are you doing?' he screams at us as he wipes blood from his eyes. He doesn't look like he's going to put up any kind of fight.

I peer at him. It's definitely the man I saw earlier when I passed the car coming out of Bédoin when he purposefully looked the other way and when he strode past us in the car park.

'Patrick Brennan?' I ask, my heart hammering in my chest.

'Who?' the man says with a confused expression as he looks up from his knees, swaying as he tries to stand. He's got a trace of a London accent.

'Are you Patrick Brennan?' I ask, although it does strike me that he's not likely to admit to it.

'Who the fuck is Patrick Brennan?' he groans as he finally gets to his feet.

Tom raises the rifle and points it at him. 'Stay there or I'm going to shoot you.'

The man raises his hands nervously. His face flushes with anger and fear. 'Jesus Christ! I don't know who the hell you think I am, but I can explain! You just ran me off the fucking road!'

'You've been following her today. And her friends. Up on the mountain. One of her friends was killed up there. So, you'd better start talking right now before I start shooting,' Tom thunders loudly.

'I didn't know that anyone had been killed,' the man babbles anxiously. 'Not until I got a phone call from our London office an hour ago. Fuck's sake, my car is totalled! Do you have any idea what you've done?'

I look at him. 'Your London office? What the hell are you talking about?' I snap angrily.

Tom grits his teeth. 'Why have you been following them?'

'I'm a press photographer,' he says with his hands held up, shaking slightly. His breathing is ragged, and there's a thin trickle of blood from a cut on his forehead. 'I'm following Darcie Miller. This is insane! You could have killed me!'

I'm confused by what he's saying and the way he's saying it.

'You're her stalker?' Tom asks.

'No, I'm not her stalker.' The man groans and shakes his head. 'My paper is running a series of stories on her husband next week. I'm here to get photos of her as part of the story. The long-suffering wife. We had a tip-off that Hugo was going to fly out here today to try and get out of the UK and hide for a few days. And now I've got a busted rib and no car because of you lunatics!'

'For fuck's sake,' I growl at him. But everything he's saying fits. I saw him putting a big camera into his rucksack down in the car park. If he was Patrick Brennan, there is no way he would know all this stuff. And it fits in with the phone call I got the other day from a journalist looking for dirt on Hugo.

Tom looks at me with a raised eyebrow. 'What do you think?'

'Yeah, I think that he's telling the truth,' I sigh.

The photographer looks over at the car, running a trembling hand through his hair. 'What a fucking mess. My editor is going to have my head for this. I'm supposed to be keeping a low profile!'

'What was with the whole "Have a nice walk, Darcie"?' I ask with a frown.

'My little joke,' he says, wincing as he touches his bruised side. Then he looks at me with a mix of anger and resignation. 'I'm not going to press charges for you running me off the road. And I'm genuinely sorry about what's happened to your friend today. But I promise that I didn't have anything to do with it, and I'd appreciate it if you'd put that fucking gun down now.'

I can hear the sound of police sirens.

Tom glares at him. 'Why did you drive off like that?'

'I saw you in my rear-view mirror coming out of that house with a gun. I thought you were going to shoot me.'

The police sirens are getting louder.

Tom gestures to the rifle. 'I'd better go and hide this in the car before Five-O get here.'

I nod and watch as he jogs away.

Patrick Brennan is still out there somewhere.

THIRTY-SIX
RUBY

It's dark and Ruby is sitting at the ornate iron table under the wooden canopy. It's been three hours since Steph and Tom returned with news of the car crash and the revelation that the 'creepy man' in the Fiat on the mountain was a bloody paparazzi photographer! They are all so angry. Darcie has sworn to divorce Hugo and never speak to him again. If Ruby is honest, the shocking news about the photographer had been a welcome distraction, even if it didn't last that long. And then what had happened to Katie hit them all again.

As Ruby shifts her feet under the table, she gets a sharp twinge in her ankle where she twisted it earlier. She remembers Katie's laugh in the car, the way the sunlight played normally on everything.

Ruby glances around, trying to shake off the terrible empty, dark feeling. The others are all inside. There is an intense silence inside the farmhouse. No one is talking except for the odd muttering of "Are you all right?" to each other. Of course they aren't all right. They will never get over what happened to their friend today.

Ruby sees the ghastly image of Katie lying inside the body

bag. The enormity of it hits. For a few seconds, her chest is so tight it's hard to draw breath. She tries to eject it from her mind's eye, but it won't go. Her lifeless, colourless face. It is going to haunt her forever.

It is now dark so that the familiarity of the outside has become strange or eerie. Maybe that's just her state of mind. White moths shuttle around the neat flowerbeds.

Then over to her right something flicks across her vision. It startles her.

Was that a bat? It's too late in the day for a bird, isn't it?

As her eyes focus, Ruby swears she sees movement in the undergrowth. Or is she just seeing things?

Tilting her head back, Ruby stares up to look at the sky. The sad magnificence of the translucent moon that looks paper thin. It's a moon that Katie will never see again. Everything Ruby looks at seems to be tinged with a melancholic significance.

Is she up there now? Ruby wonders. She's not religious, but it would be nice to think that Katie is somewhere peaceful.

'Okay if I sit out here?' asks a voice softly.

It's Abi.

She's holding a goldfish bowl of a glass of white wine.

'Of course,' Ruby says in a tone that implies that she doesn't have to ask.

Abi slides out a chair slowly and then sits down. She lifts up her glass. 'I can't seem to get drunk.'

'No,' Ruby agrees.

'What I mean is that I can't seem to drink enough to get drunk and not feel so terribly raw,' Abi sighs.

Silence. Just the noise of the cicadas which seems to be unusually quiet, possibly as a sign of reverence.

Abi looks up to the sky. 'Were you looking for her up there?'

'Sort of. It's times like this that I'm jealous that I don't have a strong faith,' Ruby admits. 'If I believed that she is now being looked after by a merciful god and has gone to a better, more peaceful place, that would make everything a tiny bit more bearable.'

Abi nods and takes a swig of wine. 'That's how I felt when my brother died.'

Ruby remembers that Abi's older brother, Peter, had died in a car crash when he was only twenty-two. That had to be thirty years ago now. It had happened just before Ruby, Abi and Katie were all due to take their finals at Oxford. The three of them had all travelled back to Hampshire for Peter's funeral.

'I remember that,' Ruby says gently.

'Remember what?' Darcie asks as she comes over with a flute of Prosecco in her hand. She has a haunted look on her face.

Ruby feels awkward and then glances over at Abi.

'Oh, am I interrupting something?' Darcie asks, stopping in her tracks.

'Don't be silly,' Ruby reassures her as she pulls out a chair. 'Just sit down.'

'We're not meant to be sitting out here, are we?' Darcie says very quietly.

Ruby shrugs. 'I'm less concerned now we know who that creepy bloody man in the Fiat was.'

'I'm not,' Darcie says with a dark expression. 'Brennan is here. I know he is.'

They fall into an uncomfortable silence.

'It's all my fault, isn't it?' Darcie whispers, shaking her head.

'No. You mustn't say that.' Abi leans forward and puts a comforting hand on Darcie's arm.

'It is,' Darcie continues. 'You heard what that detective told Steph. If you...' she takes a deep breath. 'Katie was strangled. She was either killed by someone she knew or some predatory psychopath.'

Ruby frowns. She knows what Darcie's hinting at. 'It could

have been anyone who attacked her. Some maniac lying in wait somewhere on the mountain.'

Darcie shakes her head vehemently. 'No. It was Patrick Brennan. I know it was. And Katie was wearing my stupid bloody cap. He thought she was me. So, it's my fault she's dead.' She begins to sob.

Abi leans over and gives her a hug. 'Even if that is true, how is that your fault? You didn't ask that monster to start stalking you. You're not responsible for anything that he does.'

Darcie nods as she wipes her face. She nods as if Abi's words have comforted her a little. 'Sorry,' she says with a sniff.

'You don't need to apologise,' Ruby says in a soothing tone. 'This day... Well, it's been horrific.'

Darcie looks at them and lets out a breath. 'Sorry, you guys were in the middle of talking about something.'

Abi leans forward and looks at Darcie. 'It wasn't very cheery, I'm afraid. I was just talking about when Peter died.'

'It was so awful, wasn't it?' Darcie says gently, but she's still distracted and detached. 'Such a shock. He was the closest thing I had to a brother when we grew up.'

Ruby smiles. 'You had the hots for him, didn't you, Darce?'

'Yep. Mad teenage crush,' Darcie admits as her face lights up as if she's now fully entered the conversation. 'I thought he looked like Jason Donovan with his blond curtains.'

They all laugh for a few seconds and it feels like a welcome relief.

'We were all at that funeral, weren't we?' Abi says with a frown.

'Steph wasn't,' Ruby points out. 'We hadn't even met Steph back then.'

'Oh yes.' Darcie nods as if this is such a strange thought. 'That's actually quite weird now I've thought of that.'

'Talking of which,' Abi says. 'Anyone seen Steph?'

'I guess she's recovering from chasing that bloody journalist,' Ruby says.

Darcie shakes her head and sighs. 'I can't believe he was from the press. What a way to earn a living.' Then she narrows her eyes. 'It's weird because when I spoke to Hugo earlier, he told me that it was one of my friends that had spoken to a reporter about him. And I know that none of you would do that to me. Neither would Katie. I'm just trying to work out who it is.'

Silence.

Ruby pushes the hair from her face. 'Where is Steph?'

Darcie raises her eyebrow. 'Guess?'

'Still flirting with Tom on the sofa?' Abi giggles.

'Of course,' Darcie says judgementally.

'I think it's sweet,' Ruby says, trying not to get annoyed at her sister. It's not appropriate. 'And I'm glad that Tom's here with his trusty rifle.'

Darcie pulls a face. 'I'm not. He thinks he's bloody Rambo walking around with it. And it's loaded.'

Ruby frowns. 'It's not much good unless it's loaded, is it?'

'Any sign of Shaun?' Abi asks.

But Darcie isn't listening.

She's looking at something past Ruby and in the garden.

'Darce?' Abi says with a quizzical frown.

Ruby can feel her pulse quicken. 'You okay? You're scaring me.'

Darcie points. 'I thought I saw something over there.'

They all turn to look.

Abi shrugs. 'I can't see anything.'

'It's gone now,' Darcie says sounding irritated.

'I think I saw a bat over that way earlier,' Ruby says, but she can feel a horrible creeping sensation wash over her.

'It wasn't a fucking bat, Ruby!' Darcie snaps loudly. 'It looked like someone was standing there.'

'Shit!' Abi gets up from her chair which grates noisily on the stone.

'Okay.' Ruby tries to remain calm as she scours the garden for any signs of movement. Maybe it had been someone she'd seen earlier.

'Tom? Tom?' Abi yells.

As they huddle and start to move back down the patio towards the doors that lead inside, Tom comes jogging out, carrying the hunting rifle. 'Everything okay?'

The sight of the gun doesn't make Ruby feel safer. It makes her feel very uneasy.

'Darcie thinks that she saw someone in the garden,' Abi explains.

'Right, everyone get inside,' Tom says in an assured, military-style tone as he takes control.

Steph appears, looking concerned. 'What's going on?'

'It's fine. Just get back into the house. Everyone,' Tom says, using his arms to gesticulate. 'Right now.'

Ruby's breathing is fast and shallow. She hobbles along the patio, her eyes fixed intently on the dusky light of the garden as if some maniac is going to launch himself from out of the undergrowth at them all.

She nearly trips as she's not looking where she's going but she's too scared to look away.

Tom moves quickly and methodically to shut and lock the doors that lead out to the patio.

'Keep away from the doors and the windows,' he orders them.

Then he moves swiftly away down the hallway.

Ruby spots him checking and locking the front door.

'Shit, there's the side door,' Ruby says, pointing to the door that leads from the side of the kitchen to an area where the bins are kept.

Steph races over to it and locks it.

'Jesus Christ,' Ruby sighs and blows out her cheeks. 'This is crazy.'

'Fucking hell,' Darcie growls as she goes into the kitchen. 'I'm getting another drink. Anyone else?'

'I'm fine,' Ruby says. She feels that she needs to stay alert and have her wits about her.

'No thanks,' Steph says with a wave of her hand.

Abi looks at them all. 'What the actual fuck.'

'Shouldn't we go and tell the police?' Steph asks.

Tom shakes his head. 'No. No one is to leave this house tonight. Unless there's some kind of emergency.'

THIRTY-SEVEN
STEPH

I look out of the bedroom window of the farmhouse. It's been two hours since Darcie thought that she saw something or someone in the garden. I'm starting to wonder if it wasn't just a figment of her imagination. Or maybe the sight of Tom and his hunting rifle just scared whoever it was away.

Tom is sitting at the foot of the bed looking at something on his phone. I'm propped up on pillows at the other end. There seems to be a strange distance that's developed between us since we got back to the farmhouse. I can't put my finger on it. Maybe I'm just being incredibly needy or insecure. I'm also castigating myself for even thinking about me and Tom while one of my best friends is lying in a morgue in some strange French town.

Have a word with yourself, Steph! I say to myself angrily.

My phone buzzes with another message from home. Dad, offering to fly out at seventy-eight, as if that would help. As if anything could help. Mum could barely speak through her tears when I told her. Of course they're devastated – they've known Katie since that first day they dropped me at Oxford, when she appeared in my doorway with a bottle of wine and two mugs, announcing we were going to be friends. They'd adopted her instantly, including her in every Sunday lunch, every Christmas.

The memory ambushes me: graduation day, Katie's mortar board sailing into the Oxford sky, cheap Champagne fizzing over her fingers. That smile of hers, like the whole world was opening up. My throat closes. Such a long journey from that bright afternoon to this dark day, and I can't stop seeing her face, can't stop the tears tracking down my cheeks.

Oh, Katie.

I sniff again and Tom turns to look at me. He narrows his eyes quizzically.

'Who are you texting?' he asks me. He sounds incredibly suspicious.

What the...?

I frown. I replay his question back in my head in disbelief.

I'm sitting here with tears streaming down my face and his first thought is to ask me who I'm texting. What the hell is he talking about?

'None of your business,' I snap at him. It's been a horrendous day. I'm tired and upset.

Tom just looks at me angrily. 'What?' he asks aggressively. There's something about his sudden shift in manner that suddenly scares me. He's like a wound coil.

I decide to try and pacify him. I know that I shouldn't have to, but it's my instinctive reaction to confrontation. It always has been.

I gesture to my phone. 'I'm just texting friends and family. Keeping them updated on everything that's happened today. They're all very worried and upset. That's all.'

Tom shrugs, but he looks sullen like a little boy. 'Then why didn't you just tell me that?'

His face and body are twitchy and tense.

'I'm sorry,' I say, lowering my voice to almost a whisper. I feel like I've annoyed him for some reason.

I look down at my phone again. I can see my hand is shaking. Tom is glaring at me and it's making me feel very anxious.

I'm not sure what to do. Do I make an excuse, go out into the rest of the house and tell the others about his strange behaviour? Then what?

I glance across the room and see the hunting rifle resting against the wall where he put it.

I'm paranoid. How is this happening?

I look up from my phone and force a smile. 'Is everything all right, Tom? You seem a bit upset,' I ask very gently. There is part of my brain shouting that I shouldn't have to placate him after everything I've been through today. If Tom was a decent human being, he'd be asking if I was okay. He'd be comforting me.

But there is something about the way he's acting that is incredibly unnerving. My instinct is for self-preservation over logic or pride.

'I don't know what the fuck you're on about,' Tom snarls. His voice is loud and makes me jump.

Oh God.

There is a tense silence.

'I feel like I've done something to upset you, that's all,' I say.

'Of course you have,' he hisses. 'Texting your boyfriend while I'm sitting here in your room. You're taking the piss out of me, aren't you?'

'Boyfriend? What boyfriend?' I ask. 'I haven't got a boyfriend, Tom. I wouldn't have been with you last night if I had a boyfriend.'

What the hell is he talking about? His behaviour is suddenly very strange.

'Of course you're gonna say that,' he scoffs with gritted teeth. 'That's what slags like you always say. Lying to our faces.'

I'm too scared to confront him for calling me a slag. I know it's unforgivable.

I can't understand where any of this has come from.

I hold out my phone, but my hand is trembling with fear. 'I promise you. You can check my phone if you want.'

Tom hits my hand aggressively, my phone flies across the room and smashes against the wall.

'What are you doing?' I ask in disbelief. My eyes are full of tears. It's all too much. Why is he being like this?

I stand up. I have to get out of the room and away from him.

'Sit down!' His voice drops to something low and lethal, barely above a whisper. The kind of quiet that screams danger.

'Please, Tom,' I say, trying to get my breath. 'You're really scaring me.'

'Good. I want you to be scared. It serves you right for leading me on,' he jeers furiously. 'That's what women like you do, isn't it? Little prick tease and then throw it in our faces. Who the hell do you think you are?'

'I really don't know what I've done to deserve this,' I sob. 'Why are you being like this with me?'

'Don't you get it? It's not you.' Tom laughs as if I'm an imbecile.

'What do you mean, it's not me?' I ask, wiping tears from my eyes. 'You're not making any sense.'

I stand up again and look at him with the tears hanging on my eyelashes. 'Please. I need to get a glass of water.'

Tom reaches into the pocket of his shorts and pulls out a hunting knife that has a serrated edge. 'Sit down or I'll gut you like a fucking pig!'

THIRTY-EIGHT
DARCIE

Darcie opens the fridge and takes out some water. She stopped drinking about an hour ago and now she's got a headache. She reaches into the rucksack that she took on the hike, takes two paracetamol in her hand, tosses them into her mouth and swallows them with the water.

She then goes over to the wooden table where the welcome brochure sits and puts her rucksack down there. She'll take it back upstairs later.

Looking over at the stairs, Darcie wonders what Steph and Tom are doing. They seem to have been in her room for a very long time. They can't be shagging, can they? Not after what's happened today. That would be weird, wouldn't it? Completely inappropriate.

Abi and Ruby are in the living area. There are a couple of side lamps on. Air's *Moon Safari* is playing very quietly. It's music that reminds Darcie of a moment in time. The point at the end of one millennium when the new one is looming. It was around that time that she and the others went out together. Private members' clubs, bars, club nights in west and south London. Back in the day.

The memory hits without warning: Katie dancing at Bagley's, face painted with hearts that caught the light, pink feathers from her boa clinging to her sweaty skin. So vivid Darcie could reach out and touch her – except she can't, not ever again. Pete Tong was DJ'ing. A host of club classics. They'd dropped pills that night. Mitsubishis. They were small, white, round and stamped with the Mitsubishi car logo. Darcie has no idea why. Katie is dancing like she doesn't have a care in the world. She looks so young and happy.

It's my fault that Katie is dead, Darcie thinks to herself. She can't seem to get it out of her head. It's driving her mad. The guilt is overwhelming.

Her phone rings. *Notting Hill police station.*

Are you fucking kidding me? Darcie thinks, but she knows she has to answer it.

'Darcie?' It's Detective Inspector Darren Baker.

'I assume you've heard what's happened?' Darcie says coldly.

'I have. I'm so terribly sorry,' he says in a soft voice.

'You understand that had you put Brennan in jail when you had the chance, my beautiful friend would still be alive?' Darcie asks.

Silence.

'I'm never going to forgive any of you for that,' she says venomously.

'I completely understand that this is a very difficult time for you, Darcie,' he says. 'I've been liaising with a Detective Marie Jobert. I know she's been with you today.'

Darren sounds the 't' at the end of Jobert.

'Jobert,' Darcie corrects him. *He's such a peasant.*

'We have more intel on Patrick Brennan that I need to make you aware of,' Darren says. 'And I know it's not something you really want to discuss or hear at the moment.'

'What is it?' Darcie snaps.

'We believe that Brennan is in Bédoin,' Darren says.

I knew it!

'His train got in yesterday morning at 6 a.m.'

Even though Darcie suspected that he was, she feels a horrible ball of anxiety deep in the pit of her stomach.

'Do you know where he is?'

'No, I'm afraid not.'

'Did he kill her? Did he kill Katie?' she asks.

'I think it's likely,' Darren says. 'I know that you flagged up your concerns with Detective Jobert. Your friend was dressed very similarly to you, had your baseball cap on and she's blonde.'

'He mistook Katie for me,' Darcie says. 'How am I meant to live with that?'

Silence.

'I've spoken to the British Consulate and the French police,' Darren says. 'We have you all going on a plane back to London first thing in the morning from Marseille. And you'll be taken by police escort to the airport.'

'No. That can't happen,' Darcie says. 'My friends want to see Katie in Avignon.'

'We can arrange for them to see Katie once her body is back in London,' Darren says.

His use of the word 'body' goes right through her.

'I don't think that it's safe for any of you to be in France any longer than you need to be.'

'What about tonight?' Darcie says as she looks over towards the glass patio doors and the windows. Maybe she did see Brennan in the garden earlier.

'Detective Jobert tells me that you have two police officers in a patrol car outside?' Darren asks.

'Yes. But they don't look old enough to shave,' Darcie groans.

Silence.

'I have a CCTV image of someone we think is Patrick Brennan coming out of the railway station in Bédoin,' Darren says. 'I'm going to send it over to you now.'

'Okay,' Darcie replies. 'Although knowing what he looks like isn't going to help me much when he breaks in here and cuts our throats with a knife.'

'I'm going to send you the photo,' Darren says, ignoring her last comment. 'Then I'm going to send you the details for tomorrow morning. Pickup time is 6 a.m.'

Darcie hangs up and staggers into the living area, her legs barely holding her up. The phone in her hand might as well be a live grenade.

Ruby and Abi look up sharply.

'What's wrong?' Ruby asks, already rising from her seat.

'He's here.' The words come out in a whisper. Darcie's free hand finds the doorframe for support. 'Brennan. The police say he got to Bédoin yesterday morning.' Her voice fragments on his name.

'What?' Ruby says looking horrified.

'Oh my God,' Abi gasps, putting her hand to her mouth.

'He was on the mountain?' Ruby says as if she's thinking aloud.

'They don't know,' Darcie says. 'But I do. He killed her...' She shakes her head as her eyes fill with tears. 'He killed her.'

Ruby glances over at the windows. 'Where is he now?'

Darcie gives them a dark look. 'No one knows.'

Abi sits upright as she looks over at the patio doors. 'Jesus,' she whispers. 'They can't expect us to stay here all night.'

'They've arrange for us to fly home first thing in the morning,' Darcie explains but she can see the sheer look of panic on their faces.

Darcie's phone buzzes in her hand. She looks down.

It's a text from Notting Hill police. There's an attachment

which she assumes is the photo of Patrick Brennan. It's not much use to anyone now.

Then she opens it.

The photo shows a man in his thirties, with very short hair and a rucksack over his back arriving at what she assumes is Bédoin railway station.

Except she's not looking at anything except for the man's face.

A face she knows.

Darcie feels physically sick by what she's looking at.

Her whole body reacts. She can hardly get her breath.

'Are you all right, Darce?' Ruby says, standing up and walking towards her.

Darcie looks up from the phone.

Abi stands up. 'What is it?'

'The police in London have sent me a photo of Patrick Brennan arriving at Bédoin railway station,' Darcie says trembling.

Then she turns the phone to show them both.

'Oh my God!' Abi clasps her hands over her mouth.

The man in the photo is Tom.

THIRTY-NINE

SHAUN

Six Hours Earlier

Shaun turns off the shower and grabs a towel. Drying himself, he looks at his face in the mirror. He wraps the towel around his waist. He needs to shave. Grabbing a can of shaving foam, he takes off the lid and squeezes it. There's just the noise of the pressurised gas but no foam. It's run out.

Tom shaves. Maybe he's got some in his room?

Walking along the landing, he looks down the stairs. Tom has been badly shaken by the events of the day. He's hardly said a word since they left the mountain and cycled home.

'Tom?' Shaun calls out.

'Yeah?' he replies from where he's sitting in the kitchen.

'Do you have any shaving foam?' Shaun asks.

'Yes, mate,' Tom says. 'Just on the shelf in my room. Help yourself, bruv.'

'Ta. That's grand.' Shaun makes his way down to Tom's room.

He can't seem to get the image of Katie's body at the bottom of the ridge out of his head. He's seen more than his fair share of dead bodies while he was in the army, especially in Afghanistan. He's seen the body parts of Sergeant Andy Higgins after he went to inspect a suspected roadside IED in the north of Helmand Province and it went off. But they were in a war zone. Seeing Katie was so unexpected that it was shocking. Shaun is thankful that he still has the ability to be shaken when seeing death. He knew other soldiers who had become permanently desensitised to it.

Going into Tom's room, he notices how neat it is. He wouldn't expect anything less from an ex-soldier. Being neat and tidy becomes part of your DNA when you're in the military.

There is a small set of wooden shelves on the far side of the room. Shaun spots the black can of shaving foam and walks over to get it.

He grabs it and, without thinking, flips it into the air and goes to catch it with the other hand. But his hands are still wet from the shower and the can slips and falls to the floor. It rolls along the wooden floor and disappears under the bed.

'Bollocks,' he says under his breath.

Kneeling down, Shaun looks under Tom's bed and reaches to grab the can.

To the right of where the can lies is a thick black folder of some kind.

What's that?

Even though he knows it's not appropriate for him to take a look, Shaun can't help but pull it out.

Jaysus, in the old days it would be dirty mags under the bed.

As Shaun pulls the folder from under the bed, he sees that it's not really a folder. It's more of a scrapbook.

Opening it to the first page, he sees a photograph of a woman.

It's nighttime and the woman looks like she's standing at a bedroom window, dressed only in her bra. The photo looks like someone has taken it from her garden. It's hard to make out her face clearly, but she has blonde hair.

What the feck is this? Shaun thinks as he peers at the photo, wondering if Tom is some kind of pervert who secretly takes photographs of women. He never had Tom down as that kind of bloke. *What a little prick.*

Shaun is now captivated. He turns the page.

Another photograph from the same back garden, but it's now broad daylight and a sunny day.

There's a woman sitting on a reclining garden chair wearing a white bikini and sunglasses.

Shaun immediately recognises her.

Christ, that's Darcie! What the feck!

Turning the pages frantically, Shaun sees more photos. He also sees photos of Darcie cut from magazines and newspapers. There are screenshots of Darcie from her Instagram page.

Shaun is trying to work out why Tom has this under his bed. He can't understand it.

To his horror, he remembers Steph telling the female French detective that Darcie had been the victim of a stalker in London for the past two years. And they had been told that that man had travelled to France, possibly Bédoin.

It's him. He's the bloody stalker.

'You shouldn't be looking at that,' says a voice in a calm tone.

Shaun glances up to see that Tom, or whoever he is, is standing in the doorway, glaring down at him.

'What the feck have you done?' Shaun asks in utter horror, holding up the scrapbook. 'It was you. You're a freak.'

Shaun's eyes move down to Tom's hands. He's holding a knife and hammer.

There's no way that he's leaving this room alive.

FORTY

STEPH

Now

I'm looking at the floor. I'm trying to avoid Tom's glare. How did I get him so incredibly wrong? Jesus, I slept with him this morning. It makes me feel sick just to think of it. It's like I'm sitting in a room with a completely different person. His facial expression, his body language, even the tone of his voice.

He's gripping onto the handle of the knife so hard that his knuckles are white.

My heart is pounding against my chest and my mouth is dry. I don't think I've ever been this scared before. No. I know I never have been.

Tom looks at me with utter disgust. I don't know what's wrong with him or what I've done to provoke him.

How the hell am I going to get out of this?

Suddenly, there's a knock at the door.

'Steph?' calls a voice. It's Abi.

Tom glares at me and puts his finger to his lips to tell me to be quiet.

My eyes roam around, wild with panic.

'Steph?' Abi says again, this time sounding confused.

Tom is staring right at me.

My stomach is so knotted that it's painful.

I take a nervous swallow. 'Erm, I'm just in the middle of something,' I say, trying to sound as laid-back as I can. Even though I can't work out how I'm getting out of this, I just don't want it to escalate.

'Yeah. It's just that I wanted a quick word about something,' Abi says, sounding relaxed but insistent. 'It won't take more than a minute. I promise.'

Silence. My pulse is thudding in my neck.

'Steph?' Abi calls again.

My eyes lock onto Tom's. He has a dark, intense gaze that seems to go straight through me. It's almost as if he's dead behind his eyes, like a shark.

'Yes,' I stutter. 'I... I... We're...'

Tom moves the knife as if to warn me to get rid of her.

'Erm... Look, I'll be down in a minute, okay. I'm just going to get dressed,' I say, hoping that this will buy me more time.

For a few seconds, Abi doesn't respond. I'm hoping she's just going to go downstairs.

Then another voice.

'Steph?'

It's Darcie.

Tom's head whips around as he stares at the door suspiciously.

Why are they both out there?

'Yes, it's okay. I'll be down in a minute,' I say again, praying that they will just go away before Tom reacts.

'Is Tom in there with you?' Darcie asks.

My stomach lurches.

Jesus, why did she ask that?

'Yes,' I reply, but my voice sounds a little high-pitched.

'Are you okay?' Darcie asks.

Tom sits forward on the bed.

'Yes, yes, I'm fine. Honestly,' I reply, but I can't help but sound upset.

Suddenly the door flies open.

Darcie, Abi and Ruby are standing outside.

Before I can react, Tom grabs me and puts the knife to my throat.

'Oh my God!' Ruby gasps.

'Leave her alone, you sick fucking psycho,' Darcie shouts at him. She's visibly shaking but trying to hide her fear. 'We know who you are.'

I frown. *What is she talking about?*

Tom stands up with me in front of him. He has me in a vice-like grip as he keeps moving backwards.

Darcie edges into the room and looks at me. 'He's Patrick Brennan. He killed Katie.'

What? How the hell is that possible?

'Leave her alone!' Abi shouts.

How can Tom be Patrick Brennan?

'Good to see you, Darcie,' Tom sneers as we move slowly towards the door.

'What the hell are you doing?' I croak. His forearm is hard against my windpipe.

Darcie dashes across the room, grabs the rifle and points it at us.

'Let her go!' she bellows.

Tom laughs loudly. 'Put that thing down, you stupid woman.'

Darcie squints down the sights of the rifle at her. 'Let her go, you fucking freak.'

I'm terrified. If Darcie tries to shoot him, she's got as much chance of killing me as she has of killing him.

'Darce,' Abi says sounding alarmed. 'You need to put the gun down.'

'No,' Darcie snaps. Her eyes are wild. 'This vile, pathetic excuse for a human being has ruined my life and killed our friend. Now I'm going to shoot him.'

'Darce,' I rasp, trying to get my breath.

'It's not even bloody loaded,' Tom snorts. 'Get out of my way.'

CRACK!

The air explodes with the sound of a gunshot.

I feel the bullet whistle past my right ear and hear it hammer into the wall behind us.

Suddenly Tom throws me to the ground.

It knocks the wind out of me.

I hear Darcie scream.

Tom grabs the rifle from her, tosses it to the floor.

Then he grabs Darcie by the hair and puts her in a necklock with the knife to her throat.

'Get the fuck off me!' Darcie screams.

'Come on, Darcie. Don't struggle,' he says in an unnerving, amused voice. 'It's time we spent some quality time together. I know this is what you want really.'

As I get slowly to my feet, I watch as Tom moves Darcie at knifepoint out of the bedroom door and onto the landing.

'Get out of my way!' Tom thunders to Abi and Ruby as he drags Darcie towards the stairs.

I start to move swiftly across the bedroom. I can't let Tom – or whoever he is – take Darcie from here with him. He clearly has something horrific planned for her.

'Let her go!' Ruby yells. 'The police are outside.'

I get onto the landing.

Tom is moving down the stairs with a knife held to Darcie's throat. He's looking back up at us.

'Stay there!' he hisses.

I have no intention of just standing and watching.

'Is this how you get your kicks?' Darcie taunts him. 'Pathetic.'

'Shut up!' he snaps.

'Your parents must be very proud,' Darcie snorts sarcastically.

I don't understand why she's goading him with a knife at her throat. She must have a death wish.

I push past Ruby and Abi on the landing and head for the stairs.

'Steph!' Abi says under her breath.

Tom and Darcie are now in the hallway.

'We've got to do something,' I say as I reach the top of the stairs.

Tom nods up at me. 'Where are the car keys?' he growls.

I shrug. 'I'm not sure without looking,' I say.

It's a lie. I know exactly where they are. On the welcome pack on the small table by the glass doors out to the patio.

But I'm using his question as an excuse to start to come down the stairs.

'Let me have a look around and get them for you,' I say as I move slowly down the stairs, not waiting for Tom to reply.

Darcie struggles. 'I'm not getting in a car with you,' she gasps.

'Shut up and stop struggling or I'll slit your throat,' Tom snarls.

'Go on then. I dare you!' Darcie says, but she's struggling to get her breath.

'Darcie!' Ruby calls down, trying to get her to stop provoking him.

I try to give her a reassuring look as I get to the bottom of the stairs. The air smells of honeysuckle and lavender. It's so incongruent with what's going on.

'It's okay,' I say, holding up my hands to try to pacify Tom. 'Everyone keep calm. I'm just going to get the keys.'

I'm trying to buy us time to think. I can't let that man just walk out of here with Darcie. But I have no idea how to stop him. He has a knife to her throat, for starters. Even if he didn't, I wouldn't be able to overpower him.

I walk down the short hallway. My feet are cold on the stone floor.

'Slowly does it,' Tom barks at me as he follows me, pulling Darcie with him.

I can sense him behind me as I go into the living area.

What am I going to do?

I go to a sofa and turn over a couple of cushions, pretending to look.

'Sorry,' I say very quietly as I go. 'They have to be here somewhere.'

I go over to a dark, wooden dresser where some of the glasses are stored.

I make another play at searching.

Out of the corner of my eye, I can see the small table where I put the car keys.

On one side is the welcome brochure for the farmhouse.

And next to that is Darcie's dark grey rucksack.

I have a sudden thought.

Isn't there a six-inch kitchen knife inside Darcie's bag? The one that she was waving around, threatening to shank someone with.

I have to somehow get that knife. It's the only thing I can think of. And I have to do something.

But how?

Ruby and Abi have appeared very tentatively at the doorway to the living area.

'You're not going to get away with this,' Ruby says. 'You do know that?'

'Really? Why's that?' Tom snorts.

I use the distraction of this conversation to move slowly over to the table.

'The French police know who you are. They've got a photo of you arriving at Bédoin station,' Ruby explains. 'They have guns over here. As soon as they see you, they're going to shoot you.'

I'm standing with my back to the room. The grey rucksack is right in front of me at waist height.

'You think I haven't thought of that?' Tom says in a withering tone.

I try to remember where Darcie pulled the knife from.

The right-hand side pocket, wasn't it?

'So how does this all end? What are you hoping to achieve with all this?' Abi asks, trying to distract him and keep him talking.

I reach slowly for the side pocket and touch it.

I can feel the knife inside through the material.

'It ends with me and this bitch dying somewhere beautiful together,' Tom sneers.

'Why?' I ask.

'Why?' he snaps. Then he glares at Darcie. 'Because she makes thousands of people feel inadequate, fat, poor and boring. Her perfect life, body, clothes, family, lifestyle. It's all bullshit but she makes money out of other people's misery.'

I pull the zip.

I hold my breath. He's going to notice that I've stopped moving around the room any second now.

'You know what? I think I'd prefer to die here than go anywhere with you, you little freak,' Darcie gasps.

I reach inside and grab the cold steel handle of the knife.

I pull it out very slowly.

'Fine,' Tom laughs. 'I can slit your throat right now and let your sister and your friends watch you die. That might be better, actually.'

'No,' Abi screams.

There is a momentary silence in the room.

I can feel that Tom is looking over at me.

I have the knife in my hand still.

Shit!

'Oi, what the fuck are you doing over there?' Tom snaps at me.

I freeze. Heart pounding.

What now?

'I just found the keys,' I say without turning.

'Good,' he says.

With a swift movement, I pull up the front of my T-shirt and push the knife down the front of my jean shorts. I can feel the cold steel against my stomach.

I turn around and hold the keys up high to my right and dangle them in my right hand, hoping to distract Tom for a second.

As his eyes move up to look at the keys, I use my left hand to pull my T-shirt down properly so that the handle of the knife isn't showing.

'Right, very slowly, I want you to come here and hand them to Darcie. She's going to be driving us,' Tom explains.

With a sweep of my hand, I 'accidentally' knock Darcie's rucksack to the floor.

'Sorry,' I say quietly, looking directly at Darcie, trying to make eye contact.

Darcie looks at me as I take a step towards her and Tom.

Then her eyes go down to the rucksack which now lies on the floor.

'Don't do anything stupid, Steph,' Tom snarls.

I'm now looking directly at Darcie.

She's giving me a quizzical look.

'I won't,' I say.

Darcie moves her eyes back to the rucksack and then back to me.

She knows what I've done. I can tell from her expression.

I give her the faintest of nods to signal that I have the knife.

Darcie's eyes widen.

We both know that if we are going to do something, we are going to have to do it in a split second.

I'm now five yards from where Tom and Darcie are standing.

I can see that the knife has cut into the skin on Darcie's neck and drawn blood.

My breathing is fast and shallow.

I take a couple of steps forward so I'm now an arm's length from them.

'Don't come any closer,' Tom warns me.

I nod as I look at him.

I make a big gesture of holding out the car keys with my left hand.

'Here you go,' I say.

I'm watching Tom's eyes.

Then I drop the keys to the floor.

Tom's eyes instinctively move down to watch the keys as they hit the stone flooring.

I look at Darcie and give her nod.

With my right hand, I'm already pulling the knife from my shorts.

'Now!' I shout.

Darcie stamps down on Tom's foot with everything she's got.

In the same moment, she sinks her teeth into his forearm.

'AH!' Tom yells in agony.

Darcie elbows him, pushes his arm up and moves away.

She's free of him.

Everything feels like it's in some strange slow motion.

I lunge towards Tom, gripping the knife handle.

He can see me coming for him.

He swings the hunting knife towards my face.

I duck and at the same time plunge the knife with everything I have into the middle of his chest.

The blade goes into him and I let the knife go.

And then everything seems to stop.

The knife is just protruding from Tom's chest.

There's about four inches of blade inside him.

Tom fixes me with an indignant stare as if he can't believe I've had the audacity to stab him.

I move back and away from him quickly.

Blood bubbles and froths at his mouth.

I must have hit a lung.

His hand clutches the knife handle.

He grits his teeth and winces as he pulls the knife out of his chest.

He takes a step forward.

Then he winces in pain, stops moving and sinks slowly to his knees.

His shirt is now soaked in dark blood.

Finally he crashes to the floor.

We're all frozen, petrified.

But he's not moving.

He's dead.

FORTY-ONE

The interview room clock ticks past midnight. My hand still burns where I gripped the knife, though I've scrubbed it raw in the station bathroom. Somewhere down the corridor, Darcie's sobs have finally quieted. Her screams when she realised what I'd done – what I had to do – still echo in my head. *You killed him. You actually killed him.*

Two deaths in one day. Katie this morning, Brennan tonight. The fluorescent lights flicker. How can this be the same day that started with my birthday hike?

My fingers found his neck automatically – some half-remembered first aid training kicking in. Still warm, but no pulse fluttered under my touch. Just the sticky wetness of blood seeping into the floorboards. So much blood. My hands wouldn't stop shaking as I backed away.

Darcie's screams filtered through the walls from where Abi had taken her. Ruby's voice, steady and clipped, talking to Detective Jobert on the phone. The crunch of her feet on gravel as she went to alert the police outside, then silence from the cottage when she tried to reach Shaun.

I found myself on the sofa, a bottle of cognac appearing in my hand like a magic trick. The glass clinked against my teeth as I drank. His feet stuck out at an odd angle from where he'd fallen.

The blanket was heavy in my hands as I crossed the room. Not for his dignity – he deserved none. But to erase him, to make him disappear like he'd made Katie disappear.

A door slams in the police station corridor, jolting me back. Detective Jobert explained that I wasn't under arrest. But the very fact that I had stabbed and killed somebody meant that I had to be taken to Avignon for a recorded interview to take place.

I hear some shouts and loud talking which echo down the corridor and then the sound of approaching footsteps.

The door opens and Detective Jobert comes in holding some manila folders in her hand.

As she approaches, she points to my empty cup. 'Would you like more coffee, Steph?' she asks in a friendly tone. She has been nothing but polite and amiable since we made the journey over from Bédoin.

'I'm fine, thanks,' I say with a forced smile.

'Something stronger?' she suggests as she sits down at the wooden interview table opposite me. 'I'm sure I could find you some brandy or whisky?'

I shake my head. 'That's very kind, but I'm fine. Really.'

'Okay. I have run the details of what's happened today and this evening with my boss, Commissaire Dubois,' she explains. 'There is no suggestion that you did anything wrong. I have the statements from all your friends and they all tally with what you've told us in your interview tonight.'

'Oh, that is a relief,' I sigh. Even though I'm a trained lawyer, I'd become paranoid that I was going to spend the next twenty years of my life in some squalid French women's prison.

'The law is very similar as it is in your country,' she says, meeting my gaze. 'The right to self-defence is a principle of French law. It's only complicated a little because the threat to life was to Darcie and not to you.'

I nod. It's exactly what I would have expected logically. But I haven't been thinking logically today.

'We call it justifiable homicide in the UK,' I explain, although it's been decades since I did any criminal law.

'Yes. Exactly. Patrick Brennan had a knife to Darcie's throat. He was attempting to kidnap her and there is a strong chance he was going to murder her as well,' Detective Jobert says. 'And that is justifiable homicide. We have spoken to le ministère public.'

I nod. 'It's the French equivalent of our Crown Prosecution Service, isn't it?'

'Yes. I think so.' Detective Jobert nods. 'They will not be pursuing any charges over this death. So, you are free to go.'

'What about Katie?' I ask.

'We are waiting for forensic checks to come back,' she replies. 'But our theory is that Patrick Brennan cycled over to where you were climbing this morning. He spotted Katie walking up the mountain on her own. As we've discovered, she was wearing Darcie's baseball cap, similar clothes and she has blonde hair. Visibility was very poor. And very tragically, he mistook Katie for Darcie and murdered her.' Detective Jobert looked at me with her big brown eyes. 'I cannot imagine what you and your friends are going through. I assume that you still wish to travel home in the morning?'

'Yes,' I reply. I just want to be back in my lovely flat and sleep in my own bed.

'We have been liaising with the police in London,' she explains. 'They have booked flights for you.'

'Yes, Darcie mentioned it before...' My voice trails off. 'Well, before the events of this evening.'

'Be ready at 6 a.m. You'll be driven to the airport,' Detective Jobert says.

'Thank you,' I sigh weakly. I'm just so incredibly tired and drained.

FORTY-TWO

RUBY

2 August 2022

It's morning and Ruby sits at the table out on the patio as the first hints of daylight appear. She's hardly slept at all. She and Darcie had shared a bed, like they used to during thunderstorms as girls. Ruby had felt her sister trembling in the dark, had pulled her close like she used to before teenage years and rivalry drove them apart. 'You were so brave,' she'd whispered, meaning it. The way Darcie had faced down Brennan, raw terror in her eyes. For a moment, Ruby had glimpsed the sister she'd always tried to protect, before judgements and jealousies built walls between them.

Now, watching the sun creep over the horizon, Ruby's chest tightens. They'd lost Katie, but maybe – just maybe – she and Darcie have found something they'd buried years ago. When Darcie had finally drifted off, her head on Ruby's shoulder, it felt like forgiveness. For both of them.

Ruby thinks back to twenty-four hours ago when she'd woken up with a slight twinge of a hangover. She'd sat in the same seat, nursing a cup of tea and watching the sun come up.

But in those twenty-four hours, the whole world seems to have been turned upside down. She still feels as if everything is detached and surreal. For a fleeting couple of seconds, Ruby's mind goes elsewhere. A mundane thought. And then she's hurtled back into the dark reality.

How are any of us going to get over this? she thinks. *I don't think we ever will.*

The rising sun burns a strip of orange across the horizon. There is the chatter of birds with an intermittent crow of a cockerel in the distance. Underneath this noise, the gentle lapping sound of the pool. It is already warm. The air has the promise that it is going to be another glorious Provençal day. But one without Katie.

'Can't sleep?' asks a voice.

Ruby looks up and sees Abi approaching. Ruby wipes the tears from her face and sniffs.

Abi is holding a bottle of Prosecco and a packet of cigarettes. She puts them down on the table and gives Ruby a big hug.

'Hey,' Abi says. 'We're going to get through this. Okay?'

Ruby nods, but Abi's embrace has made her unravel.

'It's so unfair,' Ruby sobs as she blows out her cheeks and tries to catch her breath.

'I know,' Abi whispers as she sits down, reaches out and takes Ruby's hand.

'Sorry.' Ruby wipes her face with the back of her hand. 'I don't know where that came from. It just suddenly hit me that Katie isn't coming home with us. And I don't understand how that can be. It's not real, is it?'

Abi takes a cigarette from the packet and puts it in her mouth. 'No, it's not real. My head feels like it's in some strange bubble.'

She lights the cigarette, takes a drag and then blows a plume of smoke up into the air.

Ruby gives her a quizzical look. 'I thought you quit?'

'I did,' Abi says shaking her head. 'But I thought "fuck it".' She offers the packet to Ruby. 'Want one?'

'Yes. Fuck it,' Ruby says with a half laugh as she reaches and takes one.

Abi leans over and lights it for her.

'Thanks,' Ruby says as she sits back and takes a long drag. 'That's good, isn't it?'

Abi smiles. 'Yeah. Reminds me of that flat in Clapham. Nipping off to that corner shop to get more wine and twenty Marlboro Lights just before it closed at ten.'

'Those were the days,' Ruby says sadly. 'Not a care in the bloody world.'

Abi puts her cigarette down on the ashtray, takes the Prosecco, pops the cork out and takes a swig from the bottle.

'Want some?' she says, holding up the bottle.

Ruby nods and holds out her hand. She swigs down a couple of mouthfuls and the fizz hits her throat. 'Fag and Prosecco. That's a proper breakfast.'

Steph comes out. Her eyes are red and puffy from where she's been crying. 'What's going on?' she asks, pointing to the cigarettes and Prosecco.

Abi shrugs. 'I'm not sure I can face today sober and without cigarettes.'

Ruby gets up and goes and hugs Steph. 'Stupid question, but how are you doing?'

'I don't know.' Steph sighs as she hugs Ruby back. 'I don't think I've even been to sleep.'

Abi offers Steph the cigarette packet. 'Want one?'

'Yes,' Steph says immediately, pulling one out and lighting it. She takes a deep drag and then blows out the smoke. 'Ah, I'd forgotten how good a cigarette first thing in the morning is.'

'We all used to smoke back in the day, didn't we?' Ruby asks.

'Katie was the worst,' Steph says softly. 'Lighting each cigarette from the last one when she was drunk.' The memory hangs in the air between them like smoke, almost solid enough to touch.

Darcie appears wheeling her suitcase. Despite the fact that the sun hasn't even risen properly yet and the sky is still a pinky-orange colour, she's wearing big seventies boho-style sunglasses.

'Anyone know what's going on across the road?' she asks, sounding serious.

Ruby shakes her head. 'What do you mean?' She wonders if she's talking about Shaun. They haven't seen him since they returned to the farmhouse yesterday afternoon. Ruby had knocked on the cottage door twice, but there had been no answer. She assumed that the police would have contacted Shaun since then.

'Have you seen Shaun?' Steph asks.

'No,' Darcie says as she looks over in the direction of the cottage. 'But the place is swarming with police officers.'

'I guess that they're going through Brennan's stuff over there?' Abi suggests.

Darcie pulls over a chair and sits down. She moves her sunglasses down and peers at them. 'Are we smoking and drinking?'

'Yes,' they all say in unison.

'Probably the only way to get through today.' Darcie shrugs as she reaches for a cigarette.

Ruby gets up. 'I'm just going to see what's going on. I think we owe it to see Shaun before we go.'

'I'm not,' Darcie snorts as she lights her cigarette.

'I'll come with you,' Steph says, getting up.

They walk across the patio, down past where their rental car is parked, and along the short driveway to the road.

There are around five police vehicles parked outside.

Several officers in full white forensic suits are by the open front door and in the front garden.

Something about the scene doesn't feel quite right.

'It might be me,' Ruby says quietly, 'but it all looks very heavy-handed if they're just going through Brennan's possessions in there?'

'I don't know.' Steph shrugs. 'My brain is too fuzzy to think clearly about anything at the moment.'

A figure emerges from the cottage, bright white against the morning shadows. Detective Jobert, Ruby realises, but transformed in her forensic suit, blue latex gloves stained dark at the fingertips. Something about the way she walks makes Ruby's stomach clench.

'We're just wondering what's going on?' Ruby gestures towards the cottage, but her voice sounds thin, wrong.

Detective Jobert stops. Behind her, more figures in white suits move like ghosts through the cottage doorway. The detective pulls off one glove, then the other, taking too long to answer.

'I'm afraid we found a body.' Each word falls like a stone. 'About an hour ago.'

'What?' Steph's hand flies to her mouth, but Ruby already knows. Already sees the truth in Jobert's careful expression.

'Shaun?' The name scrapes from Ruby's throat.

Detective Jobert's face is solemn. 'Yes. And I'm very sorry, but it looks like he's been murdered.'

FORTY-THREE
DARCIE

Four Weeks Later

Darcie pulls on her black Mulberry coat and then pauses in front of the full-length mirror in her bedroom. She can hardly bear to look at her own reflection and turns away.

Katie's funeral. Four weeks since France, and still her mind stumbles over those words. Each morning brings the same sickening wave of remembrance: Katie's gone, and it's her fault. The guilt lives in her bones now, as much a part of her as breathing.

The thoughts and recriminations that swirl around her head have crushed her very soul. And she's started to resort to booze and pills. But the nightmares are so vivid and so devastating that Darcie fears falling asleep. She can't seem to get Katie's face out of her mind. She's haunted by it.

The very thought that she will never see her friend again just hasn't sunk in. Her eyes quickly fill with tears. Her hand trembles as she reaches into her black Hermès handbag, takes out a tissue and dabs her eyes and nose.

Oh, Katie, what have I done?

Taking a deep breath to compose herself, Darcie walks out

of her bedroom, down the landing and into the kitchen. She's removed all signs of Hugo since she returned. He's now living in a hotel. The newspaper article about Hugo's inappropriate behaviour caused a media storm. Both the BBC and Channel 4 are now running internal investigations into the shows where Hugo's alleged behaviour had been covered up. Hugo has effectively been cancelled and his career is over. And so is hers.

The house feels lighter without Hugo's darkness seeping into every corner, without the constant dread of what mood he'll bring home. Last night, she'd found Bella curled up on the sofa, actually wanting to talk, like when she was little. No more tiptoeing around Hugo's passed-out form, no more making excuses for his behaviour.

DI Darren Baker visited Darcie last week. 'Employment agency rushed the background check,' he'd explained, shifting uncomfortably under her glare. 'Brennan's forgeries were good, but—'

'Good enough to get Shaun killed?' The words had come out like ice. She can still see the cottage across the road, still hear Tom's – no, Brennan's – voice. 'Good enough to let a murderer live opposite us?'

She fastens the buttons on her coat, remembering the way Baker had stared at his shoes. Pathetic. There was nothing he could do or say to make it right.

Darcie glances down at her watch. The taxi that is taking her over to the large crematorium in Chiswick is coming in ten minutes. In the past few weeks, Darcie has left the planning of Katie's funeral to Justin, Max, Sophie, Ruby, Steph and Abi. She can't bring herself to have those conversations when she's feeling this guilty about Katie's death. Abi and Ruby have been distant with Darcie since they got back from France. Or is she being paranoid? Everyone is dealing with their grief in their own way.

Steph has kept Darcie informed of the plans for the funeral

every few days. Which flowers they've picked. The readings, the eulogy and the music. Justin will read a eulogy. She feels a wave of nausea hit her. Lovely Justin who remained friends with Katie after they split. *Not like me and Hugo*, she thinks bitterly. We were never friends. Ruby is going to say a few words. Steph asked for Darcie's input, but she just didn't know what to say.

Sitting down at the kitchen table, Darcie looks around. The house feels so horribly big and empty. On the fridge, there are a couple of photos and articles secured under fridge magnets. A profile of Darcie from a Sunday supplement magazine when her book was released. A photo of Darcie doing a book reading to over a hundred fans at the Waterstones in Piccadilly. It breaks her heart to look at them. She needs to get rid of them. All of that has now gone. The irony of that thought isn't lost on her, on today of all days.

Reaching into her coat pocket, Darcie pulls out a delicate gold Soru bracelet. Katie's bracelet. It had been given to her by her daughter, Sophie. Darcie thinks that it's appropriate that this bracelet should be placed on Katie's coffin at the crematorium. Only Darcie and Katie would really understand why. It's a message and an apology. She feels tears coming but forces them back. She has to keep it together.

Placing the bracelet carefully into her bag, Darcie hears the front doorbell ring.

It's time to go.

FORTY-FOUR
STEPH

The wicker coffin sits at the front of the room, bathed in soft light. Ruby's fingers find mine and squeeze. Her mascara has left dark trails down her cheeks. To my left, Abi stares straight ahead, jaw clenched, while Darcie at the end of our row keeps dabbing at her eyes with a crumpled tissue.

Justin's voice breaks as he finishes speaking. 'She always knew exactly what to say to make everything better.' He presses his lips together, struggling to continue.

When Ruby takes the podium, her voice carries clear despite the tremor in it. 'Katie once convinced me to go skinny-dipping in Scotland. In April.' A ripple of laughter breaks through the grief. 'She jumped in first and came up screaming about her nipples freezing off, but wouldn't let me back out of it.'

A photo appears on the screen—Katie mid-laugh at some long-ago party, head thrown back, eyes crinkled. The opening notes of "Tender" by Blur fills the room. More images follow: Katie with birthday cake smeared on her face at six; Katie with that awful purple hair phase at sixteen; Katie radiant in her wedding dress; Katie with arms wrapped around her children.

I'd helped choose that particular laugh photo. I remember the moment it was taken—Ruby had just knocked over an entire pitcher of sangria at Katie's thirtieth. It was the laugh that had drawn us all to her, that full-body surrender to joy.

Row by row, people move forward with white roses. Katie's mother, Doreen, approaches the coffin first, shoulders shaking. Her husband, Steve, walks stiffly beside her, his face a mask, eyes dry and focused somewhere beyond the coffin. When Doreen stumbles slightly, it's her son, Kev, who reaches out to steady her, not Steve. Steve places his rose mechanically and steps away, while Doreen presses her palm against the wicker, lingering.

My turn approaches. The rose stem feels too thin between my fingers, too fragile a thing to carry all this grief.

I take a deep breath as our turn comes. We stand up slowly and go to take a rose from a basket. For a second, I can't bring myself to look at the coffin as I approach. But I know that I have to. And as I gaze at where Katie is lying, my eyes fill with tears and I swallow. It's all I can do to not completely break down.

Darcie and I file round to the left of the coffin while Abi and Ruby go to the right. We bow our heads and take a moment to remember our dear, beautiful friend.

'We're Going to Be Friends' by the White Stripes is now playing. I'm looking at the coffin and I know that Katie is lying there inside. And I know that I'll never see her again. I've got to say goodbye but it's so unbearably painful. My stomach is twisted and I can't get my breath.

Out of the corner of my eye, I see Darcie wiping tears from her face. I hear her sniff and sob.

I give her a reassuring glance.

Darcie places the rose on Katie's coffin.

As my eyes move back, I glance for a second at Darcie's bag which is by her feet.

It's open by a few inches.

Something glints in the light, which is what drew my eyes there.

It's gold.

I focus on it.

Then my stomach lurches.

It's a delicate gold bracelet. I've seen it before. It's Katie's.

The bracelet that Katie was wearing only ten minutes before she walked off into smoke and we never saw her alive again.

What the…? My brain is trying to make sense of it.

How has Darcie got that bracelet?

Katie was wearing that bracelet the last time I saw her alive.

Darcie appeared fifteen minutes later and told us she hadn't seen Katie.

I get a horrible, dark sinking feeling as I start to put the pieces together.

FORTY-FIVE

I sip my Champagne and glance around the function room at the Barnes Cricket Club. Justin is a member and has hired it for Katie's wake. We've been here for about an hour and I cannot get what I saw Darcie do in the crematorium out of my head. I've wracked my brains but there is no logical explanation. There's a voice that keeps telling me that there must be a simple reason why Darcie has Katie's bracelet. But there just isn't.

Since we left the crematorium and arrived at the wake, Darcie has been deep in conversation with people. I need to talk to her on her own and ask her. I can't flag it up with Ruby or Abi until I've heard what Darcie has to say. But it's making me feel sick with fear.

Over on a huge screen on the wall is Justin's video showing all the photos. A photo of the five of us comes up. We're all at Glastonbury with pints of cider in hand and mud-caked wellies.

What year was that when it rained and became a mud bath? I wonder. *2016?*

I can still remember some of the bands we saw. Adele headlined on the Saturday night. Katie and I insisted that we go off and see Two Door Cinema Club whose album we both loved.

Ruby insisted that we all go to see Gregory Porter which was far better than I feared it would be.

The photos change again and I see Katie with her arms around Sophie and Max as teenagers.

I glance around the room searching for Darcie again. My need to speak and confront her is overwhelming.

Then I see her.

She's sitting outside vaping on her own at a wooden table. Lost in her own thoughts.

Breaking into a march, I head for the double glass doors and step outside. I have to confront her with my suspicions.

It's September, but it's still balmy. The trees have changed and the leaves are now a beautiful array of orange, mustard and chocolate brown.

'Thought I'd get some fresh air,' I say to Darcie as I approach. My heart is banging and my breathing is shallow. I'm so frightened about asking her how and why she had that bracelet.

'Me too,' Darcie says sardonically holding up her black vape.

'It still doesn't feel real, does it?' I sigh, looking in at all the people drinking and talking in the wake through the giant windows.

'No. I'm not sure it ever will,' Darcie says.

Silence.

Come on, Steph. You have to do this now.

I feel sick to my stomach as I look at Darcie's handbag that's sitting on the table. It's closed.

'Have you got any tissues?' I ask, stalling for time.

'I have somewhere,' Darcie mutters, patting her pockets.

'I did have some, but I've used them all,' I say, but my eyes are still locked on the bag.

'I can't find any,' Darcie replies. Her voice is tight.

I reach across the table. 'Mind if I look in your handbag?'

Darcie yanks it back so forcefully, her glass nearly topples over. 'There aren't any in there.' Her knuckles whiten around the strap.

'Okay,' I say, holding her gaze until she looks away first.

The silence between us pulses.

Darcie's face flushes. She knows.

My heart is pounding. I can taste metal in my mouth.

I lean forward, dropping my voice. 'I want to look in your handbag, Darcie.'

'What are you talking about, Steph?' Darcie snorts, the fake laugh scraping at the air between us. 'Are you drunk?'

'I know what's in there,' I say, my eyes trying to catch hers. 'I saw it earlier.'

The tremor in her hand betrays her as she reaches for her wine glass.

I reach out to grab her handbag but she snatches it away from me.

'Why have you got Katie's bracelet?' I ask fixing her with a stare.

Silence. I can see Darcie's expression. Her mind is racing.

'What are you talking about?' Darcie laughs again but she can't hide the fact that she's completely rattled. 'It's my bracelet.'

'Your bracelet?' I ask. 'Show me then.'

Darcie fixes me with a cold stare. 'Why are you asking me this? You actually think that I—'

'Show me then,' I snap as I interrupt her.

I meet her eyes. Her face is static but I can see from her chest that her breathing is quick and shallow. She's full of anxiety.

'Is it your bracelet, Darcie?' I ask firmly.

'What?'

'It's a simple question.'

'No...' Darcie stumbles. 'It was a present from Katie.' She's lying.

'It wasn't though, was it?' I say shaking my head.

Darcie scratches her nose and shakes her head. 'What are you going on about, Steph?'

'I know what I saw. Sophie gave Katie that bracelet at the beginning of the year. She never takes it off. She wouldn't.'

'So what?' Darcie shrugs and moves as if she's going to get up. 'I just don't know what your problem is, Steph,' she snaps angrily. 'I'm going to get myself another drink.'

'Sit down right now, Darcie,' I snarl through gritted teeth.

'I don't have to listen to this,' Darcie huffs.

'You say you didn't see Katie after she left us. So how the hell did you get it?'

Darcie turns her face away.

'And if you lied about the fact that you saw her,' I say, 'you have to tell me what happened, however awful it is.'

Darcie lets out a long ragged breath, her head dropping into her hands.

There is a long, terrible silence.

I know that Darcie is building up to telling me the truth. Her whole body is collapsing in on itself.

'Darcie, you've got to tell me,' I say, trying to keep my voice calm but I feel sick with fear, with what she is going to tell me.

Darcie's eyes are full of tears but she just won't look at me. She's shaking her head very slowly.

'I can't...' she stutters, trying to get her breath.

'You have to. You know you have to.'

Then she turns her head to look at me. Her face is twisted with pain.

'I killed her,' she gasps. 'I didn't mean to, but I killed her.'

FORTY-SIX
DARCIE

1 August 2022
Four Weeks Earlier

Katie emerges from the smoke like an avenging angel, her face hardened into lines Darcie has never seen before. The sight hits Darcie like a physical blow—Katie's anger piercing straight through her carefully constructed walls. Her stomach twists with a sickening lurch of shame and longing

'What the hell are you playing at, Darcie?' Katie demands, her voice low and dangerous as she approaches.

Darcie's mouth goes dry. She wants to look away but can't. Katie's disappointment is worse than any fury—it confirms every doubt Darcie has about herself. A desperate urge to reach for Katie, to pull her close and confess everything, surges through her body with such force that Darcie has to clench her fists to stop herself. The truth hovers on her lips, but fear clamps down like a vice. She's spent too long hiding, too long protecting herself from rejection. Even now, with Katie standing before her—the one person she can't bear to lose—Darcie remains frozen, a prisoner of her own cowardice.

'I've no idea what you're talking about,' she says coldly. It's her defensive mechanism.

'What?' Katie snaps. 'Abi found us and said you were being a complete prima donna.'

Darcie rolls her eyes. 'Yeah, that's not actually what happened.'

Katie fixes her with a dismissive stare. 'Really? It's not unknown for you to lie, is it?'

Darcie spots another two cyclists whizzing past downhill through the smoke.

'Right, what is your problem, Katie? You've been giving me looks and making comments all bloody morning,' Darcie asks sharply.

'You just don't get it, do you?' Katie shakes her head.

'What don't I get? Enlighten me.'

'Darcie, you're my best friend and I love you. But you're so horribly self-absorbed that you are unable to take other people's feelings into account. It just doesn't occur to you because what you think, feel and want are the only things on this planet that matter to you.'

Who does she think she is? How dare she?

But Katie's words cut through her and Darcie can feel her eyes smarting with tears. 'I still have absolutely no idea what you're going on about, Katie.'

'You just had to sleep with that Shaun, didn't you?' Katie sounds disappointed. 'Not only was it pathetic to watch you throw yourself at him like some teenager, you did it in front of *me*.'

'So what?' Darcie snorts somewhere between a laugh and a sob.

'So what?' Katie yells. 'What the fuck is wrong with you? Are you a sociopath? We've spent the night together twice in the past two months.'

Darcie is silent. She doesn't know what to say.

'You told me that you loved me,' Katie says, her voice breaking. 'I thought we had something. And then you go and shag some bloke in front of me. What's wrong with you?'

'I told you that I loved you because I was drunk that night. That's all,' Darcie says, but it's a lie. Somehow she can't bring herself to say how she truly feels. Admit that she loves this woman standing before her like she's never loved any man before.

Katie fixes her with a cool stare, her voice suddenly even. 'If I wasn't so angry with you, I'd pity you. You're toxic. And damaged. And you'll never be happy.'

Silence.

'Have you been speaking to a journalist?' Darcie asks angrily.

'What?'

'You heard,' Darcie snaps. 'The journalist that is running a story about Hugo. What did you tell him?'

Katie raises her eyebrow. 'I told him the truth about your vile, predatory husband.'

Darcie locks eyes with Katie. The woman who has held her tenderly. The person she has shown her true self to. Been vulnerable with.

'How could you do that to me?' Darcie chokes.

Katie laughs sadly and shakes her head in disbelief. 'You're doing it again. I pour my heart out, telling you how much you've hurt me. And all you can think about is your precious reputation.'

'But you're going to destroy everything I've worked for. All these years.' Darcie feels the anger rising inside.

'Good,' Katie snorts.

'Good!' Darcie explodes. 'You've ruined my life.'

Katie smirks. 'Your fake, vacuous little life? Ah, poor you.'

Darcie is overwhelmed by a fury that just seems to

completely possess her. It feels almost childlike in its intensity. Like the time she was taunted by three girls at school and she attacked them with a pair of scissors and got suspended.

Suddenly Darcie takes a step forward and grabs Katie. She wants to teach her a lesson. How dare she smirk at what she's done? How dare she pity her?

'I loved you. I loved you,' Darcie whispers repeatedly. Her eyes are hot with tears. 'How could you do this to me!'

Suddenly she's stepping towards Katie. Her hands are on Katie, but this time she wants to hurt her. To punish her.

Katie backs away, fear in her eyes. 'What the hell are you doing?'

'I want you to shut up.'

'Get off me. You're pathetic. The person I feel most sorry for is Bella. Jesus, having you two as parents. She must be seriously damaged.'

'Don't you dare talk about Bella,' Darcie says putting both her hands around Katie's neck.

'Get off me!' Katie struggles.

'Shut up.'

'Good luck with paying for all her therapy,' Katie snarls.

'Shut the fuck up!' Darcie screams in rage.

She's shaking Katie while her hands are around her neck. It feels like someone else is doing it. As if the rage has possessed her and is now in control.

Katie makes a gurgling sound and Darcie can feel Katie's skin under her fingers.

She must stop. But she can't.

Katie's arms are flailing, hitting her. Her wrist hits Darcie in the jaw and the gold bracelet that she's wearing falls to the ground.

Darcie squeezes her throat hard.

Katie's eyes are wide with terror.

Then Katie isn't making any noise at all. She isn't moving.

Katie slumps forward, heavy and limp. All her weight on her.

Darcie pushes her away and allows Katie to drop to the ground.

She falls like a lifeless doll.

No.

'Katie?' Darcie whispers. 'Katie? Oh my God! No, no, no.'

She kneels down on the ground and puts her arms around Katie's head.

Darcie's body starts to tremble with fear.

She's going to open her eyes in a second, isn't she? Darcie tries to convince herself. But she knows she's not.

Touching Katie's face gently, she can smell her perfume. The one she bought her last Christmas. 'Hey. It's okay, Katie. It's okay,' she whispers in a reassuring tone as her eyes fill with tears. 'It's going to be all right.'

What have I done? What the hell have I done?

'Oh God...' Darcie sobs loudly as she holds her tightly. Her skin is warm and a little damp with sweat. 'I'm sorry,' she gasps. 'I'm so sorry.'

What am I going to do?

She can't just leave Katie lying there.

Darcie wipes the tears from her face, gets up and glances around to see if anyone is near. It's hard to tell in the smoke but she can't see anyone.

Walking towards the edge of the track, she looks down a steep ridge with a huge rock towards the bottom of the slope.

I have to put her down there.

Darcie can't believe that this is actually happening. She can hardly get her breath.

Taking Katie's feet, Darcie starts to drag her towards the edge. It's slow progress. She seems to weigh a ton.

Finally, Darcie manages to get Katie across to the precipice. She puts her hands under Katie's body, rolls her over the side and watches as her doll-like body tumbles and falls before smashing into the rock below.

FORTY-SEVEN
DARCIE

1 January 2023
Four Months Later

The prison officer's boots echo against the concrete floor as she approaches – fifties, long black ponytail, cold blue eyes. 'Darcie Miller?' She doesn't wait for confirmation before gesturing sharply.

'Yes.' Darcie's voice emerges as a whisper.

After two months of being shuttled between holding facilities, HMP Holloway, the largest women's prison in Europe, has become her reality for three suffocating and frightening weeks. Ten years stretch before her like an abyss. Her heart hammers against her ribs as the officer leads her across the room.

The smell hits her first when they enter the visiting area – a nauseating mix of industrial cleaner, body odour and cheap perfume. Darcie's hands twist together, the skin around her nails raw from constant picking. Plastic chairs scrape against linoleum. A child's shriek pierces the drone of conversation.

Most visiting stations are occupied – women in identical grey prison shirts leaning across tables, desperate for connection. A prisoner nearby bounces a toddler on her knee while her husband watches, his smile not quite reaching his eyes.

Then she sees Ruby.

Her sister rises from a chair, uncertainty etched in every line of her body. The hesitant wave Ruby offers makes Darcie's throat constrict. She forces her face into a smile, though her lips tremble with the effort. Each step toward Ruby feels impossibly heavy.

'Am I allowed to give you a hug?' Ruby's voice cracks on the question, her eyes darting to the guard stationed at the wall.

'Yeah.' Darcie nods, blinking rapidly as tears threaten. The simple fact that Ruby would still touch her feels like a gift she doesn't deserve. 'Just don't kiss me and pass me any drugs,' she jokes, the words scraping her throat.

Ruby's body stiffens against hers during their embrace – a momentary resistance before surrendering to the hug. Darcie inhales her sister's familiar scent, a remnant of the outside world that makes her chest ache.

'I'll try not to.' Ruby attempts a laugh that dissolves into tears.

They pull apart and sit. Ruby wipes her hand across her face and forces a smile.

'You look great,' she offers, though her gaze lingers too long on the hollows of Darcie's cheeks, the dull pallor of her skin.

'No, I don't.' Darcie runs fingers through her greasy hair. 'My roots need doing,' she says drily. 'And my nails.' She splays her fingers, bitten to the quick, a far cry from the immaculate manicures that once adorned her Instagram.

Ruby leans forward. 'I know we've spoken on the phone, but are you okay?' she asks. 'Or is that a stupid question?'

Darcie's shoulders lift into a shrug but the simple movement unleashes something inside her. 'I'm never going to be able to forgive myself.' The sob rips from her chest. 'Never.'

Ruby's silence is deafening.

'I can't stop thinking about her.' Darcie chokes as she blinks away the tears and digs her fingernails into her palms. 'It's torture.'

Ruby nods mechanically. An empty gesture of understanding. But how could she?

'I get flashes in my head. Just lying in bed with Katie watching telly, eating crisps and drinking wine.' Darcie can barely get the words out. 'How could I have done that? What kind of person does that make me?'

Her lungs constrict. Black spots dance at the edges of her vision as sobs wrack her body. She can feel other visitors staring, but can't stop the tidal wave of grief.

'Hey.' Ruby's hand hovers over Darcie's, not quite touching. 'You'll get through this.'

Darcie wipes her eyes, looks at her and blows out her cheeks. 'The thing is, I don't want to get through it. I don't want to feel okay ever again. I don't deserve any happiness or peace in my life after what I did.'

'Come on. That's not true,' Ruby says. Maybe it's Darcie's imagination, but Ruby's words sound hollow.

Darcie shakes her head, strands of hair sticking to her wet cheeks. 'I look back at my life and I'm so furious with myself. What was all that for? Taking photos of me wearing some designer clothes and thinking that it somehow mattered. Validation for my ever so fragile ego. For fuck's sake! I'm such a vacuous, selfish, narcissistic bitch.' Her voice rises, drawing a warning glance from a guard.

Ruby's silence is confirmation.

'Tell me the last time I did something for someone else that didn't have something in it for me?' Darcie leans forward. 'One selfless act.'

The silence stretches painfully.

'How's Bella?' Darcie asks. Her daughter has refused to have any contact with her.

'She's fine,' Ruby reassures her. But her smile is too quick.

'Has she asked you about me?' Hope flares, brief and desperate.

Ruby shifts in her seat, the plastic squeaking. 'She'll come round. It's just a matter of time, that's all.'

'I don't blame her.' Darcie sighs, but it's painful. 'You can imagine how all this has gone down at university and on social media.'

Ruby nods again.

'I've been going to the chaplaincy.' Darcie gives a snort. 'The bloody irony of it.'

'Have you told Dad?'

Darcie shakes her head. 'I don't think he wants me to call him for a while. I could hear the contempt in his voice.'

'I remember that,' Ruby murmurs. 'Does it help? Going to the chaplaincy?'

'Yes.' Darcie nods. The sessions with the chaplain and the religious services have become a lifeline in the darkness. 'It's the one thing stopping me going completely mad or... killing myself.'

'Please don't say that.' Ruby's face drains of colour.

'Don't worry. I'm well aware how utterly selfish that would be.' Darcie traces a scratch in the table with her fingers. 'I want to write a letter to Justin and the kids.'

'Okay,' Ruby says cautiously.

'What do you think?'

'I think if you want to write letters to them, then I think you should,' Ruby says. She's choosing her words carefully. 'Whether they will open and read them is a different matter.'

Darcie nods, swallowing the lump in her throat. She knows this but she has to try to do something to alleviate the crushing pain and guilt.

'Thank you for coming for see me,' Darcie whispers.

'It's fine.' Ruby's voice is noncommittal.

'I was scared you'd make some excuse about why you couldn't come.'

Ruby meets her gaze, unflinching at last. 'You're still my sister.'

The words hang between them – not forgiveness, not absolution, but the barest thread of connection. For now, it's all Darcie has.

FORTY-EIGHT
STEPH

1 August 2023
A Year Later

I'm standing at the top of Kilimanjaro. The views are staggering. Awe-inspiring. I can't believe that we've made it. My lungs are aching from the final ascent. Just short of twenty thousand feet! The highest mountain in Africa and I'm standing on top of it.

There's snow and rocks all around me and my breath is freezing in the icy air. If I look to the west, I can see the vast plains of Tanzania. To the east, the rolling hills of Kenya.

It's taken us seven days to get here.

'It's stunning,' says a voice.

It's Abi.

Then Ruby appears. The smile across her face is priceless. She's trained so hard to get fit enough to do this climb. All three of us have.

'She would have loved it up here, wouldn't she?' I say.

It's a year since Katie died and climbing Kilimanjaro was

always her dream. Abi, Ruby and I decided that we'd do it for her.

We stand, hug each other and have tears in our eyes in an outpouring of emotion.

I reach into my pocket and pull out a small tube. Inside are some of Katie's ashes. We told Justin, Max and Sophie what we planned to do on the anniversary and they were thrilled.

I hold up the tube. 'We got you here,' I say as I sob. 'We bloody well got you here, Katie. Our beautiful friend.'

First, I move the tube over to Abi, who reaches in and takes a little handful. Then she moves a couple of steps towards the mountain edge. She's transformed over the past year. I don't know if it's Katie's death or being away from Darcie's insidious influence, but Abi has taken life by the scruff of the neck, doing some of the things that she'd been promising herself she'd do for years. She ran the Hackney half-marathon in a relatively reasonable time.

'I love you, Katie,' Abi says as her voice breaks with emotion and she throws the ashes which catch on the wind and swirl away.

I offer the tube to Ruby. She too takes a handful of ashes and walks forward. Ruby has cut her hair short and it really suits her. She and Nigel finally split up. Ruby didn't want to waste any more time with someone she didn't love. And even though I know Ruby still visits Darcie, I know how much she truly loved Katie. Ruby has managed to make peace with both those things.

'Love you, my beautiful angel,' Ruby calls out as she tosses the ashes into the air.

Then it's my turn.

As I take the ashes, I spot the lovely Kirstie Le Marque gold bracelet that my boyfriend Mark bought me. I'm looking forward to seeing him.

My mind turns to memories of Katie. Her beautiful smiling

face. Drunken nights singing Take That songs while we sat on swings in the local playground on Clapham Common in the early hours of the morning.

I toss the ashes up and watch as they fall. Then suddenly they are snatched away by the wind as if to signal that she will be protected from here on.

'Goodbye, my beautiful friend.'

A LETTER FROM THE AUTHOR

Dear Reader,

Thank you so much for reading *Five Days in Provence*. I really hoped you enjoyed it!

If you'd like to join other readers and keep in touch, there are two options. To stay in the loop with my new releases with Storm:

www.stormpublishing.co/simon-mccleave

And if you'd like to receive two FREE novellas, along with occasional newsletters and updates about my new books:

www.simonmccleave.com/vip-email-club

If you enjoyed this book and could spare a few moments to leave a review, that would be hugely appreciated. Even a short review can make all the difference in encouraging a reader to discover my books for the first time. Thank you so much!

This book started as a conversation between myself and my editor, Claire. We talked about our experience of holidays with old friends. For me, it's always been a time to really catch up properly rather than a snatched hour or two over a coffee or a bar. I'm incredibly lucky to still have friends from school, university and those I met in the slightly blurred decade of the '90s! And often we will decide to incorporate a weekend away with a hike – Snowdon, Lake District, etc... And it's in those moments that we reveal our true selves. We've been through so much together. Football, festivals, stag dos and weddings, births and deaths.

That history and bond is very special. And it hasn't all been plain sailing. We've fallen out, argued and behaved badly or selfishly over the years but always found our way back to each other. Inspired by this, I created a set of characters who have been through a similar journey together. I'm a crime and thriller writer, so something sinister happens and this acts as a catalyst. True feelings of love, trust, resentment and anger are all heightened in friendship when something dark and tragic happens. I hope that you enjoy watching how all this plays out.

www.simonmccleave.com

facebook.com/simonmccleaveauthor
x.com/simon_mccleave
instagram.com/simonmccleaveauthor
tiktok.com/@simon.mccleaveauthor

ACKNOWLEDGMENTS

I will always be indebted to the people who have made this novel possible.

Firstly, to my incredible editor, Claire Bord. This is the second book that Claire and I have worked on. And as before, when I started to discuss the idea for this book, I could see that she shared my excitement for the story. Working with Claire on this has been a joy. We share the same sensibilities, and she has supported my vision for the book with patience, enthusiasm and some incredible notes throughout. Thank you for pushing me to deliver the best book I can.

To Oliver Rhodes and the rest of the Storm team – Alexandra Begley, Naomi Knox, Chris Lucraft, Elke Desanghere and Anna McKerrow.

To my superb agent, Millie Hoskins. Thanks for all your hard work and for championing me and my books at every opportunity.

To my stronger half, Nicola, whose initial reaction, ideas and notes on my work I trust implicitly.

To Izzy and George, who are everything.

To my mum, Pam, for her overwhelming enthusiasm for everything I write.

To Dave Gaughran for his invaluable support and advice.

And Keira Bowie for her ongoing patience and help.

Printed in Dunstable, United Kingdom